Wanting

ANGELA HUTH

An *Abacus* Book

First published in Great Britain by Harvill Press Ltd in 1994
This edition published by Abacus in 2000

Copyright © Angela Huth 1994

The moral right of the author has been asserted.

A CIP catalogue record for this book
is available from the British Library.

ISBN 0 349 11331 9

Printed and bound in Great Britain by
Clays Ltd, St Ives plc

Abacus
A Division of
Little, Brown and Company (UK)
Brettenham House
Lancaster Place
London WC2E 7EN

For James

1

On the morning of the girls' departure, Alfred Baxter woke two hours earlier than usual and dressed himself hurriedly. In the quiet hours of the night, when he had lain fretfully imagining the emptiness of the house without them, he had decided that only his best clothes would befit the occasion of their leaving. And so now he brushed at the jacket of his navy serge suit with a hand which, he noticed, seemed to be trembling, and blew at the thin ridge of dust and scurf that had gathered round the collar. He then chose a grey tie, its solemnity scarcely broken by the small crest of his old cricketing club, and he gave his lace-up shoes a quick polish on the eiderdown.

In the kitchen, it occurred to Mr Baxter that to stick to his normal routine, at least in part, might quell the pain in his heart and the tightness in his chest that made it difficult to breathe. His customary cup of tea would perhaps melt the incredulity that sat like a lump of stone on his head, and give him the strength to put on a cheerful face. He lit the gas ring under the kettle and took down the tea caddy, with its four portraits of George V, from its place on the shelf.

It was early summer. Dawn was beginning to lighten the curtains – Eileen's last curtains – and fill the kitchen with grey. This was all as Mr Baxter had planned. To say goodbye to the girls in broad daylight, he had felt, would be too harsh. Sunlight would seize upon tears, making them sparkle shamefully on his cheek. Like this, they could leave unnoticed.

Mr Baxter sat stirring his tea, his eyes imprinted with the familiar pattern of cornflowers on Eileen's last curtains drawn across the window above the sink. He remembered, as he did every day at breakfast, how in her final ailing months Eileen had taken those curtains with her everywhere, as if knowing her time to finish them was limited. Even on picnics on the beach – Mr Baxter always fearing for her warmth and com-

I

fort – she had insisted on hemming them with her arthritic hands. The process of their completion was a slow one, for her stiff and clumsy fingers could scarcely hold a needle. By autumn she was still at them, painfully concentrating as she sat by the evening fire, right up to a few days before she died. She sewed into them the last of her energy, but she had never seen them hung. Mr Baxter had taken that job upon himself as soon as the funeral guests had left – half-eaten bridge rolls and cups of tea all over the place – as the only alternative to the horrible task of clearing up.

As soon as the cornflower curtains were in place, Mr Baxter remembered, he had felt much happier. It was as if Eileen's spirit was fluttering in the room again, reminding him to be cheerful. And indeed, until the sad winding up of the business, he had been cheerful.

He was glad she had not lived to see the demise of the drapery shop. That would have broken her heart. It had been their lives, after all. Fifty-three years. Mr Baxter had started the shop, in this his father's house, in a very modest way: silks and threads, and nice sharp scissors, bone and ivory and tortoiseshell buttons. Business was as good as could be expected in a small village. Then Mr Baxter discovered a recipe for considerable success: any item that a customer required, should it not be already in stock, he would endeavour to supply as soon as possible. Thus the shop expanded far beyond the bounds of mere drapery and haberdashery, and carried such disparate items as canary seed, bundles of kindling, linen dishcloths and blackcurrant throat pastilles. Baxter's became a shop to rely upon, its reputation spread up and down the coast. Soon Mr Baxter realized he could no longer manage entirely on his own, and advertised for help.

Eileen was the first to apply. She came for her interview, one bright afternoon in 1920, tripping through the door with a measure of confidence and expectancy that Mr Baxter recognized immediately. She did not, however, display any traces of boldness or cheekiness – things that would have quickly deterred Mr Baxter. She was very young: not long eighteen, with a bonny face and brown curls that bobbed about her face. Her figure was neat and slim and Mr Baxter noticed with pleasure her highly polished brown shoes, with their

Louis heels and small twin straps, a pattern of holes punched over the toes. Within a few minutes' conversation it was apparent Eileen was full of enthusiasm – a quality Mr Baxter much admired – and he took her on at once.

Eileen filled the shop with a warmth and flurry which made Mr Baxter realize what the place had previously been missing. Along with her enthusiasm, she came bursting with suggestions. Within days she had taken it upon herself to order things appertaining to the more delicate feminine areas in which Mr Baxter admitted he had neither experience nor taste: satin hair ribbons, shell brooches and cards of spare suspenders. From there she took over the buying of the materials. Shelves that had once been stacked with dull worsteds, calicoes and coarse linens now rippled with flowered cottons and handsome lace that Eileen found in local markets. Mr Baxter came to depend on her tastes, her instincts, her constant cheerful presence and when, one afternoon – as she polished the old oak counter – Eileen suggested that life would be much easier if they married, Mr Baxter found himself flared with enthusiasm identical to her own. Soon after their tenth wedding anniversary, celebrated in the rain at Lowestoft, they finally accepted the doctor's word they would have to remain childless, and Eileen suggested the girls.

Mr Baxter finished his tea, rinsed his cup, and told himself he could not afford to postpone the moment any longer. He took the key of the shop from its place under the clock, and opened the door that led from the kitchen.

The girls were as he had left them last night, grouped in a conversation piece in the window. Lily, the oldest, but of eternal youth, stood facing him, her fluid china arm stretched, as it had always stretched over the years, in welcome. Lily's creator had bestowed her with a Mona Lisa smile which Mr Baxter had never fathomed. He had been unable to work out what went on in her mind, though sometimes – and he had never dared mention his suspicions to Eileen, who had always loved Lily best – he felt it might be a tangle of disparaging thoughts, despite the superficial kindness in her pale eyes.

To Lily's right stood Winnie – dear, stupid Winnie, disaster-prone but good-humoured in face of all trouble. Her waxen cheek was burnished with a perpetual blush. In her

3

heyday in the early thirties this had given her a coquettish look which Mr Baxter, and many others, found attractive. But for the past thirty years she had merely looked permanently ashamed, and evoked sympathy. Lily and Winnie were the only ones who still retained their original, flat-waved hair. (From real nuns, Eileen had said.) Joyce, on Lily's right, a product of the unglamorous early forties, had been refurbished by Eileen, some twenty years ago: her original wig had been replaced by one of back-combed chestnut hair. She had taken to it gallantly, but it had never suited her, and Mr Baxter often regretted the old sausage curls that had fitted neatly into the back of her chilly neck.

Joyce's special friend, Maud, stood close to her. Maud was smaller, more brittle-boned than the others. In the mid-fifties she badly chipped her heel which had never quite recovered. Mr Baxter and Eileen had laid her carefully on blankets on the counter and done their best to re-fashion a smooth curve with plaster and glue, but the operation was not wholly successful. Maud had never regained her old uprightness: no matter what the Baxters did she remained fractionally lop-sided to the knowing eye, and Mr Baxter observed a distinct downward curve on her cherry lips that had not been there before the accident.

Deborah was the newest arrival – November 1959, to be precise – and secretly Mr Baxter had never fancied her much, though he believed Eileen when she said Deborah brought a touch of real glamour to the group. Deborah had a mass of stiff blond nylon curls and blood-red nails that had often spiked a customer who brushed too close, causing her to totter perilously for a moment or so, until the customer re-established Deborah's balance on her long, thin legs. And while the other four had closed mouths, in varying degrees of smiling red, Deborah's lips were cheekily half-open, as if in permanent expectation, and revealing two small plastic upper teeth, which lodged on the full lower lip. On the first of every month, before the shop opened, it had been Eileen's habit to clean Deborah's teeth with a soft, dry brush, relieving them of the skin of dust that had formed. But that was one job Mr Baxter had never relished, and he had not been able to bring himself to attend to them more than once since Eileen's death. In the

4

intervening years of neglect, a positive frizz of dust had formed in Deborah's mouth, serving her right for all her sexiness. And yet the sight of it always filled Mr Baxter with a terrible guilt, and sometimes he prayed to his dead wife to forgive him.

'Oh, my girls,' said Mr Baxter.

It had been in his calculations to allow himself just a few silent moments alone with them before transporting them to his van. He laid his hands flat on the familiar surface of the oak counter – still shining as deeply as ever, for it had been his private memorial to Eileen to keep the counter in its accustomed pristine condition – and dragged his eyes from the girls on a weary journey round the shop.

The shelves to the ceiling – also solid oak, built by his father –'were empty now: the closed drawers empty, too. Cleared of its baskets of assorted wools, its piles of woven rugs and boxes of white candles (no salesman had ever managed to persuade Mr Baxter to experiment in a line of those silly fancy candles that cost a fortune and gave no better flame), the floor space seemed much bigger. Mr Baxter fancied for a moment the girls had been dancing there all night, but then he remembered they would have been in no mood for dancing. His eyes were drawn back to the group of them, all in their summer best, dresses that were quite out of fashion now but which Mr Baxter had recovered from the attic last night: dresses that had been Eileen's favourites. Lily herself wore Eileen's honeymoon dress, a navy silk which hung slackly over the hips. Mr Baxter could not help recalling the rustle that dress made when Eileen walked and how, in different lights, its skirt flickered with a dozen blues and silvers. On Lily it was a dead dress, but a reminder.

How pretty the girls looked, Mr Baxter thought, in the dim morning light of his dying shop. A group of fashionable ladies conversing, perhaps, at the races. He found it hard to blame them for their share of responsibility in the collapse of the business. But it was so. After Eileen's death they lost much of their sparkle. Besides which, try as he did, Mr Baxter did not have Eileen's taste. The lemon twinsets and the mournful skirts which he chose the girls to model did not appeal to the customers. Sometimes they remained unsold for months, even years. The storeroom and the shop itself became cluttered

5

with dead stock, and after a while Mr Baxter was obliged to give up altogether the clothing side of the business. And other strong lines dwindled. The fault of this was not Mr Baxter's, but the manufacturers'. Mother-of-pearl buttons were replaced by plastic copies; satin ribbons were only available at a wicked price, and Mr Baxter's old customers spurned the nylon replacements. It was the decline of quality goods he regretted, and deplored the shoddy substitutes. Thinking they would bring down his high standards, in the last year or so Mr Baxter had bought less and less, allowing stocks to run down. New generations of customers found nothing to lure them to his shop, and eventually Mr Baxter had been forced to admit to himself it was time to close down. It was, after all, the age of the decline of the small business. Its future, the country over, was black. Mr Baxter accepted these facts without bitterness. It was only the parting from his girls that caused him any active pain, and there was no way round such a measure. He could not take them with him. There would be no room for them in the small flat he had bought in the nearby town.

'Girls,' said Mr Baxter, 'it's time for your hats.'

Bending over, he took from the shelf under the counter a pile of Eileen's favourites – summer hats to go with the dresses. He carried them over to the group and gently placed one on each unmoving head – fancy concoctions of straw, feathers, ribbons and cherries.

'There,' he said. 'You look splendid. Eileen would have been proud of you.'

He stood back, admiringly, waiting for their replies, which normally jingled in his head. But this morning there was silence. They had nothing to say to Mr Baxter and he did not blame them. What is there to say at the moment of betrayal?

Behind them, the shop window was now silvered with early morning sky, a colour which, as Mr Baxter had learnt from years of such early May mornings, hinted at a fine summer ahead. Well, if it *was* a fine summer, the visitors to the village would be rewarded by the Gift Shop that this place was to become. Within weeks the old oak fittings would have been ripped out and replaced with those silly hessian wall coverings that fade and fray within a year. There would be spotlights,

6

God forbid, piercing the comfortable darkness of the corners. And as for the goods: useless little notebooks with stupid messages on their covers, tins – poor imitations of the real Victorian things – of sweets, of a price that would have made Eileen weak with disbelief, lotions and potions – all packaging, no quality – and egg cups with *legs*. Pha! The decline in standards . . . Mr Baxter passed a hand over his forehead, not liking to think.

'We must go, girls,' he said. 'It's time.'

In his mind, in all his weeks of planning this departure, Mr Baxter had imagined the girls following him in single file to the yard. He was puzzled for a moment when they did not move. Then he allowed himself a smile. Of course. They would have to be carried, one by one. For a moment Mr Baxter resented this dependence of the girls upon him. It would have been so much more dignified if they had left the shop for the last time swinging their dresses, tossing their heads, as they did in his mind's eye. It was an outrage, a terrible liberty for a man to have to lift a girl. But time was running out. Mr Baxter put his arms round Maud's waist. She was very light, a quarter of Eileen's weight. Her sad mouth bruised Mr Baxter's temple and her beautiful hat of organza roses fell over one eye.

'Easy does it,' said Mr Baxter and turned, Maud very awkward in his arms, for the door. Behind him he felt the silent fury – or was it bewilderment or distress? he couldn't be sure – in the eyes of the other four. He forced his clumsy feet to hurry, much put out by this turn of events so different from his imaginings.

A quarter of an hour later the five girls stood in the back of Mr Baxter's small van. They were wedged into secure positions by crates of homemade wine – the last of Eileen's elderberry – at their feet. Mr Baxter had intended they should have nothing but the best at the end, and he had no desire to drink dozens of bottles on his own.

It was by now light enough to see the girls quite clearly. They looked so pretty, no longer worried or afraid. They stared at the *For Sale* sign outside the shop, slashed with its scarlet *Sold* banner: how cruel were estate agents in their boastful dealings. But the girls were smiling. Perhaps they

7

knew their old friend to be right, given no alternative. Perhaps they were looking forward to their final party.

Mr Baxter turned from admiring them, got into the driving seat. There was no one about. He started the engine, quietly. He moved out into the road very gently, not wanting to dislodge his passengers. But once through the village, in a lane unlikely to be troubled by witnesses, he gave a small burst of speed, knowing that the breeze would make the girls' dresses flutter with the life he remembered, and the streamers and feathers on their hats, too, would be dancing.

The cloakroom of the old rectory, a few miles down the coast, was disproportionately large in a house of solid, square rooms with no pretensions of grandeur. But had it not existed, its contents, which represented the outdoor pursuits of its deceased owners, would have been forced to flow into other passages and rooms. As it was, there was plenty of space for Colonel Windrush's fishing rods – a huge collection, by any standard, gathered over the years – to loll in the corners against the stone walls, their spindle necks bent in downward glance at their more squat companions – leather cases of Purdy guns, canvas bags of golf clubs.

The wooden draining board of the old sink was still a-clutter with Mrs Windrush's wicker baskets, in which, in the two inconsolable years of her widowhood, she had gathered flowers with a trembling hand of manic speed. When the cut flowers outnumbered the vases she pushed them into jam jars, saucepans and old chamber pots from the attic, and fed them so little water that a premature death made it necessary for her to start culling all over again. In her husband's lifetime Mrs Windrush had no interest in gardens, and would never deign to pick any of the garish blooms that a young boy from the village chose lovingly from a catalogue, producing a border of colours so vulgar that Mrs Windrush dared not complain lest she should become too offensive in her opinion. No: all she cared about in the days of Bill was that the lawn should be permanently trim, a pleasure to bare feet under the tea table, and the yew hedge should be kept low enough to reveal the marshes beyond it, and the sea.

It was only after her husband's death that Magda Windrush

fled to her shambles of a garden, with the thought in mind that since she could never bring herself to shoot, fish or play golf, gardening would be a token gesture to the outdoor life he loved so much. The very day of the funeral she bought herself a pile of gardening books, and set about their study with a concentration that surprised even herself. Garden tools – which the wretched boy had been requesting for years – were ordered in abundance: implements with shining stainless steel blades and prongs, and smooth wooden handles comforting to the hand. Mrs Windrush dug, hoed, weeded, pruned, planted: the bleakest weather could not keep her from her labours. But she was not rewarded by speed of result, and this caused her much distress. Impatient by nature, she daily inspected plants put in some months back, and cursed them for their slow progress. Indeed, 'blast the hollyhocks' were her dying words when Viola told her, in all truth, they were still only three feet high. She died long before her garden would reach its prime and left behind, in the shape of piles of opened catalogues and books, reminders of what was still to be done.

When Viola opened the cloakroom door, early on the morning of her departure from England, she was at once assaulted by guilt at the sight of these books piled among the baskets on the draining board. For all her good intentions she had done nothing more than prune the Albertines on the south wall: although she did faithfully polish the silver from time to time, which her mother had cared about very much before her father died and affections were switched to things outdoors.

Viola looked about her, as if to seal the imprint of the place on her mind before she left. In the early light the stone flags of the floor were almost colourless, like mushrooms, and crowded with boots and shoes of many sizes. A gathering of bodyless people, Viola thought, and remembered how some of the bodies had been. Above the old black waders rose her father's long legs in mackintosh trousers: his ancient tweed coat and fishing hat with its bluish feather fly stuck in the band. Above his green gumboots, their toes a mosaic of mud from his last stroll over the marshes, she saw his thick plus-fours, and his bright eyes screwed up beneath the shaggy white brows as he scanned the sky for flighting duck. Pitifully small beside her father's gumboots was her mother's favourite

9

gardening wear: fur-lined ankle boots whose zips made a savage scar up their entire body. Their sides still bulged from Mrs Windrush's swollen feet: but there were reminders of more elegant days, too – three small pairs of pale summer sandals, worn for many years before the onslaught of arthritis.

The original owner of the vicarage, Viola often thought, must have been an exceptionally tall man, for the rows of brass hooks round the walls were so high that she had never been able to reach for her coat without tiptoeing. When she was a child her brother Gideon had let her stand on his shoulders to hang things. But since she had been grown up the acquiring of clothes from the hooks had always been a struggle, resulting in many a heap of garments being dropped to the floor.

But the coats, mackintoshes, blazers and anoraks were all in place now, and had not been touched for months. Hanging from tabs at their necks, the garments all drooped in shapes of dead poultry in a fishmonger: dullish things, their previous air of protection or warmth or even smartness – in the case of Mrs Windrush's mulberry tweed – quite gone. Only the Colonel's shooting mac seemed not to have slumped. Its wide shoulders were still hunched in memory of its owner's stoop: its cracked waterproof stuff ready defensively to crackle if touched.

Above these ranks of outdoor garments hung an assortment of hats: and it was the dead hats that kept smiling, Viola thought. Gideon's topper, unworn since his schooldays, was misty with cobwebs: her father's sou'westers gleamed as they always had, while the various golfing and shooting caps were discs of pleasing muted tweed. But it was the straw hats that retained most of their spirit: the Solar Topee that the Colonel brought back from India – where he had read the entire works of Kipling in a week – her mother's lacy sunhats of wheat-coloured straw. She would wear one of them every summer afternoon, no matter what the weather, often forgetting to take it off indoors for dinner. Viola's earliest memories of her mother's beautiful face were framed by a straw brim which threw a cobweb shadow across her pale skin. The favourite of these hats had a garland of imitation cornflowers round the brim. Their blue had not faded. Viola, looking at the hat now, remembered it so well: on how many occasions had her mother sat upright at the tea table, covered with its white cloth of drawn thread, in a cornflower blue silk shirt to match the hat's flowers, her thin arms pricked with gooseflesh, for she scorned the covering of a cardigan no matter how cool the breeze. Mrs Windrush was always bluer, brighter than the sky, which in this part of England absorbed so much grey from the sea that even on the brightest day the grey outshone the striving blue.

Viola shivered. It was quite cold. It was always cool in the house, even in the hottest summer. The flagstone floors and thick walls were impenetrable by the fiercest sun. Coming in on a very hot day, the house could be relied on to give relief. But there were always warm patches, if you knew where to find them. On spring mornings in the library the sun would fall through the windows making a fretwork on the rug that stretched as far as the Colonel's desk. As a child, Viola remembered, she would run barefoot through the patchwork of warmth, feeling it very briefly on her legs, then dash into the complete cool of the shaded part of the room by the fireplace. It was like swimming in and out of warm patches of sea: sometimes she would pretend she was in fact swimming, and make movements with her arms. But this private game was quite silent. She did not disturb her father, who kept his head bent over his desk as, unwillingly, he went through his papers.

For a moment Viola contemplated going to the library to see if the sun was on the carpet. But she knew it was several hours too early. Besides, the library distressed her, now that her father's desk was so empty and tidy that for the first time in her life she could see the Moroccan leather blotter – his wedding present from his wife. The trouble was, there were still hours to go until the taxi arrived to take her to the station, and there was nothing left to do. Her cases were packed, her sheets folded and in the laundry box at the back door, the food – except for a single egg for her breakfast – all eaten. Having got up far too early after a sleepless night, she was in no mood to read, or to wander through the empty house only to be nagged at by memories. So she had decided to go out.

With a gesture of great determination Viola reached up for her father's old mackintosh. She had been meaning to do this for ages, knowing that the longer her parents' things were left untouched the harder it would eventually be to get rid of them.

11

As she lifted it down, it creaked in her hands and smelt sourly of salt dried on plastic. Such distaste overcame her that she was tempted to put it back, postponing once again the disagreeable moment. But she fought her own battle, and won. She put on the mackintosh and, avoiding the sight of herself in the speckled mirror, jumped up to reach for her father's favourite fishing hat. It smelt of distant hair grease. Viola rammed it on her head. Then she looked at the floor to make her selection of footwear. She could not bear her mother's zipped boots that aped, so cruelly, the latterly deformed feet. She turned from them, and settled for a pair of Gideon's old gymshoes.

Thus dressed, Viola left the cloakroom and hurried across the lawn – over whose long grass her mother would have despaired – to the gate in the hedge that led to the marshes. There, she felt happier as the familiar squelch beneath her feet broke the silence and a single bird – a lark, was it? – was swooping and singing above her. It was light now, flat whitish sky showing an economy of cloud on the horizon, behind which the sun was rising. The tide was far out, leaving the beach vast and empty. But if Viola cocked her head, leaving her ear free of the noisy plastic collar, she could hear the merest whimper from the sea.

On this walk, she determined, she would go through once again in her mind the long list of reasons for not selling the house, which she would put to her brother in New York. It had been a democratic gesture, on her father's part, to leave the place jointly between them, and while Mrs Windrush was still alive there were no disputes. Now, it was different. Gideon had been in New York for a year, doing very well in Wall Street, and had no intention of returning to England for some time. When he did come home, he would be living in London, not Norfolk. To Gideon, the solution was obvious: sell the house and they would share the money. Viola, at almost thirty, could buy somewhere of her own. The alternative was helplessly to watch it fall into disrepair, unable to afford new slates for the roof or anything else that needed expensive attention. Viola saw the sense of these arguments, and agreed she herself could not hope to earn a living based in so faraway a place. Besides which, a house once so full of noisy, happy people, now empty, would be conducive to melancholy. So Gideon was right. And yet ... Viola was going to argue against him.

But try as she did the list of good reasons for keeping the place evaded her this morning. As she walked on the firm wet beach the entire compass of her eyes was filled with the soft translucent light. Feeling the ribs of sand beneath her feet she remembered that as a child she had imagined they were the imprints of the bodies of underwater monsters who liked to lie on the sea-bed when the tide was high, unseen. She had often wondered if she might one day see the monsters, woken from their sleep by the pull of an outgoing tide, scurrying after it in fright. But her father, who was so often up early duck-shooting, had never mentioned any such sight, and she had not liked to ask.

Viola made her way towards the wreck, whose jagged black outlines were the only harsh thing in view. It was a large ship, destroyed in the last war. Viola had remained uncurious about the details of the event, and had never discovered what exactly had happened. She had heard all the passengers were saved, but no one had bothered to claim it for salvage. Although at high tide only small prongs of the ship were visible, like a broken fence, when the sea was out it made a huge and ugly hulk on a ridge of slightly raised sand. Viola had never been very near it and had never felt the slightest desire to examine it closely. Gideon, as a child, had swum out to it numberless times and enjoyed diving through its glassless portholes with his friends: the competition was to see who could get through the smallest porthole. And when his gang wanted to get away from girls, it was to the wreck they went at low tide, to smoke their illicit cigarettes, quite sure Viola and her friends would never follow.

Viola knew her fear of the wreck to be childish: she knew that barnacles and slimy planks and even skeletons – should there be any of those left at the Captain's table – were all harmless, but nonetheless a nameless distaste, a real horror, seized her whenever she made a private attempt to go near to the old ship. But this morning, now surprisingly at ease in her father's mackintosh and shooting hat, fear was a distant thing, and she thought it worth trying once again for her private satisfaction.

13

Thus resolved, she stopped for a moment, and turned back to look at the distance she had come. It was quite a way. The familiar line of the village roofs and chimneys was indistinct in a thin mist that trailed across them, echoed vertically in two thin spires of smoke. Viola could just make out their own roof: from this distance the illusion was that it almost touched the church tower. She could see the smudged shapes of the copper beech and the horse chestnut in the garden, then came the swirls of marsh divided from the beach by a barricade of reeds. It was a water colourist's view: everything fluid, barely defined, insubstantial. Lowering her eyes to the sand, Viola then saw the tyre marks – parallel to the path she had been walking and aiming for the sea. She looked about her, puzzled. There was no sign of either man or vehicle on the beach.

She turned once more to the wreck. She reckoned it was not more than half a mile away: the nearest, she calculated, she had ever been. With firm step she continued on her way. She looked for more tyre tracks but could see none, and felt relieved.

Some moments later Viola stopped again. She had discovered the best way to keep herself going was to concentrate on her feet. To see the wreck looming larger with every step would have intimidated, made the journey harder. But now, instinctively, she stopped and looked up with a great effort of will. She was surprised by her proximity to the ship. She could see, which she had never seen before, ragged fringes of seaweed flapping from its sides. She could see the blackness of its gaping portholes, eyeless sockets, staring. Her heart began to race uncomfortably, and she clenched her hands in her father's pockets. It was quite a while before she could bring herself to move again, and when she did it was sideways rather than forward.

She was now not far from the sea and could hear its snarling more clearly, although the sound scarcely interrupted the huge silence. But suddenly there was a piercing squawk, and two seagulls rose from an invisible part of the wreck. The fright they gave Viola made her smile to herself, aware of her own foolishness. But all the same, her heart still beat very fast.

Stopped by the gulls, she once again willed herself to go on. Icy sweat needled down her spine, and her knees were shaking.

But inwardly she laughed herself to scorn, determined now, having got this far, to get into the *shadow* of the monster . . . even to stretch out a hand and touch its vile bark.

Viola took three uneasy paces, then clamped a wild hand over her mouth to stifle a scream. Unless she was mad, she could see, half hidden by the bows, a *naked bent arm*. When she dared to look again, a little higher, she saw half the back of a straw hat, almost identical to the hats in the cloakroom at home, from which fluttered two pink ribbon streamers.

As she felt her eyes flatten against their sockets in disbelief, Viola hoped the whirling wheel of her brain would stop at some solution. There were *people* at the wreck. They were not dead sailors, were not ghosts. They were solid figures. Who were they?

When she had recovered herself enough to step cautiously sideways once again, all was then revealed. Simply: a picnic was taking place. An early morning picnic. She was the intruder. Before turning away, hoping not to be seen, she regarded the picnickers curiously for a moment, still afraid.

It seemed a strange time of the morning for a girls' outing – which it seemed to be, for Viola could discern no men. She counted five women in summery dresses that flapped in the breeze, and all but one wore pretty hats. The bare-headed lady – her hat had flown to rest some yards away – was propped up in an uncomfortable sitting position, leaning against the dark bows of the ship. Her companion seemed to be lying down, her skirts raised over her knees. The arm Viola had first seen belonged to the tallest lady, who had her back to Viola: the other two stood opposite each other, their heels strangely dug into the sand, so that they leaned slightly backwards. There was a rug on the ground, and an open hamper. Several bottles of wine and glasses were placed on the rug between the lady who sat and the lady who lay. There was something very intense about their attitude: a silent kind of enjoyment, and there was no sound of laughter or of voices.

Viola never knew how long it was she took to realize that this was no ordinary picnic. It was only when she grew conscious of the fact that the sitting-down lady, who wore a dark gleaming dress, was staring at her, completely unmoving, that she knew she had entered upon something more horrible than she could ever have envisaged. They were dead sailors' wives she was looking at, come together for some motionless celebration, or memorial. Their limbs, their heads, remained quite, quite still. Only their skirts and floppy hats were rustled by the breeze. They stared, and behind them the tide was coming in very fast.

Viola screamed. She thought later it might have been a warning. At the time it was the only way to release her terror. Then she turned from the grotesque sight and began to run back across the miles of empty beach, throwing off her father's mackintosh as she went so that she could run faster. As she flung it across the sand the thought of its being swept away by the next tide brought tears stinging to her eyes, but she knew there was no possibility of going back.

2

Harry Antlers, pressed daily into an early rising by an abundance of nervous energy, stood in the hotel bathroom shaving. He hated this forced examination of his reflection every morning. Neither his individual features nor the overall impression of his head gave any encouragement in the hopes that he could be considered even slightly handsome. Harry was cursed by outstanding ugliness. As a child, he had thought this state was a phase that would pass. He lived in hope, scrutinizing daily the unkind assembly of features, searching for improvement. But he was never rewarded. The only changes were for the worse. And unfortunately for Harry, the unfair moulding of his countenance was not made up for by a fine and manly body. Harry was not a large man, nor finely made. He was narrow shouldered, a little stooping: a womanly back view. The legs were badly bred, bandy from the thighs down and flaring into thick, square ankles. Well cut trousers could have gone some way to disguising this ungainly shape, but Harry was a man of no taste in clothes, and remained unconscious of the fact that his ill-fitting nylon garments enhanced the unattractiveness of his body.

But for all that he had against him physically, except at shaving time Harry was not unduly depressed by his appearance. He had learned that women's tastes in men were perverse. They were completely indiscriminate – judging from his many conquests – in the matter of physical appearance. Apparently almost any man was better than no man. And provided the male specimen was just a little famous, could provide money, an air (at least) of power and some show of romantic treatment, then girls, even beautiful ones, were his for the asking. Only last night, he had proved this once again. At a cocktail party in the Plaza he had met a fluttery young thing called Susie. She had dyed blonde hair and huge eyes whose lids trembled with well-rehearsed interest in others. On hearing that Harry was in the theatre she declared that her life's ambition was to act: she would get there one day, but meantime was working for an airline.

'You're a very lovely lady,' Harry said. 'Why don't I buy you dinner and we can discuss your career?'

By his reminder that the pleasure of dinner had to be paid for, Harry left Susie in no doubt of her obligations. They ate seafood in Greenwich Village, having held hands all the way there in the taxi, and within half an hour Harry was so profoundly bored by this lovely lady's attempts at communication that he could scarcely bring himself to describe his reasons for being in New York. She was predictably impressed: her half exposed bosom quickened its anticipatory rising and falling.

'You're a very, very special man, Harry, you know that?' she said, as he paid the bill.

But the attraction was not mutual, and Harry had to be up early. He saw her home, refused to come in, but promised to call. He knew he would do no such thing. Susie, like all the rest, was not what he was looking for.

Harry carefully wiped the last of the shaving cream from his cheeks. He rinsed them with a cold wet flannel. The slapping noise echoed sullenly in his head, as it always did, reminding him of the constant thwacks of his childhood, the vicious noises that leaked through the thin walls of the bungalow telling of his father's daily anger with his mother, and the beatings she endured. One day he would meet a girl who would listen to stories of his childhood, and soothe away the memories. In the meantime, the screams, the thumps, the brutal silences and joyless meals lodged darkly in his mind, stirred – much less frequently these days – only by the dabbing of his own cheeks each morning.

He patted them dry, now, leaving the skin dull and colourless, dark shadows under the eyes. Then he brushed his hair: that, at least, was something to be proud of. It always gleamed, Harry Antlers' hair. He could not remember how many girls had run admiring fingers through it, exclaiming at its fineness. The other thing they admired was his name, and there Harry was bound to agree with them. It had a resounding clash. It evoked images of noble beasts, fighting. It was a distinguished name, a name that people remembered. *Antlers*. It was the only thing for which he could be the slightest bit grateful to his father.

Harry swung into the bedroom, impatient to be getting on with the day. He dropped on to the unmade bed and picked up the telephone all in one movement. Irritation pricked his skin, making him physically uncomfortable.

'Where's my breakfast, for Christ's sake? I ordered it half an hour ago.'

'Sorry, sir. I'll put you through – '

'Don't put me through anywhere. Just tell them to hurry up. And where's my post?'

'Post?'

'*Mail*. You know I like it sent up as soon as it arrives. I've told you a hundred times I like it – '

'One moment, sir.' Pause. 'There's no mail for you this morning, Mr Antlers.'

'*Nothing*?' Harry heard his voice turn into a whimper of incredulity. It was always a bad day, the day that started with no letters, albeit of the dullest kind. Wherever he was in the world Harry arranged that letters would follow him. They gave him a sense of being planted rather than temporarily placed. Also, a sense of importance. Without constant correspondents seeking to be in touch with him, Harry was a more easily angered man. He slammed down the telephone receiver, switched on the radio. He was always anxious to catch at least four news bulletins a day: not so much because he had an avid interest in world affairs, but because they gave a rhythm to the day. He lay back, briefly relaxed, listening to the droning American voice, and sensed a sudden nostalgia for the Britishness of the BBC's eight o'clock news. He wondered when he would be returning home.

An hour later, Harry walked down Sixth Avenue, script beneath his arm. He liked New York. He liked its speed, its punch, its lottery of fame and failure, its glinting soaring buildings of menacing glass. But the gentle sun of an early summer morning, the soft air as yet unpolluted by the day, were lost on him. He was not a man who noticed the benefits of nature, or cared for them. His chosen earth was covered with pavements, he cared not a damn for trees or unpeopled landscapes. The restlessness of cities reflected the restlessness

19

of his own blood and spurred him, occasionally, to something near contentment. And within cities his preferred places were indoors: underground theatres, small dark rooms, stuffy offices lit with neon – places that daylight could not penetrate. Sometimes he reflected that he would like all seasons but winter to be abandoned. If the sky had to show itself, it should be a dour grey sky. Only a moonlike sun, less cruel to the ugly, should be allowed. Spring, with all its vulgar promotion of newborn things, should be abolished. For many years Harry had planned his life so that he should avoid the headache-making greens of April and May. It was with gratitude, now, that the screaming yellow metal of taxi-cabs streamed past his eyes. Manmade colours held no horrors for him. Concrete soothed his nerves.

Harry stopped at a drugstore. Whenever possible, he was a two-breakfast man. His over-active adrenalin glands caused him constant hunger, and here in America his appetites were wonderfully satisfied by a diet of waffles, maple syrup and ice cream sodas.

He looked through the window, wondering whether there was time for griddle cakes and bacon. One hand on his paunch, he glanced idly at the breakfasters on their high stools – people in a hurry, eating with one hand, reading the paper with another. Office folk, there for sustenance rather than pleasure. Harry, if there was time, would eat for pleasure rather than sustenance.

About to enter the drugstore – to hell with being overweight – Harry caught sight of a girl at the far end of the counter. She, like most of the other eaters, was reading. But not for her a newspaper or magazine. The book she held, Harry could see from the cover, was Jane Austen's *Emma*. As Jane Austen was hardly a best-selling author among commuting breakfasters on Sixth Avenue, this seemed to be an unusual sight. Harry found himself looking more closely at the reader. He could not see much of her face, for a mass of corn-coloured hair fell over it. She wore a navy sweater, and jeans. Nothing in the least remarkable. And yet there was something very attractive – touching, almost – about her air of concentration. She was apparently oblivious of the noise and surroundings, totally immersed in a very different world. To escape? Harry wondered, and found himself betting his last dollar she was English. Had there been time, he would have gone and sat on the empty stool next to her and asked a few questions. He was often successful in such approaches. But there was no time. He was late already. Harry walked on, thinking suddenly of Mr Knightley. Of all fictional heroes he had always considered Mr Knightley the finest, the one with whom he would most like to be confused.

A couple of hours later Harry sat in the third row of the stalls of a small and dingy off-Broadway theatre. On the seat beside him were three empty cups of coffee and a couple of half-eaten doughnuts, which had in some part made up for the missed second breakfast. So far, he had seen eight girls: eight girls desperate for the part of Laurie, heroine of *Begone*, the play he was directing by way of a personal favour for an old producer friend, a long-time admirer of Harry's work. Laurie was a good part. The girl was on stage throughout the play. Whoever got it, should the play have any success – and Harry had no doubts about that – would make her name. No wonder they were all so nervous. But had there been any real talent, Harry would have seen it at once beneath the nerves. As it was, the right girl had not yet come forward. As the next candidate came on to the empty stage, Harry sighed. His belt was too tight, his legs ached from being in the same position so long. Miss Haley Bead, the name on the list, a short and stocky girl with a definite moustache, was not going to be any good. He could tell that at a glance. But she had to be given a chance.

Harry stood up. His benign mood of an hour ago, induced by the doughnuts, was beginning to wear off. Haley Bead came to the front of the stage, frowning against the two spotlights.

'Haley Bead, Mr Antlers,' she said.

'Hello, Haley Bead.' Harry tried to sound gentle. But judging from the way the girl winced, there must have been something gruff or unwelcoming in his voice. He tapped the open script he held in his hand. 'Now as you know, Haley Bead, this is the scene where Laurie tells her mother she's going off to live in Ohio with a truck driver.'

'Yes, Mr Antlers.'

'Good. I'm glad you understand that.'

'Oh, I do.'

'Excellent. Now, the mother is sitting there, on that chair.' He pointed to the only prop on the stage. 'See? The mother's a tiresome old cow but she loves her daughter. Laurie has a lot of good reasons for going . . .'

It was the ninth time Harry had said all this and he felt the tediousness of repetition drag in his stomach. 'Right. Let's see what you can do.'

Harry sat down. He regretted not sending Chris Heep, his assistant, out for another doughnut to keep him going through Ms. Haley Bead's performance. Chris Heep was at this moment retying his gym shoes, an act which occupied a large amount of each day, slumped in a seat two away from Harry. The familiar sight was enraging.

'For Christ's sake, Christopher Heep, concentrate,' snapped Harry.

The girl on the stage looked startled. She took a moment or two to recover herself, clenching her hefty fists, and taking a deep, audible sigh. She turned to the empty chair on which sat her invisible mother. She stared ferociously into the space as if confronting Banquo's ghost rather than a middle-aged woman from Brooklyn. Swallowing, she braced herself for the announcement. The familiar words grated in silence of the small theatre.

Laurie: I'm going, mother. I am, you know. I'm really going this time. I've had it up to here.

Haley Bead's large hand swiped across her neck in a gesture of self-execution. Her eyes never moved.

Laurie: It's no use you looking like that, mother. You don't understand. You've never understood. You've caged me all my life, telling me what to be, how to be, and now I've a chance to go and find out for myself who I really am, and you throw a *fit*.

To emphasize the word, Haley Bead, who had less talent than all the others put together, bent one knee. Harry, who had always found something faintly uneasy-making about these words, thought them particularly embarrassing as

22

spoken by the present candidate. He tapped Chris on the knee, signed that she should be cut off.

'Better let her go on down to the end of the page,' whispered the languorous Chris, whose sense of fairness was the only thing keener than Harry's.

Harry leaned back, thumbs lodged in his belt, and shut his eyes. He had envisaged Laurie as a frail blonde, steeliness beneath her frailty, and all he had seen this morning were butch, liberated girls who equated independence with aggressive unattractiveness. And Haley Bead's rendering of Laurie's anguish was the greatest mockery yet. The girl had so little observation she would not get a job picking up rubbish in Central Park. Aggrieved, Harry let her drone on to the end of the page. Then he jumped up, punching the air, cutting her off.

'Enough, enough. Thanks. I see what you're getting at.' He tried to be decent. 'Very interesting.'

The girl blinked, extricating herself from the misinterpreted skin of Laurie. She was confused by the rude shock.

'You don't want me to finish, Mr Antlers? I was just – '

'No thanks. I don't need to see any more. You'll be hearing from us.' He tried to smile. 'And now, it's goodbye Haley Bead.'

'Very well.' Crushed, the girl left the stage. Harry turned to Chris.

'And now, *we* break for lunch.'

At the most annoying times, Chris Heep could be quite firm. He flipped one of his long legs over the seat in front of him.

'No, we don't. It's only twelve-thirty. We can fit in one more. Otherwise we'll be here all night.'

'Shit,' said Harry, sitting down again.

'Next,' Chris called.

The girl with the corn-coloured hair, the reader of *Emma*, walked on to the stage. Harry looked at his list. Viola Windrush. A note said she had had a couple of small parts in plays for BBC Television, and a summer season at the Salisbury Playhouse. So he was right about her nationality.

When Harry looked up again Viola Windrush was sitting on the empty chair.

23

'That's the mother's chair, not Laurie's,' he roared. Viola turned to him.

'I was merely waiting for instructions,' she said.

Harry scratched his ear. It was the first English voice he had heard for weeks, and a very sweet one. Totally useless for playing Laurie from Brooklyn.

'What the hell are they doing sending you to audition for this part? They might have known a nice English girl like you would be the last thing I want.'

'God knows,' said Viola, with a small smile. 'I made the same point myself. But they said I might as well try.' She remained on the chair, hands folded in her lap, unmoving.

'Well, I suppose you might as well, now you're here.'

A small rise of Viola's shoulders indicated a stifled sigh.

'If you like,' she said, looking at him, 'I could save your time by not going through with it. To be honest, I should hate to get the part, even if I was suitable. I think it's a terrible play.'

Viola, who was by nature a placid creature not inclined to provoking scenes, was amazed by her own forthrightness. She had heard of Harry Antlers, of course. In the theatre he was known as a brilliant bully. Working with him was reputed to be exciting in some respects, but full of hazards due to his irrational responses. If an actor was able to stand up to the Antlers' form of treacherous behaviour, then an exceptional performance was sometimes achieved. He had his loyal followers and fans: there were those who claimed there was a kind and touching side to him. But for the most part, actors and producers who had worked for him once would never deign to do so again. He was taken on by new people confident they could handle him – only to join the ranks of those who could not. Actors who did not know him met him with a mixture of dread and hope: fear that he would use his usual bullying tactics in front of the whole company, but hope that he might use his rare magic to inspire a great performance. Viola, for her part, had felt a natural apprehension about the audition, but as she positively did not want the part of Laurie she knew she risked nothing by being honest. What mattered greatly to her was that she should not become yet another of Harry Antler's crushed victims.

Her impudence – Harry did not give himself time to think of her gesture as one of consideration – immediately angered Harry.

'Right,' he shouted, standing again. 'Right, right, right. Thank you very much for your opinion, Miss Windrush. Very grateful for it. Delighted you're not going to waste my time.'

Under the spotlights Viola was frowning, unnerved by his anger. She wished she had not been so foolish as to agree to come for the audition. Chris heaved himself to his feet, confident some sort of scene was about to take place which he had no desire to witness, or to be called upon later to give evidence.

'I'm off to a movie, back at two,' he said, and hurried away. His heart was not in the theatre, but in Hollywood. Even working, reluctantly, for Harry Antlers, he managed to see three or four films a day.

Harry and Viola remained alone in the theatre. Viola stayed in her place, unmoving on the chair. Her stillness, her calm in face of his fury, enraged Harry further.

'Well, come on down from the stage. Or are you going to stay there thinking things over all through the lunch hour?'

Harry's tone, despite himself, was less harsh. Viola stood up, moved to the steps that led down into the small auditorium. She stopped a few paces away from him. She was much shorter than Harry.

'No,' she said, 'I'm going.' Away from the spotlights, her hair was dimmer, an unburnished mass that foamed about her pale face. She had very dark eyes, but Harry could see that they were not brown. They seemed to be navy. The first navy eyes he could remember seeing.

'Right,' he said again, and felt an annoying pulse begin to beat in his temple. 'But if you change your mind I daresay we could still fit you in somehow this afternoon. It'll only be *mildly* inconvenient.'

'I'm not changing my mind, thank you.'

'Would you like something to eat?' This was not a pre-meditated question. It came without thought, surprising Harry himself. Viola shrugged.

'All right. If you like.'

Harry looked at his watch. An hour and ten minutes till he had to be back for the afternoon session. He had intended to go across the road to an excellent hamburger bar where he could seek comfort in a couple of jumbo burgers and a thick malted milk shake. But with this sudden turn of events his appetite suddenly fled. He could not bear the thought of such food eaten in upright discomfort, and quickly calculated how long it would take a taxi to get to his favourite restaurant on Third Avenue.

'We'll have to hurry,' he said. 'There'll be just time for you to give me a few of your interesting opinions on the play.'

Outside, the sun was aggressively bright. Warm. Sweat dampened Harry's armpits in instant reaction. In the blessed shade of the cab he was aware that he smelled quite pungently. Viola screwed up her nose, turning her head away, looking at the cross-town shops. Neither spoke.

In the crowded Italian restaurant, they had to wait ten minutes for a table. Harry sweated harder. He would have liked to have walked out to express his indignation at the outrageousness of keeping so regular a customer waiting. But there was no time to go elsewhere. He pouted, frowned, tapped his paunch with impatient fingers. Viola kept on looking away, as if she had nothing to do with him.

At last they were seated in a small corner table. Harry ordered himself a fillet steak with French fries, without looking at the menu.

'I always have the same,' he said. It sounded like a boast. He then suggested a whole list of American cocktails Viola might like: she politely rejected them all and asked for mineral water with her plain grilled fish. Her skin was the colour of moonstones.

'So what have you got against the play?'

'Almost everything.'

'And what makes you think you're any kind of judge?'

Viola shrugged. 'I don't ask anyone to consider my opinion. But I read a lot of plays, for pleasure, and because I'd like to write one myself one day. Reading so much, it gets easier to detect a false note, a hollow core, or just plain bad writing.'

'Ha ha! So we have here a budding writer,' Harry sneered. 'A budding writer as well as a budding actress. A multi-talented lady, indeed.'

Viola smiled slightly, ignoring his sarcasm.

'Oh, I'm not really a budding actress. I used to think I'd like to be one and I was lucky enough through *devious* means' – she smiled again – 'to get one or two parts in England. But I didn't enjoy it. And I wasn't much good. So I've returned to the original desire of writing – one day.'

'Connections,' Harry snapped, his mind still on the earlier part of her explanation, which infuriated him. 'If there's one thing I really hate, it's people who not only *have* connections, but use them.'

Viola took a sip of water. When she put it down a thin line of silvery bubbles made a jewelled moustache on her curly top lip. She blushed, her pale cheeks briefly colouring.

'Do you?' she said. 'That must cause you a lot of discomfort much of the time.'

Having prepared himself for an invigorating argument, Harry found himself mellowed by the first mouthfuls of steak and chips. He saw no point in pursuing this particular course and asked why she was in New York. He was rewarded with no more than a cursory explanation: her agent had arranged the audition, but the real reason was to talk to her brother about the future of a house they jointly owned. The very idea of such a problem annoyed Harry. He could feel irritation, a physical thing, spiking up through the cushion of food that lay heavily in his stomach.

'Ah,' he exclaimed. 'You're obviously from the privileged classes.' His voice was bright with resentment. Viola flinched. 'Well, I have no such fortune – or misfortune, whichever you like to call it. I come from a very ordinary background.'

'Ordinary backgrounds are such good excuses, aren't they?' said Viola, quietly. Harry chose to ignore this remark.

'Believe it or not, until three years ago I had never seen an avocado pear.'

Viola sighed. She tried to contain a smile. To take such chips on the shoulder seriously would be insulting to their owner.

'If that sort of revelation is designed to make me feel uncomfortable,' she said quietly, 'I'm afraid it hasn't succeeded.'

Harry said nothing. They only had five minutes for coffee, and so far things had not gone well. He had failed to intimidate this cool, arrogant young English girl, and he was unused to

27

such failures. He ordered coffee, made a great effort to quell the turbulence of feelings that clashed within him.

'Why don't you give me your address and telephone number?' he said at length.

'Whatever for? Why would you want to get hold of me? Besides, I shall be going home in a few days.'

Harry thought quickly.

'You're not entirely wrong about the play,' he said. 'I have to believe in it if I'm directing it. But there are some weaknesses, I have to admit. Perhaps you could . . . give a hand with a bit of rewriting.' He knew he had played skilfully upon Viola's vanity, and was rewarded with an encouraging smile.

'I could try,' she said, and gave Harry the address of her brother' apartment.

In the taxi he said:

'Are you going anywhere special? Because if you're not doing anything I'd be very grateful if you'd sit in on the rest of the auditions this afternoon. I'd like your opinion.'

Viola's eyebrows rose under her hair.

'Very well. But I'm no judge of an actress, really. It'd be interesting, though.'

'Thanks,' said Harry, with his most charming smile.

Back in the theatre, stuffy and airless in the afternoon heat, Viola refused to sit with Harry next to Chris in the front row. Instead she took a place at the back, a little guilty at having agreed to this privilege. She enjoyed watching the actresses do their best with Laurie's clumsy speech, and wondered why Harry made so little effort to put each one of them at her ease. Mid-afternoon, a girl from California appeared on the stage. She seemed without doubt to be the best. Viola wondered if Harry would agree. She wrote the actress's name on the back of her cheque book, and began to think how she could improve Laurie's part by some rewriting. It would be exciting to be given the chance. A modest beginning, but a beginning. At five o'clock – the hours had passed uncommonly fast – Viola remembered she had promised her brother she would be back early for an uninterrupted talk before his girl-friend came home. She left the theatre unnoticed.

Harry, too, was surprised by the enjoyment of the afternoon. The fact that Viola sat silently ten rows behind him caused a

28

peculiar sense of well-being he had no time to define. Without articulating the idea very clearly to himself, he imagined discussing the afternoon's candidates with her over a drink . . . perhaps dinner. In the girl from California he reckoned he had found as near a perfect Laurie as he could get, and wondered whether Viola would agree. At six, when the last girl had gone, he turned to the back of the auditorium, full of pleasurable anticipation. At first, seeing Viola had gone, he was unable to believe his eyes. He stood quite still, fingers rubbing against the bristly stuff of the seat in front of him, rage piling within. Like everyone else he had the misfortune to meet, she was a traitor. She had betrayed him – accepted his proposal happily enough, only to betray him.

'*The bitch*!' he shouted out loud, startling the sleepy Chris. 'She'll pay for this.'

He marched up the aisle to the door, to the dreaded gold light of early evening, his head flaming with plans for revenge. Outside, he hailed a cab and ordered it to drive to the nearest McDonalds. He needed several hamburgers and a thickly malted milkshake before he would be in any condition to fight for calm and give himself a chance to think.

An hour later Harry entered the dusky lobby of his hotel a placid man. The rage and disappointment of so short a time ago had ebbed away, to be replaced by an irrational optimism, a quiet acceptance of some kind of unclear but possible happiness. Such feelings in Harry were rare, and to be made the most of: he smiled extravagantly at the man behind the reception desk, who handed him a letter. A girl's writing, and sent round by hand. Thinking it could only be an instant apology from Viola for her untimely disappearance – hell, the girl needn't have apologized, he had judged her too harshly – he handed the man two dollars, murmuring 'Get yourself a huge drink, George.' (It was one of his habits to call members of the hotel staff by their Christian names, to show he was at one with them, on their side, understood their ordinary lives.) George, whose actual name was Jack, smiled gratefully.

In the dusk of his room – Harry liked shutters always to be closed – he slit open the letter with shaking fingers. At a glance, the handwriting was not that of an educated English girl.

29

He read:

Dear Harry, this is to thank you for a truly wonderful evening last night. I find it hard to put into words what I felt when I woke up this morning. It was that something really good, and unusual, had gone on between us, and I wondered if you felt like that, dearest Harry, too? It isn't often that one meets a real soulmate and such chances shouldn't be missed. I know you're a very popular man and probably have hundreds of girls at your beck and call, and perhaps only think of me as yet another blonde. But I am a blonde who really cares for you — yes, even in so short a time. I know I would like to do all sorts of things for you, like cook your breakfast and clean your windows and mend your socks. You make me feel wonderfully unliberated, which is a great relief these days. I have thought of you all day and am keeping my fingers crossed you will call me tonight and we can go on from where we left off. With great affection, and with love, Harry — Susie.

Harry owned a suitcase in which he kept all such letters and photographs of their writers. It privately entertained and comforted him to think he had so valuable a store of evidence of the love and admiration he inspired in a multitude of heterogeneous women. Sometimes he ruffled through the letters, picking them up and letting them fall over his head like overgrown confetti. Sometimes he re-read them, laughing out loud at their incompetent phrasing, the clichés they employed to try to express the passion they felt. None of them had ever been rewarded with an answer that indicated requited feelings. Harry did not write love letters. He did not love. He had never loved, though sometimes he had imagined it was a state, like a tropical storm, that might blast him one day.

Susie's letter, had Harry been in a less impatient frame of mind, would have been filed to take back to England and added to the store. As it was, he screwed it up and threw it across the room into the wastepaper basket. Clean his windows, indeed. What made her suppose he owned any windows to clean? And why *hadn't* Viola sent an apology?

Harry was uncertain what to do with his evening. He had tickets for a Broadway musical. Chris had invited him to see a film. Neither idea appealed. For some weeks, after his arrival in New York, which had been noted in a small paragraph in a gossip column, he had received many invitations from hospitable Americans. His name was still well-known, even outside theatrical circles: fame had come upon him in his early twenties with a play called *Host of Lies*. Harry had met the author, an undergraduate, in a pub. Secretly sympathetic to the subject, and recognizing an original talent in the writer, he had agreed to direct the play. It was put on at the Edinburgh Festival, where overnight it became the star show of the Fringe. Later, transferred to London, it received ecstatic reviews and ran for two years. To Harry's further amazement it then went to New York, where it had a short but successful run off-Broadway. Thus Harry's reputation was made on both sides of the Atlantic.

And the two years of the play's life had been happy ones. Harry enjoyed the fame, the recognition, the being in demand both professionally and by ambitious girls. He enjoyed the sudden money, too, though he spent little on himself. It did not occur to him to leave his unsalubrious flat, or get himself a powerful car. His pleasure was to buy a larger bungalow for his parents and realize his sister's ambition by setting her up in a shoe shop in Dibden Purlieu. The rest he spent on food, travel and flowers for the extraordinary number of beautiful girls to whom he had suddenly become desirable.

But those heydays were many years ago. Since then he had been in fairly constant demand – diminishing, of late – to direct both for the stage and minor feature films. But there had been no success similar to that first play. Harry was still known as the man who had discovered and directed *Lies*, a reputation which no longer gave him any joy – only reminded him just how long ago that single triumph had been.

'Harry Antlers, director of the controversial *Host of Lies* in the seventies, is back with a new play,' the story had run. But the novelty of English visitors of fading fame wears off quickly. A stay of more than a few weeks ensures a decline in popularity and Harry had been here for two months. Invitations were no longer forthcoming. He was reduced to engendering his own fun, or spending his evenings alone. This evening, if he could not be with Viola, Harry wished to be alone. But he was plagued by restlessness, and had no desire to sit in his airless

31

room watching television. And so when he was sure the sun had gone down behind the skyscrapers, leaving the streets in merciful shadow, he left the hotel, heading for Third Avenue. He walked slowly at first, enjoying a small breeze that had cleared the heat of the day. Then, from nowhere, an idea came to him. Spurred by the excitement of this idea, he doubled his pace, twisting skilfully in and out of the people who, unfired by love, moved more slowly on the crowded pavements.

On the few occasions in her life that Viola had been forced to spend Friday nights in a city, she had felt strangely depressed. As one brought up in the country, comforted by the rhythm of the seasons so apparent on the quiet coast where she lived with her family, she had always had a horror of Saturday mornings, and particularly Sunday afternoons, spent in parks or streets, neon-lit places, flats where time was of no consequence and Sunday lunch drifted into unnerving Sunday evening. To her, city weekends were wasted days. Even when, on leaving home, she had been forced to live in London during the week, she had always made the long journey back on Friday nights for the pleasure of two calm days on the earth, uncovered by concrete, that she loved. Given this strange quirk in her nature – which she did not bother to fight very hard – it was not surprising that here in New York, on a fine evening in May, Viola found herself dejected.

The airlessness of the theatre had given her a headache. Her limbs felt heavy, a sense of claustrophobia constrained her chest. In the mirrorless, stale lift that soughed up to her brother's apartment, she longed for the wide emptiness of the beach at home. Shutting her eyes, she imagined it. She would be there, thank God, this time next week. She had had enough of New York.

Viola let herself into Hannah Bagle's front door. Her brother Gideon had been living with Hannah since his arrival in New York, and having experienced just a week of Hannah's company, Viola hoped Gideon was not contemplating marriage. Gideon and she had always respected each other's private lives, and asked no questions. But in the case of Hannah Bagle, chief buyer in the nightwear department of a Fifth Avenue store, Viola felt apprehension on her brother's behalf. He had been changed by his liberated lady in ways which Viola could not admire, and even at the risk of angering him, she felt she should give him some warning. She had been awaiting the right time: perhaps it would be this evening when, at last, they would have a few hours alone.

In the stark white box of a kitchen – lifeless and tidy as a show kitchen in a shop window – Viola poured herself a drink of iced orange juice. She took it into the bleached living-room – glass, carpet and furniture all white, flowerless pot plants and a few shelves of books the only apologetic colours. Hannah Bagle, as she often said, hated colour, and she had drained it not only from the place in which she lived and from her own wardrobe, but also from Gideon. He had worn a cream tie and, worse, cream socks, every day. Viola had laughed at the change in his once colourful appearance, remembering his purple socks and rainbow jerseys at Oxford. He had merely replied that Viola was, as usual, too critical.

Viola sat on the white linen sofa, put her glass of orange on the low perspex table beside her. It glowed unnaturally, a single flame in the pallor of the room. In the stifling silence she recalled the events of the day, which had been no more satisfactory than any of the other days in New York.

It had been a relief not to have had to go through the audition, which she would have failed without a doubt, and she would not have enjoyed being humiliated by Harry Antlers as the others had been. He had lived up to his reputation of being a man of exceptional rudeness: boorish, chippy, charmless – except for a few moments. And ugly. Quite outstandingly ugly. On reflection, Viola could not imagine why she had accepted his invitation to lunch, except that she had been hungry and did not like eating alone in drugstores. His flattering suggestion that she should do some rewrites on the play was a very silly one. She had no experience, merely what a single producer, some years ago, had assured her was a natural ear for dialogue. If Mr Antlers was serious, of course, then she would be prepared to try. But no. She would not. It would mean staying longer in New York and associating further with the disagreeable Harry. While all she wanted was to return home very quickly.

Oppressed by the white room, Viola was relieved to hear the

key in the door. Gideon hurried in, strangely dressed in a caramel-coloured suit, white shirt and white tie. He was a tall, untidy man, clumsy and vague in some respects, infinitely skilful in others. There was a friendly clattering of ice as he poured himself a martini of American proportions. He flung himself upon a white chair, disturbing its etiolated cushions. His presence livened the room.

He smiled – what Viola used to call his front smile. While his face moved in adequate imitation of a grin, she said, the back of his mind, elsewhere, played no part in the gesture.

'Had a good day?'

'You've picked up so many American expressions.'

Gideon briefly shut his eyes, the smile gone. He had a fine, intelligent face: the temples and long nose identical to those of his father. A curved and sensuous mouth from his mother. When he was a child, and conversations bored him, he would shut his eyes for quite long spells. The habit would enrage his father. 'I'm practising in case I go blind,' Gideon would always say, shoving sausages skilfully into his mouth as his eyes screwed up with added defiance.

'Well, did you? What happened at the audition?'

'I didn't even bother to go through with it. The director saw at once I was completely unsuitable for the part, and I told him I wasn't interested anyway.'

'After all the trouble your agent took. Won't he be disappointed?'

'I don't think he cares very much.'

Gideon pushed off his shoes and wiggled his white-socked feet in the long white wool of the carpet.

'So there's nothing much to keep you in New York?'

'No. I'll be going home on Monday.'

'We'll miss you.'

'I think Hannah probably finds three rather too much in this flat, doesn't she?'

'Oh, I don't know. She's quite easy.'

Viola judged this not to be the time to disagree. They sat in silence for a while, Gideon sipping at his martini.

'I suppose we'd better talk about the house,' he said at last.

'That's the idea.'

'How on earth do you suppose you can keep it going on

34

your own?' His eyes, an opaque grey that he had inherited from no one, were suddenly tired and troubled.

'It'll be difficult, but I'll manage.' Even as she spoke Viola knew it would be impossible. The small amount of capital left by her father brought in an income that scarcely covered a frugal life of her own, but would not begin to cover the expenses of running a large and ailing house. Already she was in debt, although there were still a few hundred pounds left by her mother which would go towards outstanding bills.

Gideon sighed.

'You won't, you know.' He lit a cigarette and smiled a proper smile. 'It's hard to know what to do. You're the young sister and all that, but it's difficult to take care of you –'

'I'm quite all right, you know –'

'Well, keep an eye on you, whatever. It's hard with three thousand miles between us. And the parents would have considered it very unbrotherly to take no interest whatever, wouldn't they?'

Viola smiled in reply.

'And so, my Violetta, I've been thinking.' Viola sensed a thin thread of excitement in her spine. Whenever, in their childhood, Gideon announced he had been thinking, it was usually because the time had come to announce a good idea. 'I've been thinking, and I've changed my mind. About selling. Just yet, I mean. I don't know at all what your life is, or what you want to do, or how long you will really want to hang about by yourself with all those ghosts: but I understand you not wanting to let it go. With the present state of the economy, it can't be unwise to hang on to it for a while.' He paused, taking in his sister's face. 'And, no, you won't have to worry about the money. I'm making a ridiculous amount over here. I can take care of all that.'

'*Gideon.*'

'So you can organize getting the roof done as soon as you get back.'

'Oh heavens. Thank you, Gid.'

'Well, I'm not being entirely altruistic.'

'You mean, one day, you might . . . ?'

Gideon nodded. He held up his empty glass.

'I shouldn't be drinking this stuff for a start. Milk is

doctor's orders. I've got an ulcer. One gets ulcers, making so much money.'

Viola laughed.

'Would you come back soon? And Hannah?'

'A year or two, perhaps.' He paused. 'Hannah wouldn't be keen on a change of environment.'

'No.'

Gideon was mellow now for the first time during her stay in New York. As he curled his long legs under him on the sofa, indicating in some unspoken way that the comfortable position would not have been permitted in Hannah's presence, for fear of the white socks blemishing the white covers, Viola was reminded of the long night hours he spent thus on the library sofa at home. In vacations from Oxford he would bring two or three friends to stay, and they would hardly appear by daylight, but come out at night with bottles of port to sustain their endless philosophical discussions. Viola, only understanding half they said, would listen but not join in. Now, recognizing the same mellowness of those evenings, she ventured an old joke.

'Maisie's still waiting in Docking,' she said.

'Ah, Maisie! Is she still the same shape?'

'She's thinner, I've heard, in memory of you.'

'Dear fat obliging Maisie. Maybe I shall be bound to look her up one day. But you, Violetta, what about you? You never write real news. Any plans? Isn't it about time you settled down? Babies and all that. Who's been in your life of late?'

'Brief visitations. No more.'

'You'd be quite hard to love, I suppose.'

'Thank you!'

'By that I mean merely that it would take a lot of perseverance to see the point of you. Once somebody had, of course, they'd never let you go.'

They both laughed. The whiteness of the room was less alien now. Outside Viola could see pink clouds with underskirts of silver. They cast blue shadows on the floor.

Gideon stood up, stretching, huge.

'Hannah rang me to say she was going to be so late we should get ourselves some food. Shall we go down to the Village and eat raw fish in a Japanese restaurant? Hannah hates it.

36

But that would be nice, Letta, wouldn't it?'

'Wonderful,' said Viola, gulping her forgotten orange juice. She knew that for the first time in New York she would enjoy her evening.

3

Viola was walking on the beach, familiar in all but colour: it had been blanched white. Above her was a white cloudless sky and in the distance, on shining wet sand, the wreck. She could see the picnickers, their dresses blowing in the breeze. She could see them beckoning to her. But fast though she walked she came no nearer to them. Then she heard a scream, her name.

Viola woke. The scream again. She opened her eyes to the dazzling whiteness of her small room, and saw the anguished face of Hannah Bagle, baring white teeth that had been chiselled to an unnerving uniformity in California.

'Viola! For heaven's sake! Look what's come for you.'

She threw on to the bed a huge cellophane package. Struggling against drowsiness, Viola saw it contained a bunch of dark red roses.

'And that's just the beginning,' Hannah shouted. 'The porter's gone down to get the rest. There are *dozens* more, apparently. What the hell are we going to do with them? You'd better come.'

Dazed, Viola got out of bed. Following Hannah to the small doorway, she tried to think clearly. Who was the sender of the roses? The porter stood at the open front door, arms spread wide to hold another five packages of flowers.

'And this isn't all,' he snarled. 'What, someone died in here, something?'

Hannah relieved him of the two top packages. Viola took the other three. They crackled in her arms, the red of the flowers flaming through the transparent paper. Together they went to the sitting-room and without saying anything lay the packages in a neat line on the bleached floor, like a row of corpses.

'For heaven's sake,' Hannah said again. She stood back surveying them, arms folded in her white towelling robe,

38

stiff with disapproval. 'If there's one thing I really can't abide it's roses. Especially red.'

'I'm sorry,' said Viola.

'What dumb idiot sent them?' She smiled briefly. 'You must have captured some New York heart, I'll say that.'

'Can't think who it can be,' said Viola, honestly.

'Better set about finding a card, then.' Hannah bent down and tore at the window of cellophane paper on one of the packages. Her hand was long and pale, fretted with blue veins, older than the rest of her. The paper tore easily. Hannah pulled out a rose, sniffed. 'Doesn't even smell.'

She threw it to the floor with distaste. For a moment Viola could see the flower through Hannah's eyes: a globe of searing red that bloodied the carpet and violated the careful whiteness of the room. Hannah began to scrabble at other packages, randomly. Soon floor and sofas were gashed by dozens of roses. Viola stood helplessly by, scrunching up the paper, pressing crackling balls of it to her chest. She apologized many times, eyes on Hannah's tight mouth.

'We'll have to put them in the bathtub for the moment,' said Hannah, 'then take the goddam lot of them round to a hospital. We can't have them here.'

By now in an icy rage, her hands snooped through the flowers in search of a card. A thorn tore her finger. She watched impatiently for the bead of blood to rise, then sucked at the finger, moaning. At that moment, Gideon, in pyjamas, appeared at the door holding three more packages of flowers. Incredulous, he looked down at his sister and girlfriend huddled in their red sea, and laughed.

Hannah snapped the wounded finger from her mouth and glared up at him.

'So glad you think it's funny. Have you ever seen such a mess? Well, she's your sister. The two of you can deal with it. But I'll tell you one thing: if these flowers aren't gone by tonight, there'll be real trouble.'

'Now, Hannah, really.' Gideon was good-humoured. He threw his packages on to one of the sofas. They slithered about like enclosed shoals of bright fish, landed on the floor by Viola. Hannah stood, tightening the sash of her robe as she did so, thereby increasing the size of her breasts. She paused

39

briefly in front of Gideon, both angry and provocative, then made much of tiptoeing her barefoot way among the flowers to the kitchen door. It slammed behind her. Gideon shrugged.

'Well, well,' he said. 'Suppose she's never been bunched on quite this scale. Who the hell are they from?'

'I honestly can't imagine.'

Viola unpinned a small white envelope from the last of the packages. She took out the card and read the message: *One hundred red roses for Viola Windrush from Harry Antlers, in admiration.* The handwriting was pleasingly firm, masculine. Viola handed the card to Gideon.

'The director I had lunch with yesterday.'

'What on earth did you do to him?'

'Nothing.'

'Rubbish. He's either fallen dottily in love, or is the master of the flashy gesture.'

'He must be mad. I didn't like him, and I made it quite plain.'

'The feeling can't have been reciprocal. He'll have succeeded in making himself remembered, if only for all this.'

Gideon looked round in some despair at the galaxies of roses, reflecting on just how much trouble they would cause. But when Hannah then entered, carrying a tray of orange juice and coffee, her previous bad humour seemed to have gone. Clearing a space between the flowers, she put the tray on the low white table, and made herself a place between the roses on the sofa.

'Well, I guess this is all a hell of a nuisance,' she said, quite nicely, 'but seeing it's happened and we're flooded out with the things, I've been thinking we perhaps ought to make some use of them. Why don't we ask some people over, Gideon? Tonight? We could have a farewell party for Viola.'

This was forgiveness. Viola smiled gratefully. She did not care what happened, now that the house was secured and in two days she would be going home.

'You could ask the suitor,' said Hannah. 'I'd sure like to meet the suitor.'

'I don't know where to find him.' Viola knew she would have to locate Harry Antlers in order to send a polite note of thanks, but she had no desire for a reunion.

'Easy,' said Gideon. 'Get a message to him through your agent.'

Viola realized she would have to do this. She agreed reluctantly, and also agreed to spend the day arranging the hundred red roses in places least likely to annoy Hannah. A bright sun came through the window then, burnishing the flowers so brightly that Viola feared for Hannah's peace of mind. But Hannah, engrossed in plans for the sudden party, was now unaffected by the colour that splattered the savagely guarded white of her room. She stroked a clutch of scentless petals on her knee, her gentle touch indicating surrender, even if temporary. Viola did not miss Gideon's loving look, and imagined her brother's break from this strange, uneasy girl would not be imminent.

When Harry Antlers received an invitation to the party, later that day, he was attacked by such a weakness of relief and joy that his dash to the nearest drugstore for a celebratory milkshake was achieved on very wobbly legs. He had trembled all day in nervous anticipation of no word of response from Viola – although surely none but a real bitch would accept such roses unacclaimed. Now he trembled more violently. His hand shook on the tall icy glass of frosted pink froth that was his balming drink. When he wiped away the moustache of pink bubbles that it made on his upper lip with his other hand, he could feel the vibrations of his wrist. Somewhere among the manifestations of extreme elation struck a cold and nagging thought: he was ill. He had been struck with some fever, or unmentionable disease. Typical of his luck, at what might be the most important turning point of his life.

But with the downing of the milkshake – sweet, soothing strawberry, gentle on the stomach, the horror of such a thought evaporated. He was not ill. Definitely not ill. He was never ill. There was a simple solution which for some absurd reason had taken twenty-four hours to become clear to him. But now it was abundantly, wonderfully, gloriously clear: there was no more doubt. He had been claimed by a force which he had always suspected might exist, and here was the proof that it did. There was no more doubt. There would never be doubt again. Harry, swallowing the last threads of pink froth, acknowledged himself a man possessed. Yes, thank God, he was at last a man possessed. He ordered another strawberry milkshake.

In the ghost train of his mind Harry had journeyed his whole life in fearful anticipation. Things had sprung out at him from the darkness – bright things which faded even as he passed them by. Things had goaded him, prodding him in incomprehensible directions, urging him on, he knew not where. Sometimes he imagined he saw the faintest light at the end of the haunted tunnel, and would hurry faster, crushing anything that blocked his path. But the light was as evasive as every horizon. He came no closer to it. With despairing regularity it faded altogether, leaving him to thrash about in total, angry darkness.

But within Harry's turbulent heart there was a calm always trying to escape. He thought of this calm (for surely it must exist) as his Sleeping Prince. One day, if there was any truth in legends, some Princess would come to awake the calm: to unlock the prison and set him free. Spooning the creamy depths of his second milkshake, Harry remembered the old metaphor and smiled to himself. Well, here he was at last, awake. The Princess approached. Now all he had to do was to possess her, for life, with the promise of undying love. In considering the gifts he had to offer, it did not occur to Harry that the girl of his choice (or, rather, the more skilful choice of Fate) would deign to refuse them. He stood, rubbing at his contented stomach, happy in his innocence, his limbs throbbing with a tiger energy that made it hard not to yell and shake himself in ecstatic pleasure. With great effort he walked quietly from the drugstore.

At 7.25 precisely that evening, Harry entered the uptown apartment block wherein he would find the girl who was now the point of his life. To celebrate the occasion he had bought a new jacket of seersucker stripes in varying shades of blue. It was not a comfortable jacket, as he had learned within minutes of leaving the hotel. Its sharp cuffs stung his wrists, its hard collar rubbed the back of his neck. But it was a jacket of distinction. In a room full of beautiful New York people, who Harry had no doubt of finding at the party, eyes might veer from his face but they would not be able to ignore his jacket.

42

In the hours that had chafed between the arrival of the invitation and the journey to the party itself, Harry had contemplated the purchase of a further hundred roses. But on reflection the excess of this idea troubled him. He did not want to arrive ridiculously laden with cellophane packages, and it was possible Viola's brother's girlfriend was not the owner of enough vases to contain two hundred roses. Instead, Harry settled for the acceptable gesture of just one further flower. He chose it with infinite care, thrusting his nose among dozens of proffered petals, dizzying himself with all the scents, before at last declaring a deep blackish-red rose to be the one he required. At his request it was laid in a transparent box and tied with spotted ribbon. But it looked naked there, a corpse in an unadorned coffin. Patiently, the shop assistant undid the bow and bedded the box with crumpled tinfoil. On this small silver sea, the rose appeared to Harry's satisfaction, and he complimented the girl on her imagination and good taste. Her attentions cost him five dollars.

Harry rang the apartment bell, holding the box to his chest. He felt no sense of foolishness. As a man setting off for a journey might check his wallet, his passport and his ticket, so, in that last moment of aloneness behind the closed door, Harry checked his heart, his desire, his determination. They were all there, ready, waiting.

The door was opened by a tall blonde of some thirty years. She wore silk: the palest silk Harry ever saw, and yet not so drained of colour as to be called pure white. It looped in a complicated fashion across her breasts, leaving much of them efflorescently exposed. Impressed, Harry met her eyes: the whites unskeined as those of a child, while the density of black mascara signalled their maturity. Had his heart not been entirely captured so recently, it might have occurred to him that here was a woman upon whose numinous bosom he would like to comfort his raging head for a while. As it was he looked at her so sternly, to indicate her attractions moved him not one bit, that she clutched the door quite nervously.

'Why, you must be Harry Antlers,' she said at last.

'Yes.'

'I'm Hannah Bagle. Come on in, won't you? Heavens above, you've brought another rose.'

She laughed a tinkling laugh that was like sun on ice, disguising the essential chill. Harry followed her into a white room lit by tall windows filled with green sky. It was crowded with people, the kind of faces he had expected. No sign of Viola. His red roses were on every shelf and table, rows of them in jugs and vases and buckets and empty beer cans, their heads stiff and lustreless, disappointing in their masses.

'Here's our hero,' Hannah Bagle was saying. Her hand rested lightly on his arm. 'This is the rose man, Harry Antlers, Viola's friend. Now Harry, what can I get you to drink? Martini?' Harry nodded. Hannah went away, leaving Harry with Gideon. They shook hands, which meant Harry had to change the transparent box from his right hand to his left. Gideon smiled, glancing at the lying-in-state rose. His mouth was a coarser version of Viola's.

'I'm Gideon Windrush. Really, we're giving this party in honour of your roses. It was brave of you to bring one more.' He watched Harry's impassive face. 'I've never sent a girl so much as a bunch of daisies myself.'

'Really.'

'Your gesture was quite something.'

'I make gestures, sometimes,' said Harry, curtly. 'Where's your sister?'

Gideon nodded towards the window. Harry saw Viola. She must have moved there when he was talking to Gideon, his back to her. She was listening to a tall young man with a beard. He held a glass of wine to his cheek as if seeking its coolness. Viola's profile, against the darkening green sky, was very simple in its perfection. She wore a dress of lavender, or grey, which hung straight from a gathered yoke, an ageless dress that made no concessions to current fashion. Her companion, who was tall, stooped to emphasize some point. Viola nodded, oblivious of anyone else. Harry clutched his box, feeling its sides bend. Hannah returned with his drink. He moved away from Gideon, led by her, and was introduced to a professor at Columbia.

The news had somehow travelled that Harry was the provider of the roses. It soon became apparent that he was the hero of the party, and he found himself greeted everywhere with exclamations of wonder and admiration.

44

'*One hundred* roses?'

'One hundred roses,' Harry conceded.

'Gee. You must be in love.'

Harry allowed this observation to go unchallenged. After three quick martinis his head felt as if it were choreographed by Busby Berkeley: a dazzling silver globe in which girls high-kicked their legs and jostled with feathered fans, causing him to sway a little. Somewhere beyond this fluttering vision, real ladies, stout and eager, plucked at his successful jacket.

'Harry! Really. You're terrific.'

'Thanks.'

'No, I mean it.'

'Thanks.'

'Are you over long?'

'A while.'

'You must come and visit with us, mustn't he, Ed? Mustn't Harry come and visit with us?'

'Sure.'

'Thanks.'

'No, I mean it.'

'Yes, yes.'

'We'd like to have you over. Ed, my husband, he's away a lot on business, aren't you, Ed? But that wouldn't matter. Now this, Harry, is my friend Martha.'

A tall approaching girl opened her huge mouth as if to swallow the entire chorus line within his head.

'Martha, this is Harry of the roses. He *sent* all these roses. Imagine.'

'For heaven's sake.' Pure green voice of jealousy.

'Now, Harry, why don't we all sit down?'

'Really – '

'No, I mean it.'

Propelled between the two women to a small white corner of three empty chairs, it occurred to Harry he was probably the most attractive man in New York. Roses were a passport to anywhere, it seemed. But where was Viola?

His bodyguard of keen ladies were plunging forks into risotto. They had not managed to persuade him to eat, even though the one who meant everything she said assured him that brown rice was an aphrodisiac. Harry's icy glass stung his

45

fingertips, their voices volleyed back and forth across him. Eventually they accepted his silence as being part of his attraction, and talked about him as if he was not there, as visitors do across the bed of a very ill patient.

'He's quite a guy, Martha. Harry here is quite something.'

'He sure is.'

'He's enjoying himself, anyway.'

'He is, too.'

'He's promised to visit with us.'

'Has he?'

'Maybe he'd even send me some roses, then. What d'you say, Harry? Daresay he sends roses all over town.'

Hyena laughter. Through its hideous waves Viola walked towards Harry, alone. Her glass had gone, her hands were at her sides. Harry stood. The music-hall in his head vanished instantly. He was firm on his feet, quite clear. If the women behind him kept up their chatter, he did not hear them.

'Thank you,' said Viola. 'I've never had such flowers. They were . . . overwhelming.'

'Listen,' Harry said, 'when all this business is over, will you have dinner with me? It's important.'

The question seemed to shock. Viola took a step back.

'I'm sorry,' she said, 'but I can't possibly. This is my farewell party. I must stay and help clear up.'

'Farewell?'

'I leave Monday morning.'

'*Leave*?'

Viola shrugged. She could have no notion of the powerful dagger she had thrust into Harry Antlers' heart.

'I must get home.'

'What for?'

'Things to settle. Besides, I've had enough of New York.'

'But you agreed to help me on the rewrites of the play. *You agreed*.'

Viola frowned, puzzled.

'Agreed? I don't remember doing that. I said I could try, but I wasn't being very serious. Besides, I wouldn't have a clue.' She noted Harry's look of confused fury. 'I'm sorry,' she added. Harry went on staring at her.

'You agreed,' he said again.

46

'*I didn't.*' Viola raised her voice slightly, annoyed by the false accusation. 'Look, I'm terribly grateful for all these lovely roses' – she glanced round the room – 'and it was very sweet and generous of you – '

'I'm a "sweet and generous" person,' Harry mimicked.

'. . . and I'm flattered. But I'm going home on Monday, that's definite, and I can't help you with the play.'

She met his eye. Her corn-coloured hair, full of green shadows from the sky, clouded the contours of her innocent face. Harry rapidly sifted through the next lines that came to him: *You are the most beautiful girl I've ever met, Viola Windrush, and I love you entirely. Come away with me now, for ever. Please just have dinner with me.*

'Bitch,' he said.

The word hit Viola between the eyes, a well-aimed bullet. The next moment she was aware of Harry Antlers crashing through the room towards the door. People turned, aware of some impending drama. He was a man who could impress his own feelings tangibly into a room. Viola followed him. In the hall she found Hannah was with him. Confused by his sudden insistence on leaving, Hannah seemed to be urging him to stay.

'Please, Harry. What's happened?'

Harry saw Viola.

'That bitch your lover's sister has betrayed me, that's all,' he said, and turned to Viola. She stood bewildered in the doorway. 'Bitch, bitch, bitch,' he said again. Then he turned back to Hannah, took her face formally into his hands, and kissed her on the cheek. 'Thank you for your party,' he said. 'You're lovely.'

He was gone.

'Christ, he's a nutter.' Hannah wiped her cheek with the back of her hand. 'What happened?'

'God knows,' said Viola.

Following Hannah back into the crowded room, she hardly cared. Harry Antlers' extreme gesture of the roses was merely the one event she could laugh about in her week in New York. And yet, as she concentrated her attentions on a group of people who were still congratulating her on being the receiver of such flowers, a small feeling of guilt began a persistent

47

ticking, which is the nature of guilt, somewhere within her. She was unused to upsetting people, on purpose or inadvertently, and if she did so it troubled her greatly. She would like to have apologized for the misunderstanding over the so-called agreement. But where was Harry Antlers now?

As the party guests clustered round her in all their friendly amazement at her good fortune, Viola began to feel claustrophobic. She wanted desperately to leave the small white crowded room, the interested inquiries about her plans, her flight, her life in England. She wanted, inexplicably, to follow Harry, to smooth things over before she left New York, to be left with a clear conscience. Though *why* he should have stirred such guilt, she knew not.

'Here Violetta, have a proper drink.'

Gideon, perhaps understanding her dilemma, was handing her a bourbon on the rocks. Gratefully she sipped it, knowing he would not mind if she left for a short while. She would simply drop in at Harry's hotel, and if she found him there, would apologize and leave. Hannah was suddenly at her side.

'Seems Harry left you this,' she said, and handed Viola the transparent box holding the last single rose, forlorn on its silver foil sea.

Viola thanked her and took the box with distaste. In the privacy of her bedroom she dropped it, unopened, into the waste paper basket. She collected her coat, bag and enough money for the journey downtown, and slipped away unnoticed.

Half an hour later, Viola rang Harry Antlers' bell. After a long moment he let her into his hotel room. It was lit only by a dim light on the desk. There were papers everywhere, as if several scripts had just been flung into the air and let fall at random. Harry backed into the room, sat in the only armchair. He was pale, sweat glistened on his brow.

'So you've come,' he said in a monotone.

'Just to apologize.'

'You shouldn't have bothered.'

'I didn't like the thought of a misunderstanding.'

'There wasn't a misunderstanding. You simply betrayed me.'

Viola sighed, not prepared to argue. She sat on the bed.

'You could take off your coat,' said Harry.

48

'I'm only staying a moment.'

'As you like.'

They sat in silence for a while. Harry's hands were crossed in his lap. There was something both pathetic and repellent about his state of abjection.

'Well,' said Viola, eventually, wishing she had not come, 'I'm sorry if I've offended you.'

'Offended me!' Harry snorted, an obscene, rumbling noise. 'If you had merely offended me, that would be quite bearable. As it is, you shone a torch in the blackness of my life and now, immediately, before any chance of warmth for us both in its light, you're determined to extinguish it. I hope you know what that means.'

Viola looked at him carefully. She wondered if he was mad. She also felt some impatience with his elaborate accusation.

'I'm sorry,' she said again. 'To me, you were simply someone I met by chance, and had you not sent me the roses I should probably never have thought of you again.'

'I'm glad you're able to feel like that.' Harry gave a small, sneering smile. 'That's very fortunate for you.'

It was then he began to tremble violently, alarmingly. Viola leaned over, put a hand on his bare forearm. The skin felt waxy, icy cold.

'Are you ill?' she asked.

'Probably. You could call it an illness.'

'Can I get anything for you? Should we call a doctor?'

'No.'

His arm was trembling harder under Viola's hand. She withdrew it, stood up.

'I think I should go back now.'

'I think you should. To your important friends.'

Viola went to the door.

'Order yourself some hot soup,' she said, hopelessly. Harry gave her a look of utter loathing.

'Hot . . . soup,' he repeated, mimicking. 'Remember this, Viola Windrush, on your escapist plane back to England: I, Harry Antlers, have entered your life now in a way that's far too profound to be shaken off by apologies, and suggestions of *hot soup*.' He spat out the words, gripping his trembling arms to his chest. 'So as you go about your petty little life, you

49

should bear in mind that here's a man who, for reasons of his own, won't give you up, come what may.'

Harry's look was changed momentarily to one of hope. But Viola laughed and the look was dashed to pieces.

'God, you're melodramatic,' she said. 'No wonder you choose bad plays. You've an incredible penchant for bad lines.'

She left, then, slamming the door behind her. He had angered her, irritated her, embarrassed her. He had also, ridiculously, frightened her. Viola realized this in the stuffy warmth of the taxi as it sped her back to safety. Beneath her scorn were intimations of the fear of having become a victim, a terrible feeling that she might be hunted and not manage to escape.

But, back at the party, Viola's fears soon evaporated, and the idea of the Atlantic coming between her and Harry Antlers was reassuring. It was with great relief and pleasure that she left New York on Monday morning. On the aeroplane, drinking champagne in celebration, she gave no thought to his preposterous warnings, but concentrated instead on plans for her future. Somewhere on the journey the idea came to her that she should find a caretaker for the house, to keep it from disintegrating, and also so that she would not be entirely alone. This small domestic plan filled her with unaccountable happiness, and she ordered more champagne in further celebration.

4

Alfred Baxter, settled physically in his small bright flat over-looking the promenade of a seaside town along the coast from the old shop, was, as he put it to himself, out of sorts.

To begin with, all had been well. There had been so much to organize: moving, unpacking, painting the two small rooms, putting up Eileen's curtains and finding a place for all the clutter he could not bear to throw away, that his mind and time had been kept fully occupied. But at the end of six weeks there was nothing further to do. The place was in as much order as it ever would be: the pictures up, the old wedding photographs in their oval frames arranged along the fireplace, the bars of soap and tins of dried milk to last his lifetime (left over from the shop) stored away, suits all cleaned and checked for loose buttons before being squashed into the small bed-room cupboard. Now, time hung heavy about him.

The hours were hard to fill, the days surprisingly sluggish. In the past, a busy morning behind the counter would pass with amazing speed, and no sooner had he finished his lunch than Eileen's delicious high tea was upon him, the hours be-tween having flown by while he checked stock, sharpened his cutting scissors and polished the mahogany drawers between serving customers. But in the last few idle days in his seaside flat, Alfred had learned the sharp lesson of the hours that all those who live alone must become acquainted with. For the first time in his life he was aware of the precise difference between ten o'clock – a chilly time when the whole morning lies bleakly ahead – and eleven o'clock, which brings with it a little more warmth if only because preparation of lunch, a sparse midday meal, is not far away. He learned about the pangs of mid-afternoon, the zero hour of three o'clock when all those fortunate enough to be employed are about their business, and all those with no well-defined occupation are drained of ideas as to how to pass the afternoon before the

51

merciful relief of early evening television. He learned how approaching night can loom like a great black mountain, to be climbed alone. When Eileen was alive, bedtime was always a happy ritual: the damping down of the small wood fire, the checking of the back door while Eileen made two mugs of cocoa, the climb of the steep stairs to their small bedroom under the eaves, skilfully balancing the mugs on a tin tray. And finally, the quiet pleasure of a hot drink, propped comfortably against their pillows, before Eileen read a few verses from the Bible and put out the light. Tired out by their busy day, they both slept instantly. They took sleep for granted.

It was only now that Alfred Baxter realized how fortunate he had been all those years. A considerable worry on his mind was the fact that Eileen's Bible had disappeared in the move. For it was the nightly verses, he began to believe, that had induced their good sleep. He searched for the Bible everywhere, and eventually, despairing, gave up. Buying a new one was an idea soon discarded; it would not be the same. He was forced to face the truth to himself: should he not find the Bible, easy sleep would never come again.

In the days of his marriage to Eileen, on the rare occasions there was time to imagine their retirement (which naturally Alfred had never envisaged would be spent on his own), they had painted for themselves some pretty pictures. They would spend much time cultivating a small garden, both vegetables and flowers, and while Eileen made herself useful in whatever way she could in the village, Alfred would at last take up his old ambition of becoming a bowls player. For years he had dreamed of treading the emerald turf of the green, smooth and shining ball in hand, white flannels scarcely creasing as he bent to cast his accurate eye on the target . . . Then the splatter of applause, that muted English sound of spectators on a summer's day – he had heard it so many times in his mind's ear. Retired, he would also listen to the music of brass bands on a fine new record player, and buy himself a bumper book of crossword puzzles, and perhaps invest in a couple of Khaki Campbell ducks. In spring and summer he and Eileen would travel to some of the places they had always meant to see: not to anywhere fancy, abroad, but short trips in their immaculate Austin 30 to the cathedral cities of England and unexplored beaches on their own east coast. Thus they would fill their years before death most agreeably. And each was convinced that as soon as one died the other would follow very quickly.

In reality, such pictures were smashed beyond all repair. For a start, despite the adequate radiators and a cheerful sun that shone through the south-facing windows, Alfred felt permanently chilly. He never remembered feeling cold when Eileen was alive and this particular, unreasonable chill – which often caused him to tremble quite violently, and would not disappear even after a hot bath – depressed him. It seemed to drain him of energy. Purpose, he realized, is warming, and he had no real purpose now. But he did try. He established some kind of routine to divide up the days – walk to the newsagent after breakfast, walk to the pub for a single pint at one o'clock, walk along the Front after tea. He even went to the Bowls Club, but then lacked the impetus to apply for membership. Without Eileen there to watch, there would be little point in his becoming a champion. He managed a crossword puzzle a day, and he acquired a taste for Afternoon Theatre on the radio, but still there were many hours in between. He received several letters from friends left behind in the village, urging him to come and visit them. But the car had been sold – Alfred had no desire for cathedrals without Eileen – and a dull apathy, caused by the permanent gooseflesh on his skin, meant the journey on rural buses was quite beyond his declining ability.

On a fine morning in late May he sat in his armchair at the window reading the local paper, which he had fetched at seven, having been awake since five. There was a warm smell of burnt toast and fried egg in the room. He had not had the heart to wash the breakfast things: procrastination, he noticed, was beginning to afflict him. Something he would have to fight.

Now, after a bad night, Alfred was feeling pleasantly sleepy. (Heavens above, what a time to feel sleepy, he thought. Mornings are for hard work. Have been all my life.) His eyes were closing over reports of local fêtes and council meetings. Then a headline caught his attention. *Models Washed up on Shore*, it said. At once Alfred was quite awake. His heart began to thump violently. The chill on his skin fled, to be replaced by an uncomfortable sense of burning on cheeks and chest.

'Oh no,' he moaned out loud. 'God, let my girls rest in peace.'

He read the paragraph several times. It seemed that earlier this week five 'corpses' had been sighted washed up on a nearby beach. The man who had seen them through his field glasses, fearing a major disaster, had alerted coast guard, police and ambulance before approaching them. Accompanied by two policemen and six ambulancemen bearing stretchers, the man had walked over the sands to the pathetic huddle of beached ladies. It was not until they were a few yards away from them they discovered the corpses were 'models', as the reporter called them. 'One of them was wearing a straw hat trimmed with cherries,' he wrote. (Trust the vain little minx Deborah to keep her hat on in a crisis, thought Alfred.) 'Police and ambulancemen put on a show of very good humour in face of loss of precious time.'

There the story ended. No mention of what happened to the girls. Had they been callously flung back into the sea? Buried deep beneath the sand? Or flung on to a municipal tip?

The thought of an ignominious end, after all his efforts to speed them on their way with dignity, brought tears to Alfred's eyes. In all his plans for their final picnic it had not occurred to him what might happen when the tide came in. He had not liked to picture a scene of floating bodies, pretty dresses adrift in the sea. Now he came to think of it he had had some unclear notion that a boat of merry sailors would pass by, join the girls in their revelries, and carry them off to a South Seas island to live happily ever after. But on reflection Alfred knew this piece of fanciful thinking was only to disguise the thought of the reality: and it had always been hard to put his finger on reality in the case of the girls.

He sat with the paper folded on his knee, mild sun fiery on flushed cheeks fretted with hot tears, feeling the weight of anguish roll from the edges of his body to some painful depth in its centre. He had let the girls down, after all. He had drowned them. Would to God in heaven that he had kept them with him, here, to share his retirement. Life might have been much better, then.

The day was a terrible struggle for Alfred. Every hour was haunted by visions of how the girls might have met their final end. Perhaps they had been *chopped up*, or *melted down*, their wigs donated as spare parts, their beautiful clothes washed and ironed for a jumble sale. As the ghastly imaginings crowded his mind, Alfred felt the burning of his skin die away and the old chill return. He sat by his window all day. He could not eat. In the evening he forced himself out for his stroll along the Front, but there the sight of the sea that had been so cruel to the girls filled him with further despair. Once he stopped at a telephone booth, determined to ring the newspaper and inquire what had happened to the 'models'. (He could scarcely bring himself to mouth the word in his mind.) But it occurred to him his inquiries might lead to further publicity. They might even send a reporter round to write a mocking little story: that, he could not have tolerated.

Some time after midnight he went to bed, dreading the sleepless hours ahead, hungry, but still with no desire to eat. He could not face the darkness, so decided to read every single small advertisement in the paper. Perhaps that would do the trick, dull the turmoil of his wretched mind.

An hour later – Alfred was not a fast reader – he discovered he had read one particular advertisement several times over. 'Take a grip on yourself, Mr Baxter,' he said out loud, in imitation of Eileen on the rare occasions she was slightly cross with him, 'and read it again.'

Wanted, it said, *friendly competent caretaker/odd job man to live in wing of old rectory. Suitable someone who would find overgrown garden a challenge and who would like to help look after a much loved house that was once full of people.*

A different ring, that advertisement has, thought Alfred to himself. A decidedly different ring. He lay back, closing his eyes, saying the words over to himself, letting their message seep into the chill of his body. If anyone in the world was suitable for such a job, surely it was he. To be able, so soon, to abandon this nasty little flat, to live in a village again, and above all to have something to do, to care for once more, would be a chance he would never have dared to imagine.

He did not like to think of the possibility too hard. But, cast in hope, the mind runs happy riot, and as dawn pressed through his window in his imagination Alfred found himself firmly established as caretaker of the rectory. Full of such bright new thoughts, his worries about the girls rested for the time being.

Three days later Alfred boarded a bus bound for the village of the old rectory. He wore his navy serge suit and his grey tie. He had had a haircut and polished his shoes. There was a clean white handkerchief in his breast pocket and a dab of Old Spice behind his left ear. Eileen would have been proud of him.

Since making the date for this interview – which Alfred had arranged early in the morning after his sleepless night – he had been blessed with a revival of energy, so that he found himself doing quite unnecessary things like ironing his underpants and sewing up the small tear in the lining of his jacket. He felt both anticipation and apprehension. Never before had he experienced an interview, having been a self-employed man all his life. But he knew quite well what a prospective employer found impressive in a prospective employee, and he spent many hours in his chair by the window working out what to say that would best convince Miss Windrush of his suitability for the job. He also wondered whether Miss Windrush might be any relation to a good customer of the same name who came to the shop years ago, sometimes with two small children.

Walking up the drive to the rectory – a fine old house, he immediately thought, but needs a bit of work on it – Alfred could hear the beating of his own heart. His nervousness amused him. At my age, he reflected. Ridiculous. But fear was reasonable enough. If he failed to get the job, then he would be forced back to the new life he hated. He did not like to dwell on such a prospect. God be with me, he said to himself, and rang the bell.

The door was answered by a young lady with a pale face and untidy hair. She wore a fisherman's jersey that was far too large for her and cradled her arms under her breasts as if, for all the fineness of the morning, she was cold.

'Miss Windrush?'

'Mr Baxter! Come in.'

They shook hands. She smiled. The smile seemed vaguely familiar. He followed her along a darkish passage to the

56

kitchen. It was a high-ceilinged old room that rambled at large towards its thick walls. Plainly it had received little attention for many years, and yet it had the air of being loved. There were faded patchwork cushions on the chairs, rows of pickled fruits and vegetables on the dresser, a crowd of potted sweet geraniums on the window ledge. The table, it seemed to Alfred, had been built for a giant. It could surely seat twenty, made from enormous slabs of solid pine. The high-backed chairs all round it spread their arms widely. The whole scene reminded Alfred of *Jack and the Beanstalk*, his first panto-mime, in Lowestoft, when he was a child. The giant's kitchen had impressed him with its enormous proportions – ten cups the size of teapots, a table a small man could walk under with-out bending his head. And here it was again, in real life. The image was further heightened when Miss Windrush sat in the huge chair at one end of the table. Curled up, legs beneath her, within it she looked tiny. Alfred chose the chair next to her. Viola dragged towards her a giant tea pot made of brown tin, and two enormous pottery cups. She poured. It was then Alfred remembered.

'You're not by any chance – excuse my asking . . . But could you be the daughter of a Mrs William Windrush? I had a very good customer in Mrs Windrush, years ago. We were Baxter's, you see. Baxter's, the drapers, though of course we ended up with many other lines.'

The light of recognition filled Viola's face. She smiled again, delighted.

'Mr Baxter of *Baxter's*? Of course I remember you! I used to come in with my mother quite often. She used to buy all my dress materials from you, and all her sewing things. You were the only shop for a hundred miles, she said, that kept a supply of bone thimbles.'

'We did, too.'

'How extraordinary.'

Alfred smiled, touched his head.

'My memory . . . but of course, I remember you as a child. I remember Eileen saying Miss Windrush had very definite opinions for one so young, when it came to ribbons and that.'

He smiled. Viola remembered him as a lean and upright man, always in a starched brown overall.

57

'And your wife . . . Eileen?'

'Eileen. She passed on some time ago. So I was forced to sell up and go into retirement. But I don't like being retired. I've got a good few years of usefulness in me yet. Silly to waste them.'

Viola passed him his tea. They both drank, thinking of their meetings in the past, and of the changes in their appearances.

'Both my parents are dead, too,' said Viola at last. 'And my brother Gideon – he used to come into the shop sometimes, remember? – he lives in America now. So it's a struggle to keep the house on. But I don't want to sell it if I can help it.'

'A very natural feeling, Miss Windrush. No one in their right mind would want to sell a place like this.'

Viola's hot strong tea had warmed Alfred right through, he was warm as he had not been for weeks. And extraordinarily at home. It was as though he had sat in this room for years. Already the ticking clock, the faded curtains, the framed engravings of snipe and teal on the copper-coloured walls were wonderfully familiar. He had not had such a happy morning since Eileen died.

'Your mother, Mrs Windrush, was an exceptional lady,' he said. 'Such style, Eileen used to say. You could tell she was a great English lady before she ever opened her mouth. She was one of our most treasured customers.'

Alfred hoped this would not sound like flattery. For it was the truth. Mrs Windrush had had a *presence*, as Eileen called it, that was unforgettable. A calm and dignified presence although she always maintained her distance. Alfred respected that. He could not abide a gushing woman, but admired friendly reticence. A great English quality, he often thought.

Viola and Alfred reminisced for a while, listening to each other as one memory sparked off another. They mused over the coincidence of this meeting. They drank several pots of tea.

An hour went by and still Viola made no mention of the job. It occurred to Alfred, at last, that perhaps she would find broaching the subject difficult. So he decided to take matters into his own hands. Give her an idea of the sort of thing he would be willing and able to do for her.

Viola sat back gratefully listening while he outlined his

58

plans. Alfred volunteered to be in charge of the garden, the fires, the rough work and polishing in the house ('Nothing I like better than to kindle a polish on an old piece of furniture'). He would care for the place when she was away: see that the larder was well stocked when she came back. He would patch the roof, clean the gutters, stoke the boiler, do any decorating that needed to be done. Would that be the sort of thing she had in mind? And, in return, all he would require was the pleasure of occupying his wing, and a little pocket money, whatever she felt she could afford. He was not interested in money: he had enough put by for his needs, and his needs were minimal. If Miss Windrush would allow him to take the liberty, he would like to try raising a few bantams, and some Khaki Campbell ducks: something he had always wanted to do, and of course she would be welcome to unlimited eggs.

As he spoke, a look of relief began visibly to gleam in Viola's face. A shaft of sunlight backlit her hair. There was a quality of goldness about her. Alfred Baxter found himself touched by her appearance of vulnerability. She seemed a somewhat helpless young thing – Alfred tried but failed to guess her age – although there was strength beneath her fragile appearance. With great passion, Alfred found himself wishing to help her: end his days in this house. Even as he spoke of the birds and the eggs he prayed to God that Viola would offer him the job. He did not often call upon his maker's aid, though he had always intended to spend much of his retirement thanking Him for the blessings of his life, kneeling beside Eileen beneath the soaring roof of an English cathedral. But Eileen's death and the sale of the car had forced him to abandon that form of thanks, and now Alfred felt acutely neglectful, and speedily prayed for forgiveness as well as for help.

He was rewarded. As Viola sat, hand on her chin, thoughtful, Alfred could see she had made up her mind.

'Well,' she said at last. 'There doesn't seem to be much doubt about it, does there? You are obviously the right man.'

Alfred made no effort to control his delight. He stood up, shook her hand, assured her of his undying service.

'Unexpected blessings, Miss Windrush,' he said, 'are what can save a man.'

Viola saw his eyes were sparkling with tears. She hastily

began to discuss practical matters concerning his instalment the following week. Then she showed him the wing, joined to the main house by a door from the kitchen. It consisted of two good rooms, a bathroom and small kitchen. They smelled of damp, and had not been painted for many years. But Alfred immediately saw their potential, and delighted in the thought of refurnishing them. Eileen's cornflower curtains, he fancied, would fit the kitchen windows to perfection.

It was not until well past midday Alfred eventually braced himself to leave. At the front door he shook Viola warmly by the hand again, not trusting himself to speak of the pleasure of his anticipation. Viola, whose feelings were very similar, gave him a smile that was so like that of her poor dear mother that Alfred, ungrounded by looking both at the past and the future simultaneously, found himself weaving down the drive with the unsteady gait of a man incredulous of his good fortune.

It was almost fifteen years ago that Gideon had brought home Richard Almond from Oxford for the weekend. Viola, aged sixteen, was eating scones at the kitchen table and studying *King Lear*. Her concentration having been interrupted by the arrival of her brother and his friend, she pushed away both book and food and turned her attention upon them. In Gideon's friends, though she barely admitted it to herself, she was constantly on the look-out for potential lovers, or at least loves, and in Richard Almond she at once recognized a possible candidate.

He was a tall, thin Irishman with fierce green eyes and wild black hair: a restless traveller, a compulsive reader, a man beset by small misadventures which he turned into hilarious anecdotes. He was reading Classics at Oxford, intending to go on to read medicine and ultimately become a neuro-surgeon. Viola, noticing his immensely long and tapering fingers, judged they would be calm and skilful with a scalpel, in contrast to the sometimes irritable movements of the rest of his body.

In his first weekend at the house Richard Almond charmed the Windrush family, not least Viola. Unlike many other of Gideon's friends, who regarded her merely as a younger sister, he helped her with *The Wife of Bath*, he took her sailing on Sunday morning while Gideon remained in bed with a hangover. By the time he left on Sunday evening, Viola was in love. *I aspire to him*, she wrote in her diary that night. *If this is my first real love, and comes to nothing, then I shall wait until this quality of feeling strikes again before I commit myself to any other man.*

Viola lived in exhilaration with her secret. She worked with new energy for her exams: there was now someone she felt a vital need to impress with her results. In between his frequent visits – Gideon seemed particularly attached to Richard and brought him often – she lived in a kaleidoscope of memories of his last visit: small, rewarding moments such as his smile to her at breakfast, his listening seriously to her views, his remembering to bring her a copy of *Isis* in which he had written an article. And when he was gone, beyond the brightness within of all such memories, the solid things of every day took on an ethereal quality that made them unrecognizable. The scintillant that is the magic product of first love scattered Viola's small quiet world, and she feared that the glitter of her exhilaration would be visible for all to see.

But she made a great effort to contain herself, and if Richard or the others guessed at her feelings they kept their thoughts to themselves. Richard, for all his friendliness, never made the slightest gesture that Viola could interpret as requited love. But she was happy enough, for the time being, that he should be her friend, and flattered that he should treat her as a contemporary rather than Gideon's schoolgirl sister.

One summer weekend in June, by which time Richard had been a frequent visitor for six months, there was to be a dance to celebrate the twenty-first birthday of Maisie Fanshawe, who lived nearby, and who had loved Gideon fiercely since childhood. Viola had not been invited, Maisie considering her too young. But at lunch on the Saturday of the party Richard suddenly declared that it was unfair that Viola should be left behind, and he would refuse to go unless she came with them.

Viola's parents quietly argued the matter. Mrs Windrush thought the idea delightful, especially as her daughter would be so responsibly chaperoned. But Colonel Windrush foresaw many a danger to his young daughter once exposed to 'wild young blood' in a Norfolk marquee. He abandoned his favourite rice pudding to make his points against young girls being thrust into the lascivious world too soon, but was mellowed by several glasses of port pressed upon him by Richard and Gideon. They made promises to protect her from all conceivable dangers, and Mrs Windrush wondered, with a sweet smile, at her husband's lack of trust in Viola. The argument was won. The Colonel conceded with dignity and went to find solace in an afternoon on the golf course.

There then arose the problem of what Viola should wear. Her own wardrobe contained nothing suitable for a dance. The only possibility was to sift through the mothball cupboards of Mrs Windrush's old clothes. This prospect all but crushed Viola's excitement: it was with many misgivings she followed her mother – all enthusiasm and optimism – into her bedroom whose window overlooked the sea.

They spent the afternoon untying plastic bags, so old that they had turned a dull opalescence, through which flaming silks and satins shone grey as shadows. As they untied bows of tape the bags crackled quietly, brittle in their age – the only sound in the quiet room. Mrs Windrush pulled out dozens of dresses – she never threw old clothes away – and for all Viola's worry as to whether they would find anything suitable for her, she enjoyed seeing them for the first time, each one a piercing memory of her mother's past.

Beautiful they were indeed: the sheerest, flimsiest fabrics, hand-embroidered and hand-made: sprigged cottons Mrs Windrush had bought in her youth in India, striped taffetas, sequined chiffons and bruised glowing velvets, soft as feathers. But none seemed right on Viola. They fitted her, for she had inherited her mother's slimness, but she looked as if she was dressed up – as indeed she was – from a store of clothes kept nowadays for charades. In dress after dress she surveyed herself in the long looking-glass: the sky had become overcast and a light rain speckled the windows, throwing a grey despairing light into the room. Mrs Windrush sat on the end of the bed in gumboots and fisherman's jersey, her arms filled with a bright writhing snake of multi-coloured dresses, her voice sing-songing with pleasure as each one of them brought back to her another event of her youth.

62

'And this one, the peacock blue, was for a ball at the Savoy. But perhaps this watered silk would suit you better – *livelier*, don't you think, darling? That was for a dance at Skindles, the banks of the Thames lit by candles for miles and miles . . .'

'It won't do, Mama. I'm sorry. I won't be able to go after all.'

Finally, there was only one dress left. Mrs Windrush pulled it reluctantly from the bag. It was very simple. White satin, sleeveless. Thin silver shoulder straps to hold up the camisole bodice. The hem was embroidered with lilies, delicate trumpet heads, picked out in silver thread.

Mrs Windrush stood up. She held the dress in front of herself, dark jerseyed arms sticking incongruously out at its sides, gumboots peeping beneath the twinkling hem. Viola made room for her at the mirror. Mrs Windrush smiled at her reflection.

'I was wearing this when I first met your father,' she said. She turned to her daughter. The silvery light of the bodice reflected kindly up into her face, bleaching out the lines, burnishing the fine bones and magnificent eyes. Viola could see exactly how beautiful she must have looked.

'Then I can't possibly wear it,' she said.

'No, I suppose not.' Mrs Windrush, rocking the skirt of the dress from side to side, was dreamily transported to a private world of long ago. Then she said:

'Though I don't see why not, really. In fact, I think you probably should. After all, it's the best one there is. It would suit you.'

She handed the dress to Viola, instantly transformed once more, in her old clothes, to her real age. The summer rain jittered more darkly against the window, and in the strange light of that late afternoon Viola agreed: they had found the perfect dress.

To the sophisticated eyes of Richard and Gideon the party was not a very imaginative affair: salmon pink gladioli propped stiffly as guns in their bowls, the sides of the marquee bunched fatly with yellow net, personifying the essence of debutantes themselves, the aged orchestra fatigued and slow. But to Viola, watching the dancing strangers, listening to the ho-ho-ho of

63

the privileged laughter and feeling the ice of a champagne glass in her hand, it was a wondrous occasion. She feared only that Richard would leave her side and she would be humiliatingly alone. But he seemed to have no intention of doing that. Taking her elbow, he guided her through the silken crowds to the dance floor.

'I'm terrified, Richard,' she whispered, feeling the spring of the temporary parquet floor beneath her feet.

'No need to be. You look, eh, how can I put this? All right.'

He gave her what she knew in her heart was an avuncular twinkle, but tried to believe was more than that. She was grateful to him and enjoyed their dance, his hand firm on her back, their legs entwined, spinning with no mistakes.

Later, moments or hours, Viola had no idea which, they walked in the garden, keeping their distance. The rain had stopped now. It had left the grass glittering like melted frost under a clouded moon. The briny air was warm but damp. There was a smell of roses and tobacco plants.

'Only the nightingale missing,' observed Richard, with a quality of laughter in his voice which did not reflect the seriousness of Viola's thoughts. 'In fifty years' time, you know, there's a good chance he'll be quite extinct. Imagine that.'

Viola was more inclined to imagine Richard's motives for coming into the garden at all. Had it been in his mind to declare the undying love for her that she felt for him? Followed up, of course, with sensible suggestions about patience in the face of youth, but promises of some kind of permanence in the future? In all her sixteen years Viola had never known such steeliness of conviction in her veins: she had been blessed very early with the kind of love that lasts a lifetime, and knew better than to endanger it with silly games of inaccessibility.

'When I eventually retire from neurology,' Richard was saying, 'I shall have a garden like this.'

Too soon their path was returning them to the house. The sleepy music was loud again. Chance was fleeing. Despite herself, Viola stopped. Richard, a pace or two ahead of her, sensed her reluctance to return indoors. He turned, looked at her for a long time in silence, compassionate. She was silver, serious, sad in the moonlight.

64

'Look what the wet grass has done to the hem of your dress! I'm so sorry. Those beautiful lilies. Come on, you'll get cold.' He gave her his arm. 'I shall never forget that dress, you know. Never, never.'

They were walking with a swift sense of purpose up a gravel path, now chequered with lights from windows of the house. Viola felt herself being swept reluctantly along, not daring to hesitate again. Richard was being *nannyish*, she thought, and it was only a surge of all-forgiving love that squashed her disappointment. Then suddenly there was a girl before them, a huge great looming girl in swathes of ill-fitting green stuff whose folds did not disguise its essential limpness.

'Oh, Richard,' she said heartily, 'I've been looking for you everywhere.'

She had long black hair, middle parted. She pushed it back from her face with both hands, lodging it behind sticking out ears, and grinned. There was a wide gap between her middle teeth. She did not look at Viola, but her ignoring intimidated.

'We were on our way back,' he said, more friendly than he need have been, thought Viola; but she loved him for his lack of explanation as to why they had been out at all. She hoped the giant would imagine they had been making love in the orchard.

'This is Viola Windrush,' he was saying. 'Viola, Sonia Heel. We meet in Oxford.'

A vast hand was reaching out for Viola's: clasped it without interest. Had Richard only said *met*, not *meet*, with all its horrible implications of regularity, Viola would have been happier. And now they were moving along together, all three of them in step, Richard in the middle, his arm withdrawn from Viola. She knew with each eternal second she was the one whose turn it was to be dropped. The keen bounce in Richard's new stride – surely not her imagination – conveyed a desire which in truth had been lacking in his reaction towards herself. It was, of course, all a matter of age. The disadvantage at the moment was in being Gideon's younger sister. Untouchable, inaccessible. But how unenlightened of him not to foresee the growing . . . The giant was laughing about something, tossing her awful hair. The marquee, now just a yard or so away, bulging with its light and music, looked down on Viola

65

like a firing squad. Her time was up: she wondered how the slaughter would take place.

Richard, helped by the immediate sight of Gideon at the bar, managed everything with a skill that suggested in the matter of shuffling ladies he was not unpractised, and to cause them the least pain in the process of repositing was his utmost desire. Viola could never precisely remember the words with which Richard suggested Viola should have a drink with her brother while he took a whirl with the giant. Perhaps she chose not to hear. Certainly she did not respond to the gap-toothed smile of triumph as the massive green hulk strode away, hand possessively on Richard's shoulder. Viola, deliberately turning her back to the dance floor, watched her brother's eyes follow the couple. 'Sonia Heel,' he said, 'is not just in love with Richard. She's unhealthily obsessed by him.'

Viola managed a smile. 'Will she get him?'

'I doubt it. Being the object of somebody's obsession is dreadfully tedious.'

Encouraged, Viola turned to look. But the sight of Richard and the giant dancing did not encourage her hopes: he seemed to be willingly imprisoned in a clumsy embrace, head buried (easily, for he was a couple of inches shorter) in the dark cavernous places beneath the swilling hair, while one rapturous hand idled about the vast green landscape of her back. Viola, craving to die, felt an unsteadiness in her legs that warned of impending death. Gideon noted her stricken face and thumped down his glass.

'Well, this isn't much of a party, is it?' he said. 'Three *Rock Around the Clocks* with Maisie and a scintillating waltz with her aunt. The band's almost asleep, I'd say, and I wouldn't mind going to bed. How about you?' Viola nodded. 'Sonia will no doubt drop Richard home in her nasty little car, and he'll be very sorry in the morning he didn't come with us.'

Viola approved the tone of her brother's disapprobation. It was the only consolation. She followed him from the marquee, head held high and face set into a rigid smile lest Richard should glance up from his nesting place and see her. On the way home in the car Gideon patted her on the knee and said:

'Don't worry, Violetta. It's only a passing lust.'

Later, very awake in bed, dawn bleaching the windows, she

66

realized the wisdom of Gideon's observation. It was sex, of course: all sex. How could it be anything else in the case of a plain giant such as Sonia Heel? Her advantage was that she was twenty or more, and was available. She would sleep with Richard. Well, Viola would patiently wait until Richard's appetite, surfeited, would sicken and so die. Then he would return to her, for love. Sonia would be relegated to the category of a woman of no importance in his life. The surety of such notions consoled. Eventually Viola slept.

In more positive form comfort came next day, too. Richard described the party to Mrs Windrush as 'a bit of a disaster, though Viola and I had a lovely dance', then did not refer to it again. Nor did he mention Sonia Heel, and Viola asked no questions. She trusted her expression did not convey her feelings, and judging by Richard's behaviour had reason to believe she had succeeded in her efforts. He was warm and friendly as ever to her, courteous and attentive. Before leaving, he invited her to his farewell party in Oxford and said he would be very disappointed if she did not come.

Viola spent eight weeks imagining all the possible horrors of another party haunted by the permissive giant. When the time came, she made a great effort to look her best and did not much enjoy herself. This was because, apart from her brother and Richard, she knew no one, and the hundred strange under-graduates showed little interest or even politeness to someone outside their world. But one cheering fact made up for the disappointment of the occasion: Sonia Heel was not present. Viola spent much of her time surreptitiously scanning the room, but her rival was quite definitely not there. Viola did not like to interpret this sign too hopefully, but found it hard not to imagine that perhaps Sonia, already, had outlived her welcome.

Three months later her speculations were to be ruthlessly dashed. Gideon gently broke the news that Richard and Sonia were to be married. Sonia was pregnant.

'Then he's an honourable man,' Viola managed to say.

'Honourable, my foot!' shouted Gideon, extraordinarily upset. 'He's an honourable fool! He doesn't love her, he never has. She was out to catch him and now she'll ruin his life. I've done my best to dissuade him but he won't change his mind. Perhaps you could –'

'Me? Don't be ridiculous. He wouldn't listen to me.'

'He might,' said Gideon, curiously.

But Viola, after much reflection, could not bring herself to write to Richard either in congratulation or condemnation. His marriage was none of her business. To try to persuade him against his course might mean losing his friendship and reveal the feelings which now more than ever she was anxious to conceal. With reluctant composure she went to the wedding, a small affair of little ceremony, and returned with double concentration to her studies. She had little faith in the idea of time as a healer, but was left with no choice other than to give it a chance.

Richard and his pregnant bride moved into a small cottage a few miles up the coast. They planned to leave for London, where Richard would begin his medical studies after the birth of the baby. Gideon visited them occasionally and once Richard came to the rectory, without his wife, wearing an expression which did not wholly convey newly-married bliss. It was impossible not to hear news of them, although Viola never allowed herself to ask questions.

The baby was born three months prematurely, and died almost immediately. Some weeks later the Windrushes heard Sonia had had a nervous breakdown and had been sent to a psychiatric home. Gideon reported that Richard was much distressed but when Sonia 'recovered', some months later, and came home, difficulties multiplied. Eventually she was re-admitted, and had now spent some twelve years in various homes. She did not recover again nor, apparently, regress: but lived in a dark and stagnant world that veered regularly between apathy and violent paranoia. Richard visited her dutifully, though over the years he admitted his visits were less frequent. Once it was established his wife would not be coming home he returned to his old habit of seeing the Windrushes frequently. He never spoke of Sonia: merely explained, that in order to be near her, he had given up his plans to study to be a neurologist. His ambition in that direction seemed to have withered. Instead, his medical training over, he became a general practitioner, continuing to live in his cottage near the Windrushes.

Viola let the rest of the morning drift by, sitting in her

kitchen chair, when Alfred Baxter had departed. She wondered if Richard, as he always seemed to, would hear of her return from America, and come and see her. She hoped he would. She was always pleased to see him. If too many months went by without a visit from him she felt a curious sense of loss, a wintry bleakness of the soul that did not decrease with the years.

5

The day that Viola left New York for England Hannah Bagle was surprised and delighted to receive her own flowers from Harry Antlers. In comparison with Viola's roses it was but a modest bunch of two dozen orchids, representing an expensive amount of care in their choosing. They were delivered to Hannah's office (in her flurry of pleasure she had no time to wonder how Harry had managed to discover where she worked) with a note of apology for his sudden departure from the party. An hour after their arrival, Harry telephoned Hannah with an invitation to lunch next day.

'My lady's left me, as you no doubt know,' said Harry. 'I'm a desperate man. I must talk. Please come. I want very much to see you.'

Hannah agreed. She put aside the fact that Harry's reasons for wanting to lunch with her were not wholly flattering, and concentrated on the pleasurable idea of his choosing her bosom to cry upon. To watch strong men crumble beneath her sympathy, so that she could then concentrate on a magnificent job of restoration, was her speciality. She knew from secret reverberations in the depths of her promiscuous flesh that she fancied Harry, and if it was his choice to begin things with a moan about a faraway English girl, well, that was fine with her.

Swinging round on her leather chair, Hannah looked at the afternoon sky, toothy with skyscrapers, and wondered how Gideon would react to Harry's invitation. It then occurred to her that this was one of those occasions about which it would be wiser to say nothing. Gideon rarely talked about his sister, but Hannah was aware of his loyalty to her – a loyalty Hannah herself had never experienced towards any member of her own family. He might not understand. Silence rather than an issue, therefore, she thought. Besides, it would be by way of a *business* lunch really – Viola being their business. This justification for intended silence pleased Hannah greatly. She swept a self-approving hand through her blonde hair, and buzzed her secretary to make an appointment with the hairdresser. The afternoon trembled with anticipation.

Knowing the restaurant Harry had chosen was a dark and ill-lit place, Hannah decided to appear her most bleached: white silk shirt, under which bra-less breasts would glow with the gold of a carefully maintained tan; cream skirt, silver nails, ashy hair. In the midday dusk she would palely shine, demure, soft, irresistibly sympathetic. She arrived early, for unlike most beautiful women she did not consider unpunctuality either forgivable or an aphrodisiac. Indeed, to be there settled and waiting, so that an instant apology was required, had often meant the scoring of the first point.

She shimmied into her place at the reserved table, sat facing the room. She felt no need to hide non-existent awkwardness in the pretence of studying a menu. Her lighting of a cigarette was only so that she should appear almost ghostly in her tranquility behind the blue smoke. Hannah had often thought of herself as a wood nymph, whatever that was.

Harry arrived ten minutes later. He strode across the room, ignoring all waiters on seeing her, a fat and anxious man. His plump and womanly hands clasped both of Hannah's including the cigarette, while his eyes roved tragically from her face to her breasts, where the tragedy turned to appreciation. Hannah suggested he needed a daiquiri very fast. She could see his tired body slump with gratitude at her instant sensitivity to his condition.

'My God, you're a lovely woman, Hannah Bagle,' he said with a charming smile, so that the ugliness of his face disappeared for a moment. 'I'm overwhelmed by your loveliness.'

Hannah, unused to such coarse compliments – Gideon, in his rare observations, would never stoop to the vulgarity of the word 'lovely' – was for a moment caught off her guard. But with a sip of the fierce cold drink she re-established her equilibrium and softened her face into a smile that reflected Harry's own.

'I thought,' she said, 'it was Viola you were overwhelmed by.'

'Oh. *That*. Her. That is an entirely different matter. That's

71

a matter of total, passionate, eternal love, such as not many men are blessed with. Or cursed, perhaps.'

'I don't know her very well. She was only with us a week. She seemed a nice enough girl. Quiet. Very English.'

'Then you missed getting to know one of the most remarkable ladies of our time.'

Hannah, determined not to be irritated by such hyperbole, stubbed out her cigarette so that Harry should now have an unclouded view of her sympathetic eyes.

'I'm sorry about that.'

'Does your lover Gideon talk about her a lot?'

'I'd rather you didn't refer to Gideon as my lover.'

'I thought that's what he was.'

'The acquisition of a label indicates a fixed position. I don't like fixed positions.'

'Oh.' Harry gave the merest smile. 'Anyway, what do you know about my lady? Through Gideon or otherwise?'

'Very little. Could we order? I'm ravenous.'

'Ah! I'm sorry. You can see at every turn I'm not a gentleman.'

Harry summoned the waiter and the business of ordering was accomplished fast, without interest.

'You must know something,' Harry persisted.

'Honestly. I don't.' Hannah shrugged. 'Apparently she tried her hand at acting – wasn't bad. But since the death of her parents she likes sticking around in some old family house miles from anywhere on a cold bleak coast. That's all Gideon said.'

'If my only rival is a house, then I've a good chance. Hasn't she got any lovers?'

'Not that I know of.'

Harry sighed. Hannah's lack of help exacerbated the frenzy in his stomach. He signalled to a waiter to hurry with the steak.

'I shouldn't worry so,' said Hannah. 'You'll get her.' She did not believe what she said, but it was time for the subject of Viola to be abandoned in favour of the subject of themselves. But Harry persisted.

'How?' he asked. 'There are three thousand miles between us. That doesn't make for a good start.'

'Precisely,' cooed Hannah in her most soothing tones,

72

wonderfully disguising the irritation she felt. 'The Atlantic Ocean is quite a little impediment to courting. You'll have to go over.'

'I have to stay another month till the play's safely on its feet.'

'I daresay you'll survive.' Hannah gave an encouraging smile.

'I doubt it,' said Harry, shoving large quantities of mashed potatoes into his mouth. 'The very fact it's impossible to see the girl is tearing my heart out.'

'Then I'll have to lend a comforting shoulder,' answered Hannah, eyes down, and giving a small shudder so that she could feel the silk of her shirt tremble against her breasts.

'Thanks. You're terrific.' Harry paused. 'Have you never felt like this? Blasted, *totally blasted* by love?'

Hannah looked up, cool. 'No.'

'Ah. Then I must be speaking a foreign language to you.'

'You are.'

'You've missed a lot.'

'I'm not sure I'd want the discomfort you seem to be suffering.'

'I like to think it's only temporary. It'll all be worth it, fantastic in the end.'

'I hope so.'

At last Harry paid her some attention. She enjoyed the way his eyes seemed to penetrate the superficial gloss of her appearance. She suspected his understanding of her was accurate, without having to ask any questions. He did ask some questions, though, with flattering interest, probably knowing the answers in advance.

'Aren't you waiting to be totally consumed by some wonderful man? To give yourself completely?'

'Good Lord, no.' Hannah looked quite shocked. 'I should hate that. That would be the end. I'm a dilettante, so far as affections are concerned.'

'I'm not, unfortunately,' said Harry, downcast again. 'I always knew it in my bones, and meeting Viola confirmed it for ever.'

'Very bad luck,' murmured Hannah.

The food tranquillized Harry. By the time he was halfway

73

through a vast concoction of chestnut and cream, he felt quite mellow. He sensed a certain weakness of the flesh come upon him: they had drunk many glasses of wine.

'If it wasn't for the fact that my heart is so utterly cast in other directions,' he said, with an apologetic laugh, 'then I'd probably find myself suggesting you and I – '

' – and I might agree at once,' said Hannah quickly. They joined in sudden laughter.

'Ridiculous.' Harry shrugged. 'As it is, maybe I will take up your offer to cry on your shoulder sometimes.'

'With pleasure.'

Harry took her hand. They were locked together in that hopeless gaze that binds millions of lunching companions bent on flirtation: they felt the sexual thrill that comes with the coffee – doomed not to be consummated because of work in the afternoon – turn to the cold flat shiver of postponement.

'There's one thing, perhaps, you could do for me.' One of Harry's soft hands still held one of Hannah's.

'Anything. I'll do anything I can.' In a swift calculation Hannah juggled her afternoon appointments, prepared to accept.

'You could find me Viola's address in the country.' He noticed Hannah's sigh: tightened his grip on her hand. 'I'd do almost anything in return.' He gave a smile that was as near to charming as the ugly set of his mouth could achieve.

'Thanks,' said Hannah, pulling away her hand, drawing herself up and back. She was irritated with herself for not having handled the lunch better. Normally, she would have some definite – albeit unspoken – plan agreed upon by now. Harry Antlers, for all his probing feelers, had proved elusive. Something of a challenge.

They parted quickly in the street, neither satisfied. Hannah promised to contact him as soon as she had the information he wanted. Harry pecked her without interest on the cheek (wondering if he had imagined the desirous feeling of only half an hour ago) and strode a little dizzily down the street. He was not accustomed to wine at lunch.

The prospect of the afternoon's rehearsals held no cheer for him. There was an ache all through his body, powerful and solid, making his legs difficult to manipulate with any firmness of step. In his mind's eye Viola twisted herself from man to man in an obscene orgy: he could not slay the men because in his horrible vision they had no heads. That jealousy spurred by fantasy, that is near to madness, tore at Harry with its lacerating nails: with wild heart and sweating brow, he stumbled into a drug store, collapsed on to a high stool at the counter, and in a scarcely audible voice ordered a double strawberry malt milkshake.

At the same time, back in her office, Hannah Bagle said to herself: Harry Antlers, you'll pay for using me this way, you'll see.

By the time Alfred Baxter returned to his flat after his interview with Viola Windrush, the afternoon was completely topsy-turvy. He knew that both good news and bad news played havoc with habitual timings, and could even change the look of a room or a place that you were used to seeing on an ordinary day. Full of his good fortune, therefore, Alfred found it no surprise that the afternoon had turned into an unrecognizable mess, so that he felt as if he were walking on air, a sensation he remembered the day he took off work many years ago to attend the wedding of Eileen's niece.

He enjoyed the feeling. As one who was punctilious about mealtimes, he now found himself cooking fish fingers and a tin of carrots at five past three, and looking forward to them with pleasure. Perhaps, having eaten so little over the last few weeks, he had been hungry all along but had not realized it, and his happy morning had released the pangs. Or perhaps this sudden flexibility in his ways was all part of the unexpected bonuses of the day.

When he had eaten his hot food on a plate at the kitchen table, Mr Baxter took a plastic carton of Caramel Dessert from the fridge, and a teaspoon from the drawer. With not a flicker of guilt he then made for his armchair at the window of the sitting-room, tore the foil lid from the carton, and with great relish proceeded to peck the spoon into the golden top of the dessert, and feed himself minute helpings, throwing back his head to savour the taste of each one, reminding himself of a blue-tit stealing cream from a milk bottle.

In her lifetime, Eileen would not have abided such behaviour, any more than Alfred would have considered acting thus. But, he thought now, from her place in heaven she would be looking down on him with compassion and understanding, and probably that funny smile of hers that she gave him when occasional moments of disapproval fought with the great love in her heart for her husband. She would understand. He had need to celebrate. Small, private celebrations were essential to the well-being of those who live alone. Eileen would not begrudge him his enjoyment of the Caramel Dessert on his knee.

When the last small spoonful was licked clean, Alfred lay back with a contented sigh and contemplated the view he had never liked and soon would never have to see again. He began to plan in his mind all the things that would have to be done: possessions to be packed up, transport of the few pieces of furniture to be arranged, the flat to be let. The prospect of days ahead busily engaged in such activities was very pleasing. 'I must thank the good Lord, Eileen, for falling on my feet,' he said.

Alfred often spoke to Eileen, still: sometimes out loud, sometimes what seemed to be out loud but was really a voice in his head. He knew this because his lips did not move, although the voice was as clear as if he had spoken. On such occasions he always imagined Eileen. He could see her, luminous in his mind, almost tangible, sitting or standing before him, usually with a piece of sewing in her hand. He supposed that this was what was meant by death not being that much of a divider from life, the force of the spirit living on, especially in the case of a loved one. Certainly, for all her bodily absence, since Eileen's death Alfred had never felt she was far from him. He had never had trouble in conjuring her vision before him.

But this afternoon the trick, the magic – whatever it was – didn't work. The picture did not come. He spoke to Eileen but could not see her. At first Alfred thought it was a trick of the light, confusing his mind. There was a bright afternoon sun in the sky: its dazzling rays might have bleached out the picture of her. Alfred turned his head from the window and closed his eyes. Now there was blackness beneath his lids, but still no sign of Eileen. Alfred concentrated very hard. He felt his fingers gripping his knees as he willed a sight of her. After a while, to his relief, she began to unfurl, something in the manner of those Japanese flowers that you put in water and they bloom before your eyes. (A very successful line at Baxter's one Christmas.) Eileen materialized feet first: her small brown shoes with the delicately punched holes and the double straps, that she had preserved for twenty years or so: her blue skirt with the daisies embroidered on the hem, her yellow blouse with the mother-of-pearl buttons acquired in the days when buttons *were* buttons – and her lacy blue cardigan, painfully knitted not long before she died. But then Eileen stopped. At her shoulders. There was no neck, no head, no more of her. Alfred concentrated again, afraid, but there was no blooming of her dear face. And for all his efforts, Alfred could not remember anything about that face: the face he knew best in the world, stamped so deeply within him it was surely indelible.

He opened his eyes, heart thumping, and looked about the room. On the fireplace stood their wedding picture in its curly silver frame, a little tarnished, for Alfred had not felt like polishing in the last few weeks. There was Eileen's face as it had been that overcast morning in Lowestoft, as a shower of rain caught them as they came out of the church, and Alfred wondering if the effect of powdered diamonds on her nose would come out in the photographs. (The fact that it did not was always a regret.) Nevertheless, there was a radiance about her, the hallmark of happy brides, that shone through the photographer's static pose and brought a pricking dryness to Alfred's eyes that he would have liked to have relieved with tears. As he stared at the photograph the years fell over backwards, catapulting him back to that day: the memory of Eileen's warm and trembling hand in his so vivid that Alfred released the grip of his own knee for fear of hurting her. Time plays funny tricks on ageing men, he thought. With unblinking sore eyes, staring at the photograph, he remembered, he remembered – how he remembered that day.

But although the picture of Eileen gave back to Alfred the sight of her face as it was then, a picture of her more recent face still would not re-blossom. Eventually, exhausted by his efforts of hopeless recall, Alfred stirred himself and decided he would further confuse the afternoon by having his tea an hour early.

As he stood, rubbing with one hand at a painful shoulder, he had the strange impression that he was not alone, but that the presence near him was not Eileen. Then he heard – he could swear it was not a jest of his imagination – a soft, familiar laugh: Winnie's. Dear, stupid, disaster-prone Winnie. Shutting up the shop, winter evenings, while Eileen was out in the kitchen cooking the tea, Alfred had often heard Winnie laugh at his meticulous ways, straightening things on the counter so all would be shipshape for the morning, checking every bolt on the shutters twice. Alfred enjoyed her amusement. She kept him in touch with his own absurdities, reminding him that even in our striving for perfection we stand accused of foibles.

And now here was Winnie laughing at him again, although she was, in reality, on a South Seas island, eloped with a sailor, picnicking for the rest of her life. Further confused, Alfred rubbed his eyes, and then his ears, and listened to the accustomed silence that proved he was alone.

Suddenly businesslike, and rubbing his hands in the manner that often encouraged his customers to remember the very thing they had forgotten, Alfred hurried to the stove and toasted himself two tea cakes. He also opened a tin of whisky fruit cake and, for the first time since Eileen's death, took out the large teapot. He ate and drank slowly, at the kitchen table, enjoying the food, feeling strength return to him. He looked forward to the evening: he would pack a tea-chest full of books and papers, polish the old pair of boots that would do him nicely for work in Miss Windrush's garden. He would see to it that everything was efficiently organized by the time of the move next week: efficiency was his second nature.

As he washed the tea things, Alfred gave little thought to his recent unnerving experience. Being a man of good common sense he put it down to fatigue, worry, simple hunger (which affects the mind). These last few weeks had not been easy and now, today, with his change in fortune, there was naturally a feeling of considerable excitement. All these elements might well contribute to hallucinations. They were nothing to worry about.

Thus satisfied with his own explanation, Alfred set happily about his tasks. He fell asleep at once that night and dreamed of Eileen. Her face returned, clear as always, smiling at him.

In her chair in the kitchen, the real world obliterated by her memories, Viola was unaware of the rapid passing of the hours. It was only when she noticed the brightness of the afternoon had faded and the shadows of things on the window-sill had changed, that she stirred herself. She stretched her stiff legs and looked round the room.

Her eyes drifted first to the huge dresser which soared high as the ceiling, dominating the kitchen, and which was laden with plates, mugs, dishes, glasses, straw baskets, postcards, jars of herbs and spaghetti and beans, balls of string – all the things that people dump down in kitchens and, becoming used to them, have no desire to move or put away more tidily. An old shopping list hung from a hook. Viola saw that it was in her mother's writing and the paper had turned to pale gold, indicating its age. Next she observed with some shock that the two yellow candles, always the colour of sunlight, had faded to a dull cream, and their copper holders were tarnished. Things had slipped a little, thought Viola, since the death of her mother: and that would have made Mrs Windrush sad. But for the moment she could not summon the will to change anything, though perhaps with Alfred Baxter's help the house would gleam again. For the moment, the preservation of things just as they were was a comfort.

When she was away from home, the kitchen was the place Viola remembered most often. In her mind its every detail was so clear that, when she returned, she had the strange sensation that reality was merely a transparency which slipped over the imaginative picture, confirming it. Places she loved were ingrained within her more strongly than people. It was to them she turned, in solitude, or despair, and found tranquillity.

The door bell rang. Its old-fashioned clanging, reverbera-ting along the passages, interrupted her reveries and forced her to make the effort of getting up from her chair. She went slowly to the hall – the bell rang impatiently again – expecting no visitors and resenting the intrusion of an unexpected caller.

79

A florist's van stood in the driveway. Its driver, at the door, was scratching his head, his face awry with indignation.

'Windrush the name? Roses for you. Bloody van full. They'll take a bit of carrying.'

He went to the van, flung open the double doors. Viola followed him. She saw the entire interior was filled with cellophane packages of red roses.

'Oh, no,' she said.

'One hundred, apparently,' said the man. 'Better get them shifted.' He lifted up a package, but Viola called out, restraining him.

'Please don't. I don't want them. I don't want a single one.'

'*Don't want them?*'

'I'd be very grateful if you could deliver the whole lot to the hospital on your way back.'

'That would be very irregular. But then an order like this isn't exactly regular, is it?' He threw the roses back into the van and slammed shut the doors. 'Still, if that's what you want. Here, you better have the card.' He handed her a small envelope. 'Look, I'll have to cover myself in this matter, you understand. Would you mind signing something to say I've delivered the roses to the hospital on your orders?'

Smiling, Viola obliged him with a note to that effect, written on a bill from the florist. Then she watched gratefully as the van drove away with its unwelcome cargo.

Back in the kitchen, Viola opened the envelope and reluctantly took out the card. *From your ardent admirer, Harry Antlers, with love*, it said, in florist's biro writing. With sudden anger she tore it into small pieces and threw it into the fireplace. The idea of Harry Antlers discovering where she lived filled her with unaccountable fury. She had not thought about him since leaving New York, and did not care to think of him again. His second ridiculous gesture, absurd in its extravagance, did not strike her as flattering. She did not think of it as a measure of passion or love, but merely as an intrusion into her private world. Enraged, she made herself a new pot of tea and switched on her portable radio. She determined not to acknowledge these flowers: all she desired was no further contact with the flamboyant Mr Antlers.

A Brahms symphony filled the room. Viola returned to her

80

chair. After a while, calmer, and the tea finished, she got up and went to the larder. She was hungry, but there was little to eat. She stood looking at the almost empty stone shelves, smelling the familiar scents of cold stone and slabs of strong cheese and apples: smells which had clustered so thickly in the small space over the years that they had permeated the air for ever, even though the food itself had gone. Viola sighed. In her mother's time the shelves were always crowded with home-made jams and bottled fruits, cold pies and hollowed Stiltons. Now, there were six eggs, some tins of fruit and a jar of pickled onions. Viola picked up two of the eggs, and the door bell rang again.

In an instant she decided not to answer it, knowing it must be the return of the man from the florist. The hospital, too, had rejected the roses. Nobody wanted Harry Antlers' wretched flowers. As the bell clanged impatiently again, Viola shut the larder door. Silence. Then she heard footsteps outside. The window was too high to see through, but Viola could tell it was the heavy tread of a man.

Remembering the back door was open, she prayed whoever it was would not come in. Unmoving, she listened. Someone was tapping on the window. Then there was a voice calling her name.

Viola dashed back into the kitchen at the same moment as Richard Almond came through the back door. They fell into each other's arms, hugging, laughing. Viola drew back first.

'I was hiding in the larder. I didn't want any visitors.'

'Not even me?'

'I wasn't expecting you. Of course I want you.'

'I heard you were back.'

'You hear things very quickly.'

'Thought I'd come to dinner.'

'*Dinner*? Is it dinner time?'

'It's five past eight precisely.'

'But I've only six eggs and a jar of pickled onions . . .'

'I took precautions. There's a whole basketful of stuff in the car. I'll get it.'

When he had gone Viola stood, dazed, by the table. She made vague movements, trying to clear a space, to remove the tea mugs and teapot and newspapers. What had unnerved her

81

was not just Richard's unexpected arrival, but the sudden age in his face. She knew that after the age of thirty, if you do not see someone for several months the rapid change comes as a shock; new lines, a puckering of skin not observed before, a gathering of wisdom in the eye. Richard, for the first time, had prominent grey hairs at his temples. His unclouded young face, forever in her mind, was now the face of a middle-aged man. The reality and the mental image did not fit, and it was disturbing.

But such thoughts evaporated on Richard's return with the basket. The fact that he was here, his familiar presence filling the kitchen just as it used to, so that all the solid things trembled as if seen through a heat haze, was all that mattered. Filled with the sudden luxurious sense of being looked after, Viola watched while he unpacked the food and laid it on the table. He put two bottles of cold, greeny-yellow wine in the fridge, fetched knives and forks and spoons from their places, remembering where everything was. Weakly, Viola's only contribution was to take the two faded candles from the dresser, put them on the table and light them. Outside, gold clouds curled about the setting sun like honeysuckle. Opening the window, Viola could smell the sea of a high tide, and the paler smell of her mother's early roses.

They ate hungrily the delicious things Richard had brought: mackerel smoked locally, bread (which he warmed in the oven), tomatoes from his greenhouse, and home-made ice cream from his mother's deep freeze. Although food had never been of particular importance in Viola's life, she was conscious of enjoying this unexpected meal more than any eating she had done for many weeks. The food filled her with a new sense of optimism, though what there was to be optimistic about did not concern her for the moment. In high spirits she found herself telling Richard about New York, the saving of the house (about which he rejoiced) and the finding of Alfred Baxter. Finally, she described the puzzling antics of Harry Antlers. The return of the second lot of roses caused Richard much amusement.

'You've always been a one for inspiring such extravagant gestures,' he said. 'Orchids from Hong Kong, remember? God knows how many smoked salmon from Scotland arriving at Kings Lynn. That diamond heart from Cartier, a return first-class ticket to Bermuda . . . I remember them all.' He smiled. Viola wondered whether it was the wine that made her think there was wistfulness in his smile.

'I returned the airline tickets, don't forget.'

'So you did. I mustn't malign you. But you were always so wickedly funny about your suitors. I sometimes wondered if any of them were aware of the scrutiny you subjected them to. Poor wretches: they lost you through such innocent things. Do you remember that one upon whom you turned your scorn because he pulled a muscle blackberrying?'

'Oh, *him*. The essence of feebleness.' Viola laughed.

'Perhaps this Mr Antlers, then, with all his strength of passion, will be the one to win you.'

'Mr Antlers doesn't stand a chance.'

They had finished eating. A full but pale moon shone through the window. The sky was deepening, but far from dark, as if it found the brightness of the day hard to absorb in its shades. Richard opened the second bottle of wine.

'Don't let's move from here,' said Viola. 'The sitting-room's very unlived in, these days. And I still don't really like to go into Father's study.'

'No. We'll stay here.' Richard sat down at the table again. Her own news over, Viola waited for Richard to begin. He gave a small, reflective smile which, Viola knew of old, was prelude to some piece of self-criticism.

'I must have been the only one not to make you grand gestures,' he said.

Viola laughed. 'For a start, you were never my suitor, but my brother's friend, very kind to the younger sister. Secondly, over the years, you gave me the entire works of Dostoevsky, remember?'

'In paperback. Yes.'

'Which have given me much more pleasure than a diamond brooch.'

'Good, good. You've always been appreciative of small things.'

He was silent for a long time. They listened to the ticking of the clock on the wall. As a child, Viola had thought a minute man lived in its works. His duty as caretaker meant he paced round and round it, checking all was well, and the ticking was the sound of his regular footsteps. They never faltered, and the clock never went wrong. Now, suddenly remembering her image of the clock-keeper, Viola tried to recall how she had imagined him able to stick to the vertical face of the clock: but she could not remember. Eventually, she said to Richard:

'How's your life?'

'Busy. There's been a flu epidemic.' It was Richard's way to be both honest but brusque when asked such questions. Viola let a few more silent moments pass.

'And Sonia?'

Richard briefly closed his eyes. The deep lids, the colour of violet bruises, trembled very slightly, disturbing a fan of small lines at the corner of each eye that Viola had not observed before. She thought she had never seen him look so old or so tired. But when he looked at her again he was quite cheerful, and sipped his wine.

'I saw her yesterday, as a matter of fact. She's been quite ill. Flu turned into bronchial pneumonia. But she's better now.'

'But how . . . in general?'

'Much the same, I suppose. No great developments for the worse of late. Terribly depressed and pretty confused. Yesterday she thought I was a doctor, but had no idea I was her husband. Usually, she refers to me as "husband" all the time. I sometimes think she doesn't any longer know my name.'

His unusually detailed revelations gave Viola reason to think it would be in order, for once, to risk a further question.

'Perhaps, I shouldn't ask you this . . . the wine. But do you ever think of leaving her?'

Again Richard was cheerful, making the forbidden subject easier than it had ever been.

'Oh yes. Heavens, yes. Of course I think about ending it all, divorce, whatever. I think about it every day of my life.' He sat back, hands in pockets. 'But I made her those promises, you see. I may have made them for foolish reasons – and looking back I see I was certainly more foolish than honourable – but nonetheless I made them. How can I go back on my word?' He sighed. 'There's just a chance, one day, she may recover, and be returned to a normal life. If that happened,

84

she would need someone to be there waiting for her. She wouldn't survive on her own.'

'You wouldn't survive with her.'

'I'd have to try.'

'You're too noble, sometimes, for your own good.'

'I believe in constancy.' Viola smiled in silent agreement. 'Some of us, I suppose, are just born constant, and there's nothing much we can do about it.'

'But what are the chances of her recovery? Of her coming out? You ought to be practical.' Viola was aware that her voice had risen.

'Very small, I must admit. No, it'll all end in its own time.'

'You mean, she'll stay in that place her whole life and die of old age?'

'I very much doubt *that*. No, one day she'll kill herself.'

Richard watched the surprise in Viola's face. He knew that of all the solutions she had contemplated as an end to his predicament, that particular one had never occurred to her.

'She had anorexia as a teenager and first felt death "looming", as she called it, then. I've never known her threaten to kill herself, exactly, but she's got this awful Keatsian phrase she keeps on producing out of the blue. "Now more than ever it seems ripe to die," she says, quite conversationally, while we're having a cup of tea or something. Very menacing. In her maddest moments she screams it out loud over and over again.'

'I'm sorry,' said Viola, after a while. 'I didn't really mean to ask about Sonia.'

'I don't mind *your* asking,' Richard said, quietly. 'I'm loath to bring up the subject myself, simply because it's a subject without news one way of the other. It's just there. The odd small changes, but basically it's the same. Sonia exists, mad. I have a mad wife who exists. I await her in case one day she needs me. What else is there to be said?'

'Nothing,' said Viola.

Richard got up and went to the sink, poured himself a glass of water. When he turned back to Viola she saw a look of such old, resigned sadness in his eyes that she did not trust herself to speak.

'But you,' he said, jolting himself from whatever the private

85

reverie, 'what about you, Violetta? Any plans? What are you going to do?'

'I'm trying to decide.'

'You can't just sit here, stagnating.'

'No. I suppose I'll go to London, find some kind of job. But I'll be here for a while, settling Mr Baxter in and organizing the roof.'

'So I'll be able to call on you.'

'Whenever you like. Of course.'

'We could do some sailing. Picnics. Do you remember Gideon's loathing of picnics?' He smiled, looked at the clock. It was almost midnight. 'I must be off.'

Viola went on sitting at the table, unmoving, watching him approach her. She relived the old longing felt all those years ago in the garden at Maisie Fanshawe's dance. She wanted him to enclose her in his arms, ravish her, take her away for ever. But of course nowadays she allowed no such desires to show. Richard's view of her was of an impassive young woman whose stern pale face was only mellowed by the light of the candles.

'Thank you for coming,' she said, standing.

In the shadowy light he looked quite young again, green Irish eyes fired with things Viola could only guess at – regret, possibly, and the strain of his self-admitted constancy. He was within a few inches of her now. Viola, rigid to disguise her trembling, waited for the repeat bear hug of their greeting. Instead, Richard drew the back of his hand over one of her cheeks, feeling the bone, almost as if searching for an ache or a pain in his professional capacity. He bent his head, as if to kiss her, then changed his mind, and drew himself upright.

'I'll be back,' he said.

When he had gone, Viola went straight to bed, leaving the mess in the kitchen. She slept fitfully, dreaming of Richard, a kaleidoscope of events in their past: sailing, walking, reading, arguing at the kitchen table. The only thing that bore no resemblance to reality was that at each event Richard was accompanied by a large mongrel dog on a lead. The dog had centrally parted shaggy hair and the mad face of Sonia.

86

6

Viola was woken by the telephone. (The only change she had made in the house since her parents' death was to move a telephone into her room.) Dawn showed bleakly through the windows. Her instant thought was that Richard was in trouble. She was at once wide awake. But it was not his voice.

'Viola?'

'Yes?'

'This is your friend Harry Antlers.'

'Oh God, Harry.'

'I'm calling you from New York.'

'How did you get my number?'

'That's no business of yours. I'm through to you, that's the main thing. Were you asleep?'

'Yes.'

'Sorry. I couldn't wait any longer. Did some flowers arrive?'

'Yes. Thank you.'

Her bare shoulders chilled by the early air, Viola had not the heart to tell him of the flowers' fate. She lay back under the bedclothes, shivering: partly cold, partly the fear of the hunted.

'Look,' she said, as gently as she could, 'you're very kind, all these flowers. But please don't send me any more. Two hundred roses is enough to last anyone a lifetime.'

'Nonsense. By the end of your life you'll have had two hundred thousand roses from me.' A terrible threat, in the early light. 'You'll see.'

Viola laughed falsely. 'Please, Harry. Don't be silly. There are plenty of flowers here in the garden.'

'Plenty of flowers here in the garden,' he mimicked. 'I'm sure there are. Some people are born into very privileged gardens, full of flowers. But is that the point, my love?'

Only great self-control stopped Viola shouting her protest

87

at being referred to as Harry Antlers' love: she was nothing of the kind. How dare he presume to refer to her as such? A jangle of answers clamoured through her head, but rejecting them all as impolite on a transatlantic phone call, she said nothing. There was a long pause. Then Harry repeated:

'That isn't the point, you idiot woman.'

He sounded so despairing that for a moment Viola was guilty of feeling unsympathetic towards so gloomy and pathetic a character. But at the same time a menacing quality in his voice clouded all clear thought and sensible answers. He had a strange capacity to make her feel in the wrong, and afraid, for all the distance between them. Hopelessly, she said:

'This call must be costing you a fortune.'

'Who cares about money?'

Viola sighed. 'How's the play going?'

'Badly. But what do I care about the play?'

'A lot, I should hope.'

'I care for nothing that keeps me on the other side of the Atlantic from you.'

'For heaven's sake, Harry . . .' Viola's irritation boiled over. 'You're suffering from a terrible fantasy about me. Quite honestly, the sooner you get over it the better it will be for us both.'

'I'm glad that's what you like to think. But I don't believe you. You're not a girl who would not recognize truth when she saw it.'

There was a long pause. Viola's mind whirled. What was he talking about? The sun was rising through her window. She wanted to slam down the receiver: his call was a loathsome intrusion into her uncontaminated room.

'I've been hearing about you,' he was saying. 'I had lunch with a mutual friend of ours. She told me a lot about you. Very interesting it was, too.'

Despite herself, Viola's curiosity was aroused.

'Who was it?'

'That doesn't matter. The point is, I learned a lot about you. About all your lovers.' There was a note of triumph in his voice.

'Lovers? What are you talking about? I don't know anyone in New York except for Gideon and Hannah, and Hannah doesn't know anything about me.'

88

'Ah.'

'So I don't know what you mean.'

'It's a possibility a friend of yours was over from London and I ran into her. New York's a very small place. And you must remember not to trust your friends.'

As Viola's mind reeled through friends who might have gone to New York, met Harry Antlers and told tales of her private life, a painful pressure of bone began to constrict her head. She felt physically sick at the thought of such betrayal. Shivering beneath the warm bedclothes, in her pain and confusion it never occurred to her Harry was so devious as to shoot poisoned arrows in order to get some reaction.

'Everyone betrays everyone,' he was saying. 'You'll learn that.'

'Look, there's not much point in continuing this conversation,' said Viola weakly.

'No. I can see it disturbs you. Must be disturbing, being reminded of old lovers so early in the morning. Are you with one of them now?'

'I'm quite alone, but it's nothing to do with you.' Viola's voice was shaking.

'I'm sorry, my love, I seem to be upsetting you. That's the last thing in the world I want to do. I'm just terribly lonely here in New York. I'll be back with you as soon as I can.'

'Please. I shan't be here.'

'Where will you be?'

'I don't know. I'm leaving here soon. I have to get a job.'

'Worry not, little one. I'll find you. I love you with my entire being. You realize that? I can't let you escape now, can I? After a life's search. I'd be mad. And don't forget I know a lot more about you than you think I know. I *love* you, woman, do you hear me? Is sending roses across the Atlantic the act of a man who doesn't – '

Viola slammed down the receiver. She buried herself beneath the bedclothes into a cocoon of complete darkness, as she used to as a child. She tried to control the shivering, to clear her mind. Much later, she heard the telephone ring again, but did not answer it. She did not get up till midday, the sun high in a summer sky, but blighted. Without warmth. Years later, looking back, she realized this had been the

89

morning the bullying had started, and the horror of dealing with an irrational man had begun.

In New York, Harry Antlers kept himself from the daylight as much as possible. When he was forced to make brief excursions into the streets the sun bored painfully through his head, adding to the many other discomforts he suffered in mind and body. He ate hamburgers and milkshakes obsessively, but their tranquillizing effects were diminishing. He was aware of putting on weight. His clothes felt tight and uncomfortable. Sleep, which had never been elusive before, was now tormented. In the noisy, muggy nights, Viola's nasty little voice, so cold on the telephone, played an endless tape in his head. By day, in the stuffy theatre, rehearsals went badly. Harry could not speak to his cast without shouting. Normally so articulate, so arrogantly fluent in his ideas, he found himself struggling to convey what he wanted. And everybody, a talentless lot, did everything wrong. Chris tied and retied his shoelaces more frequently and more sullenly. All about him people looked at Harry as if there was something the matter with him, while visions of Viola exploded endlessly in his head, obscene visions which goaded with relentless agony. It was time for revenge.

Revenge? When the idea came to Harry's mind for the first time, he was shocked. In truth, it was the last thing he wanted: he knew its dangers. But if you loved a woman who did not realize she loved you, you must fight for her, breaking all rules if necessary. In the past his only fights had been to rid himself of the many girls who – once he had become successful – crowded him with their desperate love. (Before that, there had been years of shyness on his part, rejection on theirs.) Their attentions had flattered him, given him confidence. He had used them, but not loved them in return. Now, for the first time, he was bedevilled by total passion, and this lady seemed to have no care for the havoc she was causing him. If only he could show her a glimpse of his private vision – a somewhat hazy picture of domestic peace, a state Harry had never witnessed in reality – but it included thick carpets, bowls of flowers, a chuckling baby, and the constant Viola with open arms to welcome him home each evening, dinner waiting on the table. Oh, how he would love her! Overwhelm her. That was the way to keep things going . . . overwhelming: presents, proclamations, everything. His own childhood had proved to him there was nothing to be said for emotional parsimony. There had never been a word of love uttered in his parents' house. Starved always of affection, friendship, understanding, here he was, now, a man locked in his own inadequacies – full of strange love which he could not handle. And so although the idea of revenge came unwanted from his well-meaning heart, there might be no alternative.

The play opened and was unanimously scorned by the critics. Harry did not care. He sat in his dim hotel bedroom, eating a vast breakfast as he read the papers, silently scoffing back at his detractors for not understanding the essence of the work. But their cruel jibes had no power to hurt. Nothing hurt but the absence of Viola.

The telephone rang. (It had been ominously silent for many days.) He pounced eagerly upon it, hoping against hope it would be Viola. But it was Hannah Bagle, condoling.

Harry was in no mood for sympathy, and had not given Hannah further thought since the day she rang him with Viola's English telephone number. Now, hearing her gentle voice, an idea came to him: she could help in his revenge. He asked her round that afternoon. She accepted at once.

'I have some information that might interest you, Harry,' she said. This excited him. The five long hours till she was due passed in a state of barely controlled frenzy.

When Hannah arrived, punctually at five, she saw a desperate man. Slouched in the room's one armchair, he looked pale, ill. His smile of greeting was also one of gratitude – something Gideon infrequently gave – and Hannah found his fat, ugly, pathetic state infinitely desirable. She sat on the end of the bed. Harry returned to his chair.

'I'll order drinks. What would you like? Thank God you've come.'

'Nothing for the moment. Later, thanks.'

Hannah crossed her provocative legs and fiddled with gold chains at her neck. For his part, Harry observed she was his for the taking, and was glad there would be no struggle to involve her in his plans. But for the moment he was impatient for the news of Viola.

91

'What have you heard? Tell me, quickly. Your interesting information.' He gave the small, friendly laugh of a conspirator.

Hannah shrugged, maddeningly unhurried. 'Oh, nothing *much*. I'm sorry if I gave you the impression it was very exciting. Only that Gideon let it drop the other night – I have to be very careful how I question him for fear of arousing his suspicions – that years ago Viola'd been in love with his best friend at Oxford. But nothing came of it. The friend married someone else, who's mentally disturbed, and that was that, really. Although he and Viola remain friends.'

Harry sighed, disappointed. He had expected more useful ammunition, although there were ways of utilizing even such a paltry scrap.

'Do you know his name?'

'I didn't ask.'

'Do they still meet?'

'I believe so.'

'Anything else about the man? What he does? Does she still love him?'

'He's a doctor. That's all I know.'

Harry sighed again, dissatisfied.

'Look here, Harry,' said Hannah, 'if my only use to you is one of spy, or detective, then I think I'd better go.'

'Don't be ridiculous.' He smiled so warmly Hannah's small flare of indignation was quelled. 'Look, I'm sorry. You know my feelings about Viola, even if you can't understand them. As you can imagine, I'm passionate to talk about her, to get to know more about her. But on the other hand, she's miles away, there's nothing I can do about her at the moment. And you're here, just a few feet away from me, for heaven's sake.' Pause. 'A lovely woman, Hannah Bagle . . .'

Hannah smiled, eyes down, flushed. She thought how Gideon, master in the school of British understatement, would scorn such dialogue. And she did not care. If Gideon had need of her, then he did not show it. While this strange, ugly man before her could be comforted. She could make use of her superior strength. She looked down to see he was unbuttoning her shirt.

'Is this . . . forbidden?' asked Harry, so gently that, had

Hannah been that sort of woman, tears would have come to her eyes.

'No.' She trembled.

Then her breasts were exposed, Harry's hands were upon them. He was kneeling on the ground, his head plunged between the breasts so that his hair tickled her chin, and she was cradling him like the child she would never contemplate having for fear of destroying her career. Harry was weeping. In all her various experiences, Hannah had never known a man cry in her arms before, and found it curiously stimulating. She brushed away his tears with fingers that she hoped were tender rather than nurse-like, and, surreptitiously glancing at her watch, wondered how long she would have to wait before Harry had spent his tears and would begin thinking of her pleasure. She whispered comforting words, flattered that the beauty of her body should have so devastating an effect upon a man, never guessing that his damp moaning was for himself and for the absence of Viola. The woman upon whose breasts he lay his self-pitying head for comfort was of no more significance to Harry than a hot-water bottle.

When he had finished with her, he was instantly overcome by the disagreeable state of having glutted his desire on something he had not really wanted. He lay back on the bed, listening to her having a hurried bath, watching her dress, without interest. She was flustered, late, and Harry cared not a jot for her anxiety. He did not even bother to raise himself from the bed as she prepared to leave. She knelt beside him, suffused with that temporary softness that overcomes the hardest woman after she has been seduced.

'Goodbye, Harry.'

'Forgive me for not coming down with you. They'll get you a cab. As I've told you before, I'm not a gentleman.'

'Will I see you again soon?'

'Of course.'

'I'd like to see you often, often.'

'You will. You will, you will.'

'Take care of yourself, Harry.'

She kissed him lightly on the eyes, tasting the salt of still damp lashes. He was a man who could sure worm his way into her heart, should he like to try . . .

93

When Hannah had gone, Harry breathed deeply with relief, exhausted. He dozed for a while, then woke in a calmer, happier state. The ammunition he had acquired through Hannah's cooperation was invaluable. Tricking Viola's brother meant that, in a confused way, Harry held a strong card. With a grim smile he picked up the telephone, got through to the airline and booked himself on a flight back to England the next day.

There is a rhythm to the solitary life, as Viola had discovered long ago. Many empty days go by, then comes a cluster of unexpected events. Some of these may change the whole direction of life, some may shift it just the slightest degree from the normal routine. On her return from America Viola had anticipated habitual quiet, and had already been surprised by three things: the good fortune in finding Alfred Baxter, Richard's visit, and Harry Antlers' telephone call from New York. A few days after that third, and disagreeable happening, came the fourth surprise, in the shape of a letter from her Uncle David.

Uncle David, her father's brother, was a millionaire anthropologist: an elderly and eccentric man who spent most of his time in the jungles of Brazil. On the rare occasions he was in England he had always shown a particular concern for Viola, and indeed several generous cheques since her parents' death had saved her from financial difficulties on many occasions. He now had a typically benevolent proposal to make to her.

The sitting tenant in the top-floor flat of his house in Holland Park had died, and it required complete renovation. Knowing Viola enjoyed that sort of thing, he wrote, he wondered if she would care to undertake the task for him, for which he would provide a handsome budget. In return, she could treat the flat as her own, rent free, until such time as he sold the whole house. He was returning to South America in a week's time, and would be obliged if Viola could let him know her decision before he left, so that they could arrange finances and keys. Until the flat was ready for habitation, he would be delighted if she lived in his part of the house, where she had stayed many times before. 'You may run into a quiet, scholarly fellow,' he wrote, 'son of a friend of mine, one Edwin Hardley. He's writing a book on moths – been writing it for about twelve years, and seems to prefer working in my library to his own flat or the British Museum. He's a silent sort of chap, wouldn't do a thing to hurt you. In fact, I call him Hardley There: his presence is so transparent, somehow, you're scarcely aware of him even when he's in the room. Do hope the whole plan might appeal.'

This was a cheering and unexpected solution to the menacing worries that were beginning to accumulate in Viola's mind. Amazed by such well-timed luck, her morning was suddenly sparked by plans. Once Alfred Baxter and the mending of the roof here were settled, she would go to London to convert the flat and find herself a job. The adrenalin of ideas began to flow, uncontainable. She immediately sat down to write her uncle a letter of grateful acceptance and then, still restless, jotted down the beginnings of a poem which came to her in a blinding strike of light. She had always been ashamed of her attempts at poetry, shown them to no one and hidden them away. She had no doubt they were of little merit, but she was unable to resist writing them when the Muse, or whatever, was upon her. By the end of the day she felt something was accomplished: a poem, and a letter confirming plans for a change in life. With a new peace of mind she lit the fire and sat listening to a concert on the radio. When the telephone rang she knew instinctively it was Harry Antlers, not Richard, and did not answer it. It continued to ring many times during the night. Viola ignored it with great satisfaction, and when at last she slept she dreamed of walking for miles along the empty beach with Richard. She remembered, in her dream, to tell him about the picnic she had observed at the wreck: the stillness of the ghost ladies in the fluttering dresses. But Richard's only reaction was to turn to her and say:

'Oh, Viola, *you* must be mad, too.' He looked distressed, gazing at the far-off wreck where there were no picknickers to be seen. And in her dream Viola understood his distress: he did not want two mad women in his life.

By the time Harry's plane landed at Heathrow he was in a

state of such frenzied impatience that regulations had become barriers designed for his annoyance alone. Passport control, waiting for the baggage, Customs . . . Harry stomped about gleefully noticing the effect he had upon calmer passengers. Alarmed by his audible snorts and furious face, they backed away from him, nudging, whispering, fearing attack from the apparent madman among them. Their unease further spurred Harry's mania. Free with his suitcase at last, he ran clumsily to the taxi rank. There he shouted at the driver to speed as if it were a matter of life or death.

But such disorderly emotion spends itself quickly. In the journey to London, heavy rain making the taxi a watery cage, the strength went from Harry. It left him cold and weak. He craved hot food, dreaded the silent dampness which he knew awaited him in his bleak bedsitting-room.

Heavy with self-pity, he dragged himself up the narrow staircase of the semi-detached house which had been his un-ambitious home for the past ten years. A dark passage beside the stairs led to the steamy quarters of his spinster landlady. It was her preoccupation with washing clothes – rather, boiling them in preserving pans on the stove – that Harry believed sent dampness billowing into his own quarters. Beside the clothes the landlady boiled daily quantities of vegetables and stew. The combined smells of hot soap and murky food was vile in the air. They greeted Harry with sickening familiarity. He determined to complain once more when he was next in a strong mood, loth though he was ever to enter the landlady's kitchen. But for the moment there were more urgent matters to be considered.

An hour later, from the shallows of an ugly tweed chair, Harry surveyed his aloneness. Temporary numbness of feeling had come from a packet of stale biscuits and a bowl of powdered mushroom soup. Rain continued to pour with slatey sound against the windows. The gas fire hissed, un-warming. A large pile of opened letters lay scattered on the floor. Harry recognized the false calm before another outbreak of maddened desire, and picked up the telephone.

He dialled Viola's number – a number by now indelible in his mind. It rang for a long time, the rhythmic buzz soothing, simply because it manifested some connection with the one he loved. Eventually he replaced the receiver, dispirited but not deterred. Looking at his watch, he saw that it was almost five. He calculated that by the time he had had several hamburgers at his local Wimpy, he could be in Norfolk by 8.30.

Standing, he took from his pocket a small jeweller's box and opened it. There lay a round black stone veined with white. He did not know its name but, in New York, trembling as he chose it, had thought it beautiful. The shopkeeper had said it was a most unusual brooch, and it had cost Harry far more than he could afford. But here, in this gloomy room, sodden plane leaves slapping at the windows, its magic had quite gone. Gloucester's eye, it was, now: plucked, solidified, turned to stone. The thought made Harry shiver. He hurried back down the damp stairs, slammed the warped front door and hurled the brooch far into the gutter. (One day it would be replaced with diamonds.) There was urgency upon him again. Head down, smeared glasses impeding the view, Harry charged the rain.

Richard's surprise visit had alerted Viola to more surprises. She anticipated that, in the short time she was to remain at home before going to London, he might appear several times. She determined to be more ready for him when he came again. And so each evening she tidied the kitchen a little, saw that there was enough food and wine for supper, and put his favourite Schubert on the record player.

The fact that Richard did not come for several nights left her undismayed. She was strong with the certainty of his return at some time, felt curious pleasure in exercising patience. But patience is capricious, deserts its captor without warning to leave the nerves exposed and shivering once again. On the third night of waiting Viola felt the warmth of certainty stripped from her. Such doubts and fears assailed her that despite a lighted fire she felt quite cold.

And so on this particular evening she paid especial attention to her preparations. She took the chill of her flesh to be a warning, a premonition. Tonight Richard would appear and she had no intention of letting him catch her unawares. All traces of the anguish she felt would be wholly disguised. A bath first, for warmth. Then she dressed, choosing clothes

97

with care: an old silk shirt so large it must once have belonged to Gideon, but whose soft sleeves, rolled up, gave protection: a wide belt of frayed silver leather, punched with silver studs, that emphasized the Edwardian smallness of her waist, and which Richard had often admired. Quite pleased with her appearance, and at the same time scorning her own vanity, she returned to the kitchen and lit the fire. She turned on Elgar's cello concerto, a piece she had always considered of such dignified sadness that it should be used as a remedy by anyone venturing towards the shades of self-pity. She polished apples on her skirt, studied her mother's old shopping lists hanging from the dresser. *Mince for cottage pie*, she read, and wished she could remember the forgotten day on which her family, all alive, had eaten that pie. The Colonel and his love of Worcestershire sauce . . .

There is madness in waiting, thought Viola.

At ten past nine she went to the window. It had been raining heavily all day, had now stopped. But the sky glowered over the garden ready to burst again. Viola stayed at the window, eyes searching the clouds, waiting for the first drop on the glass. But it did not come, and the music and the shuffling of the fire behind her were but rags of sound thrown over the fundamental silence. Then the front door bell rang.

Viola stirred. It rang again, and again. Viola merely went to the fire, stood so that its heat flared up her back, instantly warming the silk of her shirt. She surveyed the kitchen, defiant. For some reason, perverse even to herself, she did not wish to go to the door and open it. Rather, she would wait for Richard to come round here, as he had before.

There were footsteps in the passage outside. A pause. The kitchen door opened. Harry Antlers stood there.

'Hello, my love,' he said.

Viola felt the flames scorch her back. Her shirt pounded. She took a deep breath in the hope that it would steady her voice.

'What are you doing here?' she asked.

'Oh, I can see what kind of a greeting I am going to get. I should have imagined it, the rapturous greeting.'

Harry stepped further into the room, slamming the door behind him. Despite herself, Viola jumped. Harry's eyes scoured her nervousness. Then he cupped a hand over them as if to secure the vision of her in his mind. Viola's fingers played among the studs on her belt. When eventually he took away his hand, he smiled, as if with a great effort of self-control.

'I'm sorry if I've interrupted your evening. I'm sorry if my presence is inconvenient. Were you waiting for someone?'

'No,' answered Viola, after a long pause.

'Perhaps, then, you'd grant me the decency of the minimum of hospitality. I've come a long way to see you. I left New York this morning, only stopped in London long enough to get my car. I've been circling round your bloody Norfolk lanes for hours. I'm wet and hungry. God, I'm hungry. Would it be too much to ask for a simple piece of cheese? A glass of wine? Or milk? Anything.'

Pulling off his jacket, Harry Antlers strode to the fire. He flung the jacket on the back of a chair, turned it to the flames. Viola moved to the fridge. After some searching she took from it a saucer holding a small wedge of Brie.

'Cheese,' she said.

Harry, from his position by the fire, sneered down at it.

'I meant real cheese,' he said. 'The sort of thing people from my background call cheese. You know, or perhaps you don't, being such a grand lady. Cheddar.'

'I'm sorry . . . It's all I have.'

Even as she heard her own words, Viola cursed herself. It was ludicrous to find herself apologizing for having no Cheddar for this unwanted and unwelcome visitor. She returned the Brie to the fridge.

'There's a cold sausage,' she said.

'A cold sausage? That should keep me going for a while,' Harry scoffed.

Viola went to him, holding out a plate. Harry took the sausage. There was a long silence while he admired it intently. Viola, heart fearfully pounding as she looked upon the disagreeable mass of this ugly, bitter man, felt irrational guilt again. The sausage was undercooked.

'Very appropriate,' said Harry at last. 'Thanks. And could you, perhaps, run to a slice of bread and marge to accompany this very wonderful sausage?'

99

'Of course. And there's some wine . . .'

'*Wine*? You amaze me. Your hospitality.'

While Viola clumsily buttered a crust of stale bread – all that remained in the bin – and poured a glass of wine, Harry observed his surroundings. They did nothing to mellow his unease. Spurred by acute hunger now, he felt his old rage kindle within him. He loathed the untidy arrogance of the room: the high ceiling, the faded prints hung low on the walls, rush matting split and frayed on the stone floor – the feel and smell of a room that has housed a happy family for many years. Suddenly he stood, unable to contain himself any longer, full of the fury of one threatened by a past he has not shared. Viola handed him the bread. He snatched it from her, banged it down on the table.

'Privileged bitch,' he said quietly. 'Typical of your kind.'

He swung round to the sink, grabbed an empty milk bottle and, turning back to Viola, smashed it against the edge of a chair. The neck broke, fell to the floor with a small chink. Harry waved the rest of the bottle triumphantly, pointing the end of jagged glass at Viola. She screamed. Harry laughed.

'I come all the way from New York to see the only woman I've ever loved and I'm given a *cold sausage*!'

'Get out! Or I'll call the police!' Viola's voice was faint. She wondered how she was going to get to the telephone.

'Ah, the melodramatic little lady – '

' – and put that bottle down.'

Viola lunged unthinkingly at Harry, locked the thick wrist that held the bottle in both her hands, nails digging into his flesh. Strangely, he did not fight back. At the touch of her, all strength seemed to ebb from him. He sagged, put the bottle gently back on the table, slumped down into the chair by the fire. 'Oh, my God, my love, I'm sorry.' Sweat on his brow, tears in his eyes. 'You'll never believe me, I'm a total bastard – but I'm sorry. I don't know what came over me. Please forgive me if you can.'

Viola, shaking, handed him the bread which he ate wolf-like in one mouthful, butter smearing and glistening at the corners of his mouth. Then he drank the glass of wine. The fire spat and crackled. Viola looked at the jagged glass teeth of the broken milk bottle.

'Please,' she said. 'Just go. If you leave now, with no fuss, I won't call the police.'

Harry smiled. 'That's good of you.' He put out a hand towards her. She backed out of his reach. 'You're trembling. Don't tremble. No need. Here, come nearer to the fire. Let me hold your hand.'

Viola looked down on him. She could feel no sympathy in her heart, only a strong revulsion such as she had never known before. It froze and numbed her limbs. She did not move. Harry, wiping his mouth with a grubby handkerchief, made a soft, whimpering noise like a chained dog under a full moon.

'I don't think you can begin to conceive what I feel – the agony I've been through.'

'No.'

'And you probably don't care.'

'No.'

'But I'm not going to give up.' He smiled, almost twinkling. 'When a man has found his ultimate prize he doesn't let it go that easily. All my life, till meeting you, I've been stumbling along in the darkness. Don't you see?'

'I'm not interested. Please understand that. I'm sorry if I've caused you so much despair, but I don't want to know or hear of your feelings any more. I don't want any more to do with you, please. And I don't want you in this house. I don't want you ever to come back . . .' Her voice rose. Harry stood. 'Oh, this is ridiculous. This isn't ordinary behaviour.'

'Quite.' Full of calm sympathy now the rage was exorcized, Harry was able to laugh. 'Well, there'll be no more such behaviour, I promise, if you give up fighting. Just submit to what you know in your heart you want – '

'You're *mad*, Harry Antlers. The only thing in the world I want from you is that you should go, and never attempt to see me again.'

'Calm down, little one. I'm off. I'm looking forward to another long drive through the rain, *driven out* . . . No, don't worry: I am going. But I must eat something first. I can't drive another mile on an empty stomach. I don't believe there isn't *something* in a great house like this . . .'

He began to move about the kitchen, touching things, opening biscuit tins, tapping glass jars of rice and sultanas. It was then a new fear flared in Viola: he would find the larder and the cold chicken pie – the pastry had taken up most of her morning – which she had made in case Richard came. Even as this terror gripped her, Harry opened the larder door. Viola screamed.

'Come out of there!'

Very calm, Harry turned back into the kitchen holding the chicken pie.

'Look what I've found. Isn't this wonderful? A pie.'

'Get out, please. Go.'

Viola tried to snatch the pie from Harry, but he held it out of reach above her head.

'No fighting, now. I'll eat as fast as I can then leave you as I promised. For the moment,' he added, ominously. He sat down at the far side of the table, picked up a nearby fork and dug into the pastry.

In the silence, now that the music had stopped, the sound of Harry's eating struck every nerve in Viola's body. Unable to bear the sight of him, creamy sauce and flakes of pastry askew on his chin, she went over to the sink, folded her arms to give herself support, and stared out at the night sky. A small part of her mind could observe the absurdity of the situation: woman helpless in her own kitchen while unwanted man ravishes chicken pie made with love for another. But the humorous element was not strong enough to overcome the horror and the fear.

It was one of those summer nights when there is no denseness to the dark, when small clouds shimmy about the moon, restless in their duty of casting shade over the land till dawn. The rain had stopped, leaving a faint glitter on the leaves. The tide must have been out, for there was no whisper of the sea.

Viola heard a footstep on the path, a cautious scrunch of gravel. She tightened. Not wishing to indicate by movement that she had heard anything, she strained her eyes. She saw the shape of Richard. He seemed to stare at her, then past her. She was about to shout for his help when he backed away, over the lawn: a lithe, surprised motion. He quickly disappeared through the gate that led to the marsh.

Viola took a deep breath to help control. She turned to face Harry. He had pushed the pie away from him, entirely eaten but for a few bits of pastry that clung to the sides of the dish. He wiped his mouth with the back of his hand.

'Your lover, I suppose,' he said. 'Yes, I saw him.' Viola opened her mouth. Harry put up his hand. 'Don't bother to deny it: I know all about your lovers, past and present. Well, I'm sorry if I disturbed an assignation. I'm sorry if I've eaten the bastard's dinner, too. But it was very good, and my need was greater than his.' He stood, benign from the food, and smiling. 'I'm going now, but I warn you. I shan't be far away. Hope the thought won't disturb your screwing.'

At this word, in connection with Richard so obscene and so far from the truth, a searing rage and indignation flared in Viola so that her whole body trembled. But she managed to speak quietly.

'Harry Antlers,' she said, 'you need medical help.'

Harry smiled charmingly. 'How touching you are in your concern! But I don't need a doctor, thank you. I'm merely struck by an illness for which there's only one remedy, and that remedy will soon be mine.'

He moved clumsily to the door, flung a final look of scorn about the room. Then he turned to Viola, menacing.

'But there's one thing you must know, and never forget. When a man loves in the way that I do, there's no holding him. He's filled with a demon energy that knows no bounds. He will go to any length to get what he wants, any means. And strangely – you must believe this – it's remarkably easy to find out all one wants to know. This man, this doctor in your life – there's little I don't know about him, for instance. Loved him for years, haven't you? Perhaps you know how it feels, then: wanting. Perhaps even a beautiful girl like you knows the despair of wanting. I hope so.'

He was gone, the door banged behind him. Viola heard the muffled revving of his car. Then merciful silence, but for small shifts among the dying logs in the fire.

Viola screamed out loud, a wordless spewing forth of all the things held back since seeing Richard in the garden. Then she ran to the window, banged it with shaking hands, her fingers scrabbling among the moving clouds, calling his name, calling his name. From the window she ran to the dresser, picked up the telephone and dialled his number. It rang for a long time, but there was no answer. Shaking, she ran again, footsteps frantic on the flagstones, to both doors, making fast the old bolts and turning the huge keys in their solid locks. Turning, the sight of the empty pie dish on the table, parsley sauce solidifying on the prongs of the fork, renewed the horror. The solid comforting things of this womb kitchen, protection for a lifetime, had tonight been cracked beyond recognition, ravaged by Harry Antlers' loathsome presence. His threats savaging through her, Viola went to the fire, crouched down before it, hands stretched out to the last of the flames. Victim now of a terrible fear, the violation of her peace causing an unearthly chill to her flesh, she clutched painfully at her own arms in all her wretchedness. Escape was her only thought.

7

By late afternoon of the next day, Alfred Baxter was installed in the wing of Viola's house. He had always prided himself on his efficiency in practical matters, and the day of moving had passed with an ease which filled Alfred with retrospective content, although at the time of humping his possessions through the door there had been moments of anxiety. Would, for instance, Eileen's cornflower curtains fit the sitting-room windows? His first act, once the removal van had gone, was to try them, and he was well pleased with the result. The fact that they did not quite meet in the middle, and fell short of the window sill by some inches, was of no significance to Alfred. They were good enough to secure him from a dark night, and what they lacked in measurement they made up for by reasons of sentiment and loyalty. Eileen's last curtains would never be abandoned by Alfred in his lifetime.

He stood, now, surveying his efforts in the sitting-room, sun livening the old familiar furniture and sparkling on the brass ornaments. He had made a good beginning, but there was still much to be done: more carpet to be found – his rugs covered only small parts of the floor – and the walls to be repapered, one day. There was no hurry. It would be a pleasure to do things slowly, to take time choosing, gradually to get the place up to scratch, of an evening. But already the room had a solid, welcoming air: already it felt far more like home than the flat on the seafront had ever done. Alfred knew in his bones he would be happy here, and thanked the Lord for his good fortune.

As he stood looking about him, Alfred's thoughts naturally turned to Eileen. What would she have made of the place? Would she approve his positioning of armchairs, sofa, table? Where would she consider the best placing of their painting of Ely Cathedral? Eileen had always had such a sure touch in such matters. Arranging things – rooms, flowers, biscuits on a plate, had never been any bother to her. She placed them instinctively, to best advantage. She could, for instance, have been a top window-dresser in a large store, had she been so inclined – Alfred had often told her. But she had always said she was not interested in that kind of job. Her ambitions had never extended beyond their own shop which, with her talent for bringing life to a place, she had made as delightful as any shop you could find on the east coast. Ah, Eileen.

Hungry from his work, Alfred went to the small kitchen. This was still in considerable disorder, but it was the room Alfred cared about least. There was much to be done here: cleaning, scouring the sink, new tiles on the floor, a good gloss paint to cheer the walls. But all in good time, as he used to say to Eileen when on some occasions she would chide him for being so slow to set about things. He rummaged about in a box of food and found a tin of baked beans. He ate them with a slice of bread, untoasted as the grill would not work, and drank a mug of strong tea. Once he was settled, in a few days, he would revert to a more orderly timetable: high-tea at six, back to the old disciplined ways. He was not quite sure how he had fallen into the unsatisfactory habit, of late, of eating at odd hours, causing himself severe bouts of indigestion.

His tea over, Alfred returned to the sitting-room and the armchair that faced the window. He lay back, stretching out his legs, arms folded over his stomach, and began to accustom himself to the new view. This was, of course, made easier by Eileen's curtains which made a familiar frame: and the trees outside, thought Alfred, would soon become friends. They were good mature limes, a lovely yellow-green in all weathers, their leaves very light in the air. Pity there was no sight of the sea from this side of the house, but you couldn't have everything, and he was a very lucky man.

The next thing Alfred knew he was struggling to wake himself: through mists of sleepiness he saw Miss Windrush standing in the doorway, two glasses and a bottle of whisky in her hands.

'So sorry to disturb you,' she said, moving towards the kitchen to fill the glasses, 'but I thought you'd probably need a drink by now.'

Alfred rose in confusion. What had come over him, falling

asleep in the middle of the afternoon? He looked at his watch: half-past six. He must have been too busy to notice his weariness, which had sprung upon him as soon as he sat down.

The whisky was most welcome, restoring his spirits very quickly. Miss Windrush sat on the sofa, chatting about plans for the roof and garden, very concerned that he was comfortable and content, and begging him to let her know if there was anything he should need. She was, Alfred noticed, even in this fading light, very pale – as she had been when he arrived this morning. For all her kindness and interest in his wellbeing, Alfred felt she was distracted, there was something on her mind. Well, he could imagine: responsibility for a house like this, on young shoulders like hers, must take its toll. He hoped his presence would ease her burden.

Miss Windrush stayed half an hour, leaving Alfred with the rest of the bottle of whisky. He protested, but she insisted: a small present of welcome, she said it was. On leaving, she urged Alfred to make sure all the doors were locked last thing at night.

'We never used to do any such thing in my father's day,' she explained with a wry smile, 'but there have been cases of vandalism nearby, of late.'

'There are those who aren't respecters of other people's property,' agreed Alfred. 'I shall see to that every night, never you worry.'

'Not that locked doors are any deterrent to someone who is really set on getting in,' said Miss Windrush, 'but we might as well make it harder for them, don't you think?'

She asked the question a little nervously, Alfred thought, but things would quickly change, now. With him around to protect her and the house, she would have no more cause to be afraid.

When Miss Windrush was gone, Alfred busied himself with more unpacking for the rest of the evening. Not until it was quite dark did he draw Eileen's curtains and return to his favourite armchair. He looked slowly round the room, wondering whether his late wife would have approved his positioning of the lamps. He decided she would, and felt pleased with himself. 'Well, Eileen,' he said out loud. 'I'm nicely settled here and thank the Lord for that.'

He tried then to imagine Eileen sitting opposite him, as they had sat for so many evenings of their life together, each side of the fire. He tried in his mind's eye to see her bent head, nodding in agreement, her sweet smile with its funny way of starting one side of her mouth and slowly uncurling. But the conjuring did not work. Once again, as that bad time some weeks ago, he was able to envisage her body – clothes and shoes down to the last detail – but the picture stopped at the neck. She was a headless vision, and her going from him again made Alfred sit up in fright. It must have been the whisky, he thought. He was unaccustomed to the stuff, had never really liked it, certainly wouldn't be finishing the rest of Miss Windrush's bottle if this was the effect it had. He stood up and took the wedding photograph from the mantelpiece – he had placed it there early in the afternoon with a sense of grave priority. Eileen's face came back to him then, of course: staring at him. But only her young face as it had been on that day. The older Eileen, the one he knew better, had grown to love more, would not return.

'Dammit,' he said, putting back the photograph. 'Tricks of the mind. Cruel tricks of the mind.'

With a great effort of will he decided to stop thinking about Eileen and calm himself with a crossword puzzle. He found a book of puzzles in the kitchen. Disinclined to return to the sitting-room, he sat down at the small table in the window and took up his pencil.

For an hour or so Alfred gave himself up to the pleasure of tracking down clues and filling the blank squares with his neat answers. He had always had a good head for puzzles, Alfred, he had to admit. In the old days he had won several competitions and gathered quite a number of prize book-tokens. Eileen never knew how he did it. It was a knack, Alfred explained patiently, many times. But still she never understood, could never get the easiest clue herself. In the end, she ceased to wonder at Alfred's skill, and he stopped trying to explain. The pleasure of the occupation was something he kept to himself. He silently whipped through a puzzle most evenings while Eileen did her sewing. Enclosed in his small world of blanks and spaces and words, he was able to cast off the worries of the day before going to bed.

108

This old familiar feeling of relaxation was just beginning to seep through Alfred, reminding him it would soon be time to venture into his new bedroom, when he was disturbed by voices. At first he thought Miss Windrush must have visitors in the kitchen. But she had said she was going to bed when she left him, wanting an early night. Perhaps she had changed her mind. Alfred listened hard.

He heard a laugh. It was a thin, high, familiar laugh. No. It couldn't be. But it was. Definitely was. *Lily*'s laugh . . . Laughing at him like she used to those evenings he bolted up the shop with such care. How could it be? Lily was picnicking . . .

When she laughed again, Alfred stood up, heart beating uncommonly fast, clutching at his book of puzzles. Then he heard her voice, coming from the other room.

'Alfred! Alfred, really. You can't go on like this. Boring old memorials. Eileen's curtains again! They don't even fit. You must see they don't fit. Tear them down and throw them away. Why not? They're not the prettiest curtains, after all.'

Mocking, she sounded. She'd always had a nasty side to her, Lily. Jealous, really. He'd always thought that, privately. Alfred scratched his head.

'Come on, Alfred. Come on, love,' the voice went on, more sweetly. 'You can let your hair down a bit now, can't you? After all those sewn-up years . . . You can let your mind wander, now, can't you? Let your mind take its fancy. Be kind to yourself, love. Let yourself remember me . . .'

The voice faded away. Alfred sat down again. He sat for a while like a man stunned, his hands heavy on his knees, mouth open, eyes glazed. Then he remembered Lily.

From the start she had been a tantalizing enigma, pale and brittle-boned, her Mona Lisa smile confounding Alfred with its mystery every new day. She was beautifully dressed in those early days, Eileen saw to that – silks and satins and vague scarves round her neck that fluttered when the shop door opened. Sometimes she wore a small hat on the back of her head. Alfred recalled a damson velvet pillbox with a trailing ostrich feather that curled under Lily's beautiful chin. She had been wearing it on a particular evening, God knows how many years ago . . .

Alfred bowed his head, shutting his eyes. He asked forgiveness as he remembered.

On that particular evening, November it was, he heard a wind blowing up as he bolted the doors. He shut the windows and closed the shutters against a smell of snow in the air. He turned off the lights, leaving himself in almost complete darkness but for a shaft of light coming from the open door that led to the kitchen. He stood for a while in the middle of the shop, sniffing at the familiar smells of material and *pot pourri* and polished beeswax on the oak – all the scents enhanced by the darkness, he thought. And then he looked over at Lily, upright and alone in her corner, feathers tickling her chin but smile unbroken, and a strange sensation seized Alfred's heart. He felt great weakness at being so close to such beauty, for in this semi-darkness Lily was quite perfect. And he felt an almost overwhelming yearning to acknowledge this beauty – how, he did not know. A picture flashed through his mind of himself in the unlikely position of sitting next to a girl like Lily in a café in Paris, sipping at green drinks in long glasses. The very thought made him smile at his own absurdity: he must have seen a film with some such scene. But the smile did nothing to lessen the pain. He stretched out his hand and whispered goodnight to Lily, guiltily left the room with her eyes upon his back.

In the warm, bright kitchen, where Eileen was beating at a lump of dough on the table, the yearning did not cease. But it became more comprehensible. Alfred realized that for all their friendliness he and Eileen were quite distant in some ways, and after much abstinence he wanted to take her in his arms, dough included, if necessary, and hug her.

But Eileen's face – maybe she read his mind – deterred him from any such rash gesture. She had never shown much enthusiasm for what she called the other side of life, and anything that had to take place should be strictly confined to the bedroom. For Alfred to take her in his arms, in her apron in the kitchen, would be nothing short of an affront. It would widen their particular distance, and Alfred had no wish to risk that. So he kept his patience through their beef stew and dumplings, and refrained from offering her a glass of cider lest he should arouse her suspicions.

Later that night in bed, the Bible reading over, the light off, the bony wind rattling at their window, Alfred moved close to his wife. He pushed up the sleeve of her wool nightdress, put a hand on her arm. But the flesh which had looked so warm and soft in the kitchen felt strangely hard, cold as china. He moved his hand to her breast, Lily quite forgotten, only wanting Eileen. He felt her small hand slide over his. It lay still for a moment. Then very gently pushed him away.

'Oh, Alfred, love,' was all Eileen said.

The chill in her voice was enough. Alfred scrambled back to his side of the bed, telling her to sleep well, as always. Then, in the dark, Lily's lips smiled at him, and he ached to split that smile and crush her tantalizing little mouth and his desire twisted agonizingly through him. But he lay absolutely still for fear of waking Eileen. Thus she knew nothing of his night and made no comment on his pale face next morning.

Alfred raised his head, remembering, ashamed.

The night of Harry Antlers' visit Viola slept little. Her greatest fear was of the thing Harry had warned her, the demon energy that knows no bounds. She believed he had the cunning to gouge out things most private in her life, and the thought made her feel physically sick. How had he discovered about Richard? How? How? How? Her mind twirled, a Chinese ball of ivory rats, the useless speculations skidding round and round each other, getting nowhere. Eventually, towards dawn, she slept with the help of pills, only to wake an hour later, sweating and shaking from a nightmare.

At least there were no telephone calls the next day, and by the time she had had her drink with Alfred Baxter, Viola felt calmer. But again she worried her way through the night, wondering at what point she could go to the police and complain of harassment, and if she should elicit Gideon's aid. But what could he do? Richard would be better help, but Richard had enough concerns of his own. Besides, the thing that most shocked her, the knowledge that Harry Antlers had discovered her love of the doctor, she could never divulge to Richard.

This morning, woken from fretful sleep by bright sun, she went to the window. She surveyed the marsh, beach, thin distant line of sea, huge dome of cloudless sky, their various boundaries running into each other, translucent as water colours. In the garden Alfred Baxter was pushing a wheelbarrow towards the neglected herbaceous border. Viola could hear him whistling. She supposed it must be quite late, and did not care. The events of the last two days seemed mercifully to have receded, leaving her etiolated but composed. She returned to bed, picked up her book.

There was a knock on the door.

Immediately Viola's heart leapt like a wild thing and she cowered down under the bedclothes, saying nothing. The door opened. Richard walked into the room, carrying a breakfast tray.

'Hey, Violetta! I can't be that frightening. What's the matter?'

He put the tray on the end of the bed, took her hand and pulled her into a sitting position.

Viola managed a smile.

'I wasn't expecting – '

'Of course you weren't. I'm sorry.' He pulled a chair to the bedside, sat down. 'I should have warned you. But the idea only came to me very early this morning. Naturally I didn't want to wake you.'

'You mean you woke up this morning and thought: I must take Viola breakfast in bed?' Viola laughed, incredulous. The violent pumping of her heart was no longer caused by fear.

'To be honest, I thought, *as a doctor*, Viola could do with a morning in bed. I'm sure I was right. You look pretty worn out. Here. Look what I've brought you.'

Richard placed the tray on Viola's knee. There was a boiled egg, brown toast, homemade marmalade, coffee, a single *Rosa Mundi* in a jam jar. Richard picked up the rose and held it under Viola's nose.

'Have to admit I'm not responsible for this. Alfred insisted on the rose. Dashed off into the garden and spent a long time choosing. In fact he was so long I had to boil a second egg as the first one grew cold.'

Again Viola smiled, still unbelieving.

'Did Alfred let you in?'

'He did. Very pleased, we were, to see each other again. I

hadn't seen him since just before his wife died. He seems in much better spirits now, delighted to be here. I'm glad all that's worked out. Very good plan all round. Now, come on: the egg.'

Viola chipped at the shell with a small silver spoon. Richard peered at the rich yellow of the yolk.

'From one of my two free-range hens, I'll have you know,' he said. 'Three and a half minutes.'

'Perfect.'

'Toast all right?'

'Wonderful.'

'I'm not bad at breakfasts. But you know what I've forgotten?'

'Can't imagine – '

'*The Times*. No decent woman should ever breakfast in bed without *The Times*.'

Viola laughed again. Her hand shook as she held the coffee cup.

'Aren't you meant to be on your rounds?'

'Unusual morning, luckily. No surgery as I have an appointment at the hospital in half an hour. So I'll have to be off in a moment or two.'

But he had an unhurried look, hands clasped round a crossed knee. He observed Viola carefully, in silence as she ate. He saw her struggling.

'Don't eat any more, just to please me,' he said.

'All right. But it was lovely. Thank you.'

Gratefully Viola handed him the tray which he put down on the floor. She shifted her legs, making an uncalculated space on the bed. Richard moved to sit there.

'The other night,' he said, 'I came round to see you but there seemed to be a fraught little scene going on. It was difficult to work out whether or not I would have been welcome. Perhaps I did wrong, leaving. But I didn't want to intrude.'

'I saw you. I wanted desperately to call you to help. But then I thought there was no point in your getting involved.'

'Presumably it was your wild suitor?' Viola nodded. 'Is there anything I can do?'

Viola thought. 'Not really.'

113

'Promise to call upon me any time.'

'Promise.'

'I think you should leave here as soon as possible. There's no chance of his finding you in London. He'll soon give up. With nothing to go on, obsessives soon burn themselves out and turn their focus to something else.'

'Hope so.' Viola sighed. 'But don't let's talk about all that if you're about to go.'

'No.' Richard took her hand, smiled. 'If you were a real patient, I'd say you were a case for listening to the heart.' He glanced down. 'As it is, I can see it.'

Viola's look followed Richard's to her breast, visibly heaving beneath the thin cotton of her nightdress. Without giving herself time to think she dragged Richard's hand – curiously light and willing – to her heart, held it there for a moment or two, then flung it back on the bed.

'It's all been rather unnerving,' she said. 'But you're right. I must go very soon.'

'Shall I give you some tranquillizers?'

'Certainly not.'

'Then take care of yourself, Violetta. Eat. Sleep.' He stood. 'I'll be in touch.'

Viola held out her arms. Richard bent over her, briefly kissing her hair. She could almost have sworn, too, that for a lightning moment he stroked the back of her neck with his finger. But in a giddy state of joy mixed with hopelessness, nothing was quite certain. With a supreme effort of will she released him from her arms as soon as he began to pull away. Impeded by her own state, she could not be sure whether a fleeting look on his face was one of confusion. A moment later he seemed to be quite normal, looking down at her with affectionate eyes.

'I almost forgot,' he said. 'I ran into Maisie Fanshawe last week, happened to mention you were home. She seemed anxious to see you but said she didn't like to call after so long. I said I'd put it to you. I was sure you'd be pleased.'

Viola smiled. 'How's Maisie?'

'Definitely older.'

'Happy?'

'Who knows? She pretends to be.'

114

'Anyone in her life?'
'Not as far as I know.'
'Poor old Maisie.'
'Will you ring her?'
'Of course.'
'I'll take down the tray – '
'Please – '
'Must hurry. Bye, Violetta.'
Morning bedroom huge with sun, now. Alfred Baxter stooping over the weeds in a bright garden. Tide coming in. Richard gone. But Richard having been.

Everything was new about Maisie except her anticipation, and even this she managed to burnish quite convincingly so that people might suppose her hope of better things was not undimmed. Her frequent wearing of new clothes was her unspoken sign: she was ready, should the chance arise.

On the afternoon of her reunion with Viola she wore a new cotton dress covered in Picasso-like squiggles and new navy shoes, though their shape was one she had first been attracted to twenty years ago. She was very thin with long, shapeless legs flaring slightly at the ankle. Gaunt-faced, her eyes seemed to have been pressed under a heavy brow by the thumb of a careless sculptor – their outline indefinite, they sagged downwards at the sides. Crimson lipstick was painted meticulously on to her indeterminate mouth, which in her youth had been baggy and faintly sexy. But there was no disguising of the greying hair. Age had trammelled Maisie very fast in the last few years, thought Viola. Even her neck had not escaped its ravages. Once her best feature, exceptionally long and pale, slack skin now danced in the V of the ugly dress. Gideon had admired Maisie's neck quite genuinely. 'It's unfair that so fine a neck should support so disappointing a face,' he used to say. He would be shocked, now. Maisie's only physical attraction quite gone, she was definitely older, as Richard had said.

With little else to do, Viola had taken considerable trouble with tea for Maisie. She had laid a small table in the garden with a linen cloth and the old teatime china wild with green dragons. She cut honey sandwiches and found a packet of ginger biscuits, made China tea in a silver pot. Fearing the encounter would at best be stilted – she and Maisie had nothing in common except for their various loves for Gideon – she felt that at least if she constructed an occasion similar to bygone days it would enable them to talk about the past.

They sat, now, in attitudes of women much older than themselves, smelling the warmth of the garden and the faint salt of the sea. A breeze tugged at the lace hem of the table-cloth and blew Maisie's frizzled grey hair across her eyes. She drew her new mackintosh about her shoulders, always nervous of sea breezes. As Viola had predicted, the setting gave her the opportunity eagerly to remember.

'So many afternoons like this,' she said. 'Your mother in those wonderful hats.'

Viola smiled. If they could glide along on such trains of thought it would be quite easy.

'Things have slipped a bit, since then.'

'Oh, I don't know. It all looks very trim to me. The grass a little longer, perhaps. But that's all.'

Viola nodded in the direction of Alfred. He was tying holly-hocks to stakes at the end of the garden.

'Now Alfred Baxter's come, I'm hoping to get everything back as it was. Do you remember Baxter's, the haberdashery shop?'

'Of course I do!' Eager for small and happy memories, Maisie listed some of the good things the Baxters used to stock and which were unobtainable now, elsewhere. 'But I could never understand,' she whispered, nodding towards the distant Alfred, 'how he could stand that bossy wife.'

'Bossy? I always thought her timid.'

'That's how she liked to appear.'

Surprised by the force of her own conviction, Maisie fell into guilty silence. It was not her way to be uncharitable about people, especially the dead. A purple flush appeared on her grey cheeks. She took a long sip of tea, stamping the cup with a curve of red lipstick.

'*Lu*pins,' she said, embarrassed now and glancing across the lawn. 'I've always so loved your lupins.'

Viola tried to help.

'In her dotty gardening days,' she said, 'after my father died, my mother had a tremendous thing about delphiniums.

But in fact she wasn't much good at them. While lupins, which she hated, seemed to spring up all round her.'

Maisie smiled. Silence again. Then she said, 'Richard told me you'd been over to New York.'

'Yes.' Viola paused, judging it unkind not to give Maisie the information she craved. Her smudged eyes were desperate for news. 'I stayed with Gideon for three weeks.'

'Oh? And did you have a good time?' She sounded very old, like a great-aunt.

'I don't much like New York.'

'How does Gideon find it?'

'He enjoys making a lot of money, working long, hard hours. I think it suits his temperament.'

'Well, he's always been a hard worker.'

Viola noticed that Maisie's hand trembled on a sandwich.

'But he won't stay for ever. I think he plans to come back. He might even live here one day.'

'*Really*?' Maisie dropped the sandwich, clumsily picked it up again.

'I mean, in five or six years' time, perhaps.'

'Well, quite.'

Viola recognized the look of contrived nonchalance, as if five or six years would make no difference to Maisie.

'There was a terrible moment,' Viola went on, to give Maisie time to compose herself, 'when we thought it would be impossible to keep the house. Luckily, that crisis passed.'

'Oh, I am glad of that.' Maisie turned to Viola with a real smile. 'I mean, it's been in the family so many years, hasn't it? I always imagined that one day Gideon would want to return. Bring up his own family here,' she added.

'Yes, well, I expect he'll do that.'

Maisie bit her bottom lip, shuffling words in her mind.

'I imagine he's . . . set up with someone in New York, is he? I hate to ask, but it's very hard, not knowing.'

Viola paused, thinking about her answer. 'As you can imagine,' she said at last, 'a bachelor like Gideon is much sought after in New York. He goes to a lot of parties, gets pursued by a lot of girls. But as far as I know his heart remains untouched. He doesn't seem to have any plans for marriage, or anything like that.' She was pleased to be able to be quite truthful.

'I see,' said Maisie quietly. Fearing further questioning on this delicate ground, Viola changed the subject. She asked Maisie how she spent her time, now. Maisie drew herself up, dignified, a little defensive.

'I run a small bindery,' she said. 'We're lucky enough to have more work than we can cope with. And then, I'm pretty occupied looking after my father. He's virtually senile now. So I'm very busy. I have plenty of interests.'

She suddenly slipped her arms into the sleeves of her stiff new mackintosh and did up the belt. Viola enquired if she was cold and would like to go in. But Maisie shook her head.

'It's just that I can't afford to catch a cold, or anything like that, because I'm all my father has. He depends on me totally.'

She gave a small laugh. Her eyes swerved beyond the garden to the sea. The eyes were quite hard, as if they had become accustomed to masking despair. She looked back to Viola.

'If ever you and Gideon and Richard think of me at all, and I don't suppose you ever do, but *if* you ever do . . . I expect you must wonder why I'm still here, unmarried – ' She laughed again. 'Five years off forty and nothing much changed. Well, believe it or not, I was propositioned many times by an old boy, a widower, who lives near here. He even promised he'd take out a large life insurance, assuring me I'd benefit from it quite soon. I think he just wanted me as a nurse, though his offer of marriage was quite convincing. But of course I couldn't contemplate any such thing, could I? Though my father kept urging me, a bird in the hand and so on. There were one or two other minor interests. But it was so hard, after Gideon, you see. He set such an impossible standard. I can't imagine any other man coming anywhere near it. So here I am, still, poor old Maisie of Docking, as I believe you all used to call me.' She stood up.

'Oh, Maisie . . .'

'No, no. For heaven's sake, don't feel sorry for me. I have no pity for myself, I promise you that.' She sat down again, surprising herself by the bump on the seat, brushing away the hair from her eyes once more. 'In fact, I often feel detached enough to see the whole thing in all its absurdity: first love binding one to a standard from which one is never set free. Well, I waited quite hopefully at first. It took me ages to realize Gideon scarcely acknowledged my existence, let alone had any designs upon me. So then I slipped into waiting without hope, and the years have gone by. It's hopeless waiting that takes the toll. Look at my hair!' She pulled at a wild bit of fringe. 'Quite grey! Oh, I've aged wickedly young. I know it. I see it in people's faces. I saw it in Richard the other day. I saw it in you when we met. I see it every morning in my own mirror – '

'But you look very – '

'Don't deny it,' snapped Maisie, 'please.'

She stopped and looked out to sea again. Then she turned to Viola with a melancholy smile that must have enchanted the old boy with the plans for life insurance.

'Do you remember my dance?'

'Of course I remember your dance.'

'My parents were so worried about the rain. I didn't think it mattered at all.'

'No. It didn't at all.'

'I hated you that evening,' went on Maisie with a new smile. 'You spoiled my whole evening because Gideon took you home early.'

'I'm very sorry,' said Viola.

'He only danced with me once then he said he had to go and take care of his sister. I could have killed you. Still, I daresay if he'd stayed, and hadn't danced with me again, that would have been worse.'

'Had I known, I would never have – '

'You could never have known. I don't blame you,' interrupted Maisie. 'The young never have an inkling what their contemporaries really feel. Particularly the plain ones. They're too busy fending for themselves.'

'Quite,' said Viola. 'The young can be very cruel.'

Maisie stood up again, this time with a more determined appearance of going. She dabbed at her forehead under the tiresome hair with a transparent hand of blanched bones.

'Oh dear, one of my headaches. Brought about by all the remembering, no doubt.' She smiled wryly.

'The past can be exhausting,' agreed Viola.

'Well, goodbye dear Viola. Violetta, they used to call you, Richard and Gideon, didn't they? I'm glad you're here. Come

119

and see me one day. And thank you for the tea. I must have a word with Mr Baxter before he goes. He'll remember me, don't you think? I'll tell him to take care of those lupins, shall I?'

She was on her way towards Alfred Baxter's newly weeded border, voice petering out, grey hair tossing bravely, horribly thin beneath the bulges of her spotless mackintosh, mere ghost of the fat girl in pink tulle whose dance was spoiled by Gideon's kindness to his sister so many years ago.

In Maisie, Viola saw herself very soon, should she not take hurried steps to change things. She decided to leave tomorrow.

Alfred Baxter much enjoyed his mornings weeding in the garden, sun on his back, back soon aching but nothing serious. He had enjoyed, too, seeing Dr Almond again: fine young doctor, though he looked a mite older these days. He had been good to the Baxters through Eileen's last months: kindhearted man, pity about his troubles. Everyone knew his fondness for children. He deserved to have some himself. Life without them was not –

– *Hollyhocks*. Hollyhocks, Alfred told himself over his lunch of bread and cheese, were what he should be thinking about. He would stake them all afternoon to give his back a rest. They were almost his favourite flower, hollyhocks. At least, a close second to lilies of the valley. Eileen it was who had introduced them to their garden – yellow, pink, a lovely deep red, huge great spires that the Lord had so cleverly designed with the flowers getting smaller towards the top. Eileen went on and on about her hollyhocks, and the importance of giving them support. Once, in a summer gale, they'd all been smashed to the ground as a result of his careless staking. She hadn't half been angry, didn't get over it for days. Sometimes, Alfred tried to bring her round to other tall flowers – the sunflower, for instance, with its cheerful beaming face. But Eileen said she couldn't abide sunflowers. Only hollyhocks.

The afternoon was spent no less pleasurably than the morning, tying and restaking. It was among Miss Windrush's hollyhocks that Alfred came to the definite conclusion it had been her whisky which had given him such trouble the other night. For here in the bright sunlight there was no trouble whatsoever in recalling Eileen's face. Not that he was trying to, mind: in fact, he hadn't, for once, given her so much as a thought, and there she was grinning at him through the petals, all over the place, images of her scattered high and low, all angles, skin redder than he remembered, mouth smaller – quite confusing. She came and went all afternoon, but was no hindrance, really. He carried on with the job. He thanked his lucky stars . . . And then he saw Miss Windrush laying up tea on the terrace by the house. The sight of everything so neat gladdened his heart and Eileen disappeared. Every now and then he turned for a surreptitious glance at the two young ladies sitting there – Miss Fanshawe, he believed the other one must be, though she had changed quite a bit – pouring tea from a silver pot. Again and again he was glad. He had the definite impression life was going on here, in Miss Windrush's house. Visitors. Plans. Memories. Things he had not been able to witness, let alone share, for a good while too long. Thank the Lord, then, and now to empty the wheelbarrow. But there was a voice behind him. Calling his name. He gave a small start. Lily again? He turned and saw his own stupidity. It was Miss Fanshawe, striding towards him, a painfully thin version of her former self, but smiling and waving and coming to speak to him.

Oh yes, life was going on, here.

8

While Viola and Maisie partook of their silvery tea in Norfolk, Harry Antlers searched a London gutter. It was his belief that the fault lay in his stupid gesture of throwing away the brooch. That's where it had all gone wrong. If only – he now saw – he had arrived armed with a jewel in its smart New York box, Viola would have welcomed him. She could not possibly have refused the beautiful thing, knowing what it must have cost Harry in money and in love. And so it had to be found, for the next attempt.

He had been looking most of the afternoon, but with no luck – kicking his way up and down the seedy pavement, peering through other people's box hedges, poking at old leaves with a stick. As the hours passed his original patience turned to fury, and his fury to despair. By evening, there was nothing for it but to give up. The brooch was utterly lost. He returned to his bedsitter to console himself with a packet of chocolate biscuits.

Since his return home Harry had received one offer of work: to make a documentary film about prostitutes in Sweden. Although he had had some success making short films in the past, he regarded himself as a stage director, and the offer an insult. But an insult that should, perhaps, be given some consideration, for his finances, since the failure of the play in New York, were not in a comfortable state. The film company had suggested a very large sum for his services, and he would only need to be in Sweden for a week.

By the last chocolate biscuit Harry had come to a decision. He would do the film. It would not be shown in England and no one whose opinion he cared for would ever know. As for the money – the money would be spent more wisely this time. It would be invested in a new life.

His first purchase, of course, would be diamonds to replace the Gloucester's eye brooch. No girl could refuse diamonds.

Harry had in mind a small star, nothing too flash to begin with, which Viola could either pin on her bosom or hang round her neck. His girl in his diamonds. The thought of it . . .

On another scale altogether, he would begin to look for somewhere more salubrious to live. For it occurred to Harry, looking round his meagre room with new eyes, this would be no place to attract a girl like Viola. What she would want, as indeed would he, would be a penthouse flat in Notting Hill Gate, huge windows on to the view of London, black leather and steel chairs, television and stereo behind sliding mahogany doors, all that sort of thing. It was funny to think he had spent his grown-up life quite happily in this room with its stretch covers on the chairs, the Boots' prints and plastic mugs – and now, having met Viola, there was a great need for something better.

After the flat, the car. He would buy a great snarling lion of a car, gold or silver, two seats only, and roar about with Viola beside him. In the meantime, he would not ring her for a day or so: give her time to forget her anger and forgive him. He knew he had done wrong, very wrong, but everything had been against him – fatigue, anxiety, fear of the great arrogant house in which she seemed to be so secure. Sometimes Harry worried about his unaccountable violence. He knew that within him a loving soul struggled to be seen. But it was as if the birth channel through which it had to pass to enter the world was contaminated. Thus, the feelings that had been sown so gently, emerged full of hurt fury, forcing Harry into outrageous gestures of dismay. He knew he should never have threatened Viola with a milk bottle, but something about her haughty little face, refusing to acknowledge all his love for her, had made his hands fly up like two wild birds over which he had no control. And then the vile lover appearing in the garden, ready to pounce on her as soon as Harry turned his back – the thought of Viola being ravished by other hands had caused Harry such physical anguish on the way back to London that he had had to stop at a transport café and eat three eggs on toast.

Fired with the warmth of his plans, Harry grew impatient for morning when he could begin to put them into action. He began to pace his room, thinking of some way to release his

123

impatience. A particularly vigorous waft of Brussels sprouts and boiling clothes drifted up through the floorboards and thin carpet. That was it: now was the time.

Harry crashed down the stairs, and entered his landlady's kitchen without knocking. Marjorie Whittle, sixty-year-old spinster of scant joy, stood like a pantomime dame at her pre-war stove stirring at a pan of bubbling dishcloths. Beside it simmered a pot of rabbit stew and sprouts, while on the table a plate of lights and other innards glared up like a giant bloody eye. A scrawny cat, about to enjoy this supper, leapt in terror from the table when Harry came in.

Rage swelled in Harry. A roar thundered from him, snapping tendons all over his body.

'Marjorie fucking Whittle,' he shouted. 'This has got to stop! How many times have I told you? I pay you a bloody great rent and what do I get in return? Stench! Excruciating stench. Clouds of your filthy smells working their way up to my flat to gas me out. This can't go on, do you hear?'

He banged the kitchen table with his fist. The plate of lights quivered, glassy red. Harry charged to the stove, pushing Marjorie Whittle to one side. He crashed lids down upon the bubbling pots, damming the steam, and switched off the gas flames. The cat squawked piteously. Miss Whittle whimpered, yellow tears gathering in her eyes. Their fear spurred Harry to one final act. He picked up the bloody mess of lights from the plate, paused a moment before throwing it at his landlady's face, as if it had been funny pantomime shaving soap, and laughed at the terror in her eyes. But some minute particle of pity, rarely felt through the obscurity of his rages, overcame him. With all his force he threw the mess, instead, to the floor. where it spilt and slobbered over the cracked linoleum with a dull thwack.

'That's what I think of you, you hideous old cow,' he bellowed with some effort, for the adrenalin was draining away now, 'and I'll do a great deal worse if it happens again.'

'I'm going to fetch the police this time, Mr Antlers,' mewed Miss Whittle.

'You go and fetch the police,' smiled Harry, and left the room.

From upstairs he heard her sobs, and then the banging of

the front door. Through the window he saw her hurrying out, cat under arm, bowed. She turned out of the gate in the wrong direction for the police station – she would never report him. There had been many such scenes in the past and Miss Whittle always failed to carry out her threat. She would be going to her senile old sister down the road, and to buy more lights for the repulsive cat.

Having nicely upset his landlady's tranquil cooking, Harry felt much better. He went to his own kitchen and heated up three tins of spaghetti rings. He ate them on his knee, sluiced in brown sauce, listening to the Brahms piano quintet, temporarily at peace.

The next morning Harry gave himself a rare smile in his early shaving mirror, his mind concentrated on the important matters of his active day.

'Oh, my lovely Viola,' he said out loud. 'I have such plans for us.'

But even as he said the words, a picture of Hannah Bagle came to him. He had not given her a thought since she had left him that night in New York, and now here she was, surprising so early in the morning, golden skin palpitating beneath the silk . . . Something chafed within Harry. He needed breakfast.

A large bowl of porridge and brown sugar followed by three Chelsea buns quelled his puzzling feelings of desire for one he did not love, and before dismissing her entirely from his mind he decided it would be judicious to call her occasionally. Keep her alert. He might, after all, have need of her for vital information in the future.

Harry rang his bank. He requested that his entire savings, some two hundred pounds, should be transferred to his current account. He was saddened it could not have been two thousand, but that would come later. Next, he rang the pro- ducer of the film company and they agreed to have lunch. Then he took a taxi to a jeweller's shop.

By the end of the morning Harry had found his diamond star. It was very small, with a pearl centre, and very expensive – double his savings. But an overdraft was of no concern in such important matters. Harry paid without quibbling – the first of a whole collection of jewels for Viola, he told himself, and with a feeling of extraordinary wellbeing, set off for the Ritz to meet the film producer.

Late that afternoon, contract agreed upon, stomach stretched with quantities of food and wine, Harry's unusual sensation of peace with the world still brushed over him like fur, and he felt inclined to make some gesture to reflect his content. At the flower stall at the underground station he bought the entire stock of peonies, some half dozen bunches. Smiling to himself, he unlocked the cracked maroon front door quite eagerly. He stood in the hall calling Miss Whittle's name. No answer.

Harry went quietly into the kitchen, not wanting to frighten the old girl any further. But there was no sign of her. The pots were still on the stove, untouched since he had left them. The meat was still on the floor. The smells were horrible, though damper and less pungent than before. His benevolence thwarted, Harry felt impatience rising. He threw the bunches of peonies into the sink, called Miss Whittle once again. Still no answer: he would have woken her had she been asleep. It occurred to him, then, he had not heard her usual morning noises, shooing the cat in the garden and hoovering her carpets. Perhaps she had stayed overnight with her dotty sister. Well, it was no concern of his. Her fault if the bloody peonies died.

Harry returned upstairs. His lunch having subsided, he cooked himself a huge tea. Then he took the diamond star from its box and studied it for a long time. It was the first possession he had ever cared for in his life. There was something strangely encouraging in its small sparkle, giving him hope. Happily, he set about making his plans.

Gideon Windrush was suffering from the heat of the New York summer, and as his suffering increased so did Hannah's irritation. The sympathy she used to feel for his grumbles about her native city, and his boring views on the superiority of London summers, seemed to have evaporated entirely. Besides, she had other things on her mind.

Hannah's concept of fidelity – a thing about which she knew Gideon cared greatly – was not in strict accordance with the general meaning of the word. To her, it was loyalty of mind, while short excursions of the body were of no importance. Indeed, they were of so little significance that it was not worth recounting them, particularly to such a sensitive man as Gideon, who might find in them reasons for anger or outrage. Quite happy with her own working out of things, Hannah conducted her double life with tact and skill. Nothing would alter her admiration for Gideon's mind, and mostly she enjoyed his company. But he was a busy man, tired by evening, not always up to her demands. It was, therefore, quite reasonable to satisfy herself elsewhere, which she often did.

In fairness to Gideon, she never allowed herself to think about her short-time lovers as anything other than means of gratifying the flesh. She refused all dates with them after the initial encounter, and, lust satisfied, they were abandoned.

It was much against her will, therefore, that Hannah realized, some days after Harry's return to England, she was thinking about him quite frequently. There had been something so unsatisfactory about their three meetings that she could not put them from her mind. Besides, the fact that he had made it clear he had wanted her for nothing but quick relief was most unusual, this position being her normal privilege. She tried to put him from her mind, but to no avail. His ugly, angry face kept returning. Increasing her range of infidelity, she thought of him while making love to Gideon, and for the time being spurned other lovers. She lost considerable weight. Tension between her and Gideon grew daily.

It was Gideon who produced the appealing idea of easing things by going to England for a week. He would like to check up on his sister in Norfolk, he said: see all was well and make financial arrangements. Besides, he would like to show Hannah the house of his childhood – the beaches, the old sailing boat. They could go for a picnic on the Point. Hannah smiled sympathetically.

'Darling, it's all a wonderful idea, England. Fabulous idea. But I couldn't take the beaches bit. I mean, you know me. I'm a city girl. I'd be mooning about on beaches, now, wouldn't I?'

'Maybe.' Gideon hoped to conceal a sense of private relief at her reaction.

'So what I think is this: you go off to Viola and your

wonderful old house, I'll stay in London. Hell, I haven't been there in years. I'll have a ball looking round the shops, looking up old friends. Besides, darling, we could do with a break from each other, couldn't we? I'd say that's just what we need. Then we'll fly back together. Restored.' She cooed charmingly.

'I take your point,' said Gideon.

He poured her a large Martini on the rocks and immersed himself in pleasurable thoughts of a week at home. Hannah, for her part, was more agreeable than she had been for some time. While her mind raced with nefarious plans, she coolly made chicken salad with great care, changed into a silk kimono with nothing on beneath, and made sure it fell apart long before official bed-time.

The following day, having deliberated for hours on her plan during the night, Hannah called Harry from the office. He sounded surprised, not particularly pleased, to hear her voice.

'Well, I thought we might as well keep in touch,' she said. 'Did you have a good day?'

'Yes, yes.'

'I have news for you, Harry.'

'Oh?'

'May not be of interest to you, but I'll try it out.' She paused. 'Are you still crazy about your wonderful Viola?'

'Of course.'

'Seen her?'

'Naturally.'

'Then maybe you know what I'm going to tell you. I presume you know she's moving to London?'

Harry's turn to pause. 'Er, yes. She said something about it.'

'Did she tell you where she was going?'

'Not exactly.'

'That's where I can help. Save you any difficulty finding out.'

'What do you know, for heaven's sake?'

Taking a long drag on her cigarette, Hannah let Harry wait again. She detected an edge of anxiety in his voice.

'Oh, nothing much. Nothing important. Just her London

address and telephone number. She should be there in a few days.'

'For God's sake, woman, did you ask her brother for all this?'

'Don't be such a damn fool, Harry. So happens she wrote him a letter. He didn't say a thing. By chance, I read the letter. You know, letters lie about.'

'Quite. Well. Thanks.'

Hannah slowly dictated Viola's telephone number and address. Considering all her trouble, he sounded ungrateful.

'This is all a bit unnecessary,' he said. 'She was going to get in touch with me when she got there.'

Hannah smiled to herself. 'Well, like this, you know what you can do? You can have a whole lot of roses waiting for her when she arrives.' She laughed.

Harry did not join her laughter. It was not easy to gauge another's mood on a transatlantic call. Hannah was disappointed at Harry's apparent lack of enthusiasm. But, business over, she decided to change her tack and her voice. She could afford to be more alluring, now.

'Say, Harry. Don't go, darling. I've more news for you.' Pause. 'Gideon and I are coming over in the next couple of weeks.'

'Ah.'

'Small vacation. Gideon's going on down to Norfolk to see Viola. I'm staying in London to visit with a few friends, go round the stores, have myself some fun.'

'Re-ally?'

The minute break in the question indicated to Hannah she was doing better. She purred on an even lower note.

'So I thought, Harry, maybe you and I could get together? Just a drink or something?'

Harry was silent for a very long time. Then he, too, spoke in a lower key.

'Perhaps we could. Ring me when you get here, will you? I might be in Sweden making a film, but leave a message on the machine.'

Hannah was impressed. She squirmed in her expensive leather chair. A strange warmth, like liquid wax, seemed to be surging through her limbs.

129

'Oh Christ, Harry. You know something? I can't wait. I dunno what's got into me. I'm a tough old bird, normally. None of this sentimental stuff. But our night at the Algonquin keeps running through my mind . . .'

'You're a beautiful lady,' said Harry. 'You're a very beautiful lady. If I was with you I could show you how I felt.'

Although this last remark was roughly in the region of what she wanted to hear, Hannah found it faintly distasteful. But still, it was all the things Harry did wrong that she found so endearing. The other telephone rang, breaking her mood.

'I'll call you then, hon,' she said.

'I'll look forward to that,' said Harry. 'We'll have a drink. Or something.'

Viola went to London. At the top of her uncle's house she found the flat of four rooms in considerable disrepair, but full of sun. She saw great potential. In her practical way she set about their renovation, intending to finish the job as soon as possible. Feeling safe from Harry Antlers, and with the prospect of Gideon's visit to look forward to, she was happy. She immersed herself in the task of choosing, measuring, ordering, and thought of little else.

As her uncle had suggested, while the flat was being transformed, she stayed in the main part of the house – a house of tall, austere rooms with grand furniture and gloomy Turkish rugs. It was friendly but intimidating. Viola found herself creeping up and down the stairs and shutting the huge doors of silky wood with a strange shyness. On the fourth day of her stay, on her way up to the flat, she heard a mild cough. It came from the library, not visited since her arrival.

Viola paused, remembering, then, something about a scholar called Edwin. It would only be friendly, she thought, to make herself known to him. She walked down the dark passage. Opening the library door, she came upon the standing figure of a giant, tall as Michelangelo's David, it seemed. His head was bent, a sculptured hand at rest on the open pages of a leather-bound book.

'I am sorry,' said Viola. 'I didn't – '

The man looked up. 'Ah. That's all right. Don't go away.'

It took Viola several moments to assimilate the facts. The

speaker, at first a silhouette against the light, was no giant, no statue. The first impression melted to be replaced by a man in undistinguished clothes standing at the top of a library ladder. He snapped the book shut and returned it to its shelf. Viola noticed the bright shine on the seat of his low-crutched trousers: a spindly ankle beneath the turn-ups. She watched him feel for the step beneath him with a cautious and un-polished shoe.

'I didn't mean to disturb you,' she said.

'Oh, goodness me, you aren't disturbing me. At least, I suppose technically you are. But I love disturbances – anything to take me from my reference books. I haven't had such a good reason for *wrenching* myself from a page for weeks.'

Viola smiled. 'I'm David's niece,' she said.

'I suspected that. He told me all about his pretty niece.'

Even standing on the floor he was much taller than Viola. He wore a yellow jersey beneath his jacket which reflected on to his chin like buttercups in a child's game. His pale eyes were set far apart, divided by a wide, blubbery nose. He ran a hand through a lock of greasy hair.

'I'm Edwin Hardley,' he said.

Smiling, friendly puckers rippled through his cheeks. He must be quite old, Viola thought. At least, he had the air of one who had never been quite young.

'How do you do.' They shook hands formally, but with all the concealed pleasure of two British strangers meeting in a desert.

'Getting on all right, up there, are you?' asked Edwin.

'There's a lot to do, but it won't take long.'

Edwin sighed in admiration. He seemed fatigued for so early in the morning, perhaps by his excursion up the ladder.

'I mustn't keep you,' said Viola, making for the door.

'Oh, don't feel that.' With a surprising surge of energy, Edwin leapt ahead of her to the huge door, opened it. 'The mornings I like best are the mornings I manage to escape.' He gave a mysterious chuckle. 'If there's anything I can do to help – not that I'm much of a one with paint.'

'You must come up and see it when it's all finished.'

'That would be very nice. Meanwhile, I daresay our paths might cross on the stairs.'

'Possibly,' smiled Viola, and turned back into the dark passage.

Edwin paid his first visit to Viola that evening. He found her standing in her bare sitting-room trying out strips of different red paint on the walls. Anxious not to disturb her, he came cautiously into the room. He stood by the window, presence at once indeterminate, troubled shadows watery on his face. The lock of greasy hair fell over one eye.

'Ooh, I am sorry. Hope I'm not – '

'Course not,' said Viola, grateful for the interruption. 'Light's going, anyway.' She replaced her brush in a tin of turpentine, waved at a bare wall. 'That's going to be all bookshelves and cupboards and drinks. But I'm afraid there isn't a thing in the place to offer you at the moment.'

'How *mar*vellous,' said Edwin, 'to be able to imagine a completely bare room like this when it's furnished. I could never do that. Oh, I don't want a drink, if that's what you mean.'

'Well, I do. Let's have some gin, downstairs. I know Uncle David wouldn't mind. He said I was to help myself.'

'That would be nice.' Edwin laughed gently. 'But what I *thought*, what I *had been thinking*, this afternoon, was that perhaps it would be a good idea if we had dinner. I mean . . .'

'Well, I am hungry, I have to admit.' Viola nodded acceptance.

'Just a modest . . . I mean, I haven't a tie or anything here. Just round the corner, if that's all right.'

'Fine. Tell you what, you go and have a drink in the drawing room. I'll have a bath and put on something less covered in paint.'

Viola enjoyed her own mild bossiness to this transparent stranger. He took it well, smiling consent.

She lay in the huge Victorian bath filled with bluebell-scented bubbles, a crystal glass of gin and tonic on the rack, small sips deliciously silvering the mind, the gaunt walls of the old-fashioned bathroom beginning to sparkle behind the steam. Anticipation, out of all proportion to the forthcoming modest dinner round the corner with a scholar of moths, seized her in its wild dance . . . For all the pleasures of her solitary life, unexpected invitations were a treat. She was excited. She took unusual care with her appearance, brushing her hair until it shone, and choosing a cotton dress of pink and cream stripes in which she felt particularly comfortable.

'Oh, you do look . . .' said Edwin, standing duskily in a corner of the huge dim drawing-room, as if in fear of exposure on the wide carpet. 'I'm afraid I'm . . . Shall we go?' He tugged vaguely at his dreadful shirt.

They walked the short way to the restaurant through the tangible warmth of a London summer evening, scarcely talking. The restaurant was a dark place of green felt and well-worn hessian, Elizabethan dishes on the menu.

'Terribly pre*ten*tious, I daresay,' said Edwin, 'but rather good food.'

Studying him across the small table, Viola was of the impression that life's practicalities wafted round Edwin like underwater plants, and it was a matter of luck if he could secure anything firmly in his hands. She watched him looking about as if tangible objects and human beings were the stuff of dreams, and any negotiation with real life was a struggle. The waiters, for instance, seemed not to see his beckoning signs. His own ineffectualness was evidently a constant source of frustration: he grew quite pink waving arms and a menu. When the waiter did at last notice him, he was in a dither about ordering. The Elizabethan dishes they had chosen slid confusingly from his mind. When all was at last in hand, wine poured and tried, he sighed with relief at the end of the trauma.

'Oh dear,' he said. 'Dear me, I find the disapproval of waiters terribly unnerving, don't you?'

Edwin made so many gentle enquiries about Viola's life (to which he received well-edited replies) that it was not until the coffee that she was able to extract information about his. He admitted moths were his passionate interest and most hours of his day were spent in their study. He had begun a six-volume work on his subject some twelve years ago, and there were still five and a half volumes to go.

'But, well, time does get a little *dissipated*, doesn't it? I mean, I suppose I'm Chairman of the Moth Society of Great Britain, and that takes up far too much time. Endless meetings. A very bitchy lot, the moth people, you know. Hopelessly

133

vague, too. *Flitting* from one thing to another, never making up their minds. It's dreadful, being Chairman. And you may think, quite reasonably, due to all that silly palaver with the waiter, that I'm not chairman calibre.' He smiled disarmingly. 'But believe it or not, I'm a *very fierce* chairman. I bark and bang my fist and almost always get my way.'

Viola laughed.

'What's very nice,' he went on, 'is being able to work in your uncle's house. It's such a *refuge*. So safe. Nobody knows where I am, there. No one has my telephone number. Nobody can *get* me.'

'What sort of people are after you?'

'Well, you know what London is.' He smiled. '*Girls*, I suppose. Oh, girls. They're so tiring in their pursuits. You'll find the same with men, I daresay.'

'I don't suppose so. I don't know many men in London.'

Edwin looked a little wistful.

'You soon will. With a face like that, there's not much chance of your remaining undiscovered. Still, as the other occupant of your uncle's house, I shall consider it my prerogative occasionally to trap you into dinner.'

'Of course!'

'But no lunches, I warn you. I can't abide lunches any more. I've had a surfeit of lunches. Good heavens, if you give a girl lunch in London she wants *the whole afternoon* as well. Imagine that. Afternoons are for working, I'd always been taught. But girls don't seem to be of the same opinion. They seem to think three o'clock to five in bed' – he blushed at the word – 'is quite in order. Well, it exhausted me, I can tell you. I could scarcely summon the energy for dinner with the next girl. Luckily, your uncle's house has put a stop to all that. Oh, I'm grateful to your uncle. Marvellous library, too.'

Edwin insisted on walking back to the house with Viola, though his own flat was in the opposite direction. He took her arm, gentle fingers playing lightly on her wrist. When they came to the tall flight of steps leading to the front door, he sighed, surveying them with the dread of an exhausted climber facing the last steep slope of a mountain.

'Don't bother to come up,' said Viola, aware of his fatigue.

'Of course I'm coming up. I'd like to see you safely through the door.'

Viola smiled. They mounted the steps, clutching each other in the manner of an elderly couple. Viola unlocked the heavy studded door, pushed it open.

'Thank you so much,' she said.

'*Through* the door,' said Edwin. He went ahead of her, shutting the door behind him. For one so seemingly tired a moment earlier, he was quite firm. They were close in the darkness of the hall. Viola put out her hand, searching for a light switch. Edwin caught her hand. He pulled her tentatively towards him. She could feel him kissing her hair.

'Oh dear, you're a *dangerous* girl, I'm sure of that,' he said, and snapped on the light. 'I daresay we shall run into each other tomorrow or the next day on the stairs.'

His attempt at brusqueness made him blush: he was eager to be away. Viola did nothing to detain him. He bid her goodnight and left with the speed of the guilty.

Viola sat for a while in the brown shades of the drawing-room, reflecting on the evening. She was able now fully to understand her uncle's nickname for Edwin Hardley: Hardley There was an apt description. A most peculiar fellow, she thought: funny, particularly about himself, gentle, kind, oddly endearing. And yet not of this age, and in spirit too old for his years. She wondered if he had ever been young, or was one of those people born old. She wondered, too, why he should be the victim of such tiresome pursuit by women. They felt he needed mothering, perhaps. Or maybe his elusiveness acted as an aphrodisiac: for in the flesh he was far from the average idea of a robust sexual partner.

Unable quite to understand why, Viola felt disappointment. In her sparkling bath, possibly unconsciously, she had hoped that a strong man might march from the frail frame and devour her. But there was no hint of devouring in Hardley There. Nibbling, she thought, was more in his line. Still, he would be a friend; the quality of friendship shone about him. Viola liked the idea of his daily presence in the house. His quiet reading in the library would provide a comfortable undercurrent to the prevailing silence. And, as he said, they could meet occasionally.

When the door bell rang, soon after H.T.'s departure, Viola leapt up in sudden, renewed hope. She imagined that in his vague way he had forgotten something. She also supposed, gratefully, that he rang the bell, rather than used his key, so as not to frighten her coming upstairs. Pressing the buzzer on the entryphone, Viola shouted to him to join her in the drawing-room. She heard the front door open and close.

Returning to her old place on the huge velvet sofa, Viola wished she had a drink to occupy her hands. The excitement of earlier in the evening came back to her. She sat very still, listening to the creaks as Edwin climbed the stairs: she wondered at her state of puzzling joy as she waited.

9

Harry Antlers kept watch for several days. He parked his car some way up the street from Viola's front door and settled himself behind many a newspaper, too alert to do any real reading. His many hours of patience were rewarded by several sightings. Once he saw Viola enter the house carrying large carrier bags and tins of paint. Another time she was accompanied by a scruffy-looking man in white overalls, provoking in Harry acute agitation. It took him several moments to recover when he realized the man was a builder or painter. On a third occasion, an evening, just as Harry had started his engine to leave, Viola came running out of the house in a great hurry and hailed a passing taxi. Distant though his view of her was, Harry could see that she always looked as beautiful as he remembered, and his desire to run after her and throw himself at her feet was only quelled by the hurried swallowing of a packet of fruit drops he found in the glove compartment.

Harry had worked out that the longer he left Viola alone, the easier his next attempt to woo her would be. Surely she would at least give him a grateful smile; even that would be rewarding. And then he would be so gentle and loving to her, no matter how violent the emotions that seared him, that she would see a new man in him, and, surely, be intrigued at last.

He planned his next foray on the evening before he left for Sweden. This Harry thought a subtle piece of strategy. For if, as he supposed, this time Viola was conquered, and then started to behave like all the other girls in his life − well, telephoning him, she would find out from his answering machine he was away. Not that he wanted to play games with Viola: his love for her was much too serious for that. But in Harry's experience, a little rough treatment, a touch of un-availability every now and then, did wonders for increasing ardour. On the other hand, were she still to remain stubborn and resistant, silly bitch, then he could glut his fury on some of the nubile Swedish ladies who were to appear in his film. That, at least, would be some antidote to the physical pangs, if not to those of the heart.

Harry put great effort, all day, in preparing himself for the meeting. He had decided against asking Viola out to dinner: a girl can escape quite easily from a restaurant. By the time the bill was paid, she could have made such a good start it was impossible to catch up. He decided, instead, to approach the vast house in which she apparently lived alone, at about ten at night. Ten had always been a propitious hour for him: time when intimations of weariness in a lady can magically be transformed.

But it was a long day and evening to wait. To rid himself of excess adrenalin, Harry tried walking through Hyde Park, a way of passing the time he found particularly obnoxious. The sun beat down on his head, the bright light dazzled him, he kept tripping over lovers in the grass. In exasperation he ate a huge lunch, then a huge tea, followed by high-tea at six. In the hours between seven and ten, spent back in his room, he finally anchored himself into a peaceful state with the help of baked beans and bacon. Strangely, no more smells came from his landlady's kitchen. He had not seen her about since their little scene, and assumed she was on holiday.

By the time Harry set off in his car, in best suit and imitation silk tie, he felt unusually calm, patient and optimistic. The curtains of Viola's house were not drawn. There was a dim light on the first floor. Harry slowly mounted the stone steps to the front door. He fingered the small jeweller's box in his pocket.

To his dismay, he found there was an entryphone: should Viola recognize his voice she might not let him in. He rang, and the Gods were on his side. Amazingly, he heard her voice cheerfully asking him to come up to the drawing-room.

Harry managed to control his instant scorn at the idea of a drawing-room being 'up' in any house, and pushed open the door. He stood for a moment accustoming his eyes to the huge, lightless hall, and made his way to the grandest staircase he had ever seen. His heart continued its furious pounding, outraged that any one person should live in a house of this scale. But calmly he put his hand on the polished banister –

138

it gave a solid, comforting support – and felt with his foot for the first stair. The carpet, as far as he could tell, was either thick velvet or pure mink. *Bloody mad* . . . But, with admirable control, he began to climb.

When Harry Antlers entered the drawing-room he felt he had walked into a cavernous place full of shadows. There was only one lamp lit, on a low table beside a sofa. Viola sat in the corner of that sofa, a look of wonderful expectancy on her face. But even as he looked, silently, the radiance fled from her and she covered her face with her hands.

Harry strode across the room till he was as far from her as he could be. He turned and contemplated Viola, still hidden behind her hands, shoulders hunched. She appeared to be sobbing. Harry felt a moment's distress. But this was soon replaced by a stronger feeling of discomfort, prickling over his entire skin, that came from the scale of the room, the huge pictures, the ornate looking-glass over the marble fireplace. He said nothing, waiting.

'How could you have found me this time?' Viola cried. She looked at him through cracks in her fingers.

'I'm sorry if I've caught you at a bad time. Once again. I've come to apologize for my untoward behaviour in Norfolk.' Harry smiled.

Viola let her hands drop from her face. Her eyes were narrowed. There were no visible tears.

'I don't want an apology, or anything else from you,' she said. 'I'd just like you to go. Please. I was quite happy until you came.'

'Then I'm sorry about that. Perhaps I could try to restore your happiness before I go?'

Viola watched him take a few steps forward, pat the chestnut velvet seat of a sofa opposite her own.

'Would it be permissible,' Harry asked, 'for a humble man like me to sit on this wonderful sofa?' He did not smile.

'Of course,' snapped Viola, irritated by such absurd but serious humility. 'Sit where you like.'

That fact that she did not give him a second order to leave gave Harry courage. He sat down, made so bold as to lean back among the alien cushions, ill-shapen legs stretched out before him. He felt the small box in his pocket. It had been his intention to sit near Viola, make her shut her eyes as in a childish game, and press it into her hands. But now he saw any such move would be unwise. Her resistance seemed to be melting a little, perhaps in response to his soft voice, though her expression was not inviting. He pulled the box from the pocket and threw it across the room to Viola, surprising himself by his unpremeditated action. It landed beside her. She ducked in fear. Then she picked it up.

'What's this?'

'Just a beginning.'

Viola opened the box. She took out the diamond star.

'Very pretty,' she said. 'I love Victorian jewellery.'

'It's yours,' said Harry.

'It most certainly isn't,' Viola retorted. 'You must have a very wrong impression of me if you think I'm the kind of girl who would accept jewellery from men.' She knew she sounded pompous.

'From one who loves you. Surely that's different,' said Harry.

'Not at all.' Viola was brusque. She returned the star to its box. 'It was a kind thought, but I don't want it. I wouldn't dream of accepting it. Please take it away.'

She placed the box some distance from her. Harry did not move, watching her. They listened to the tick of the gilded clock above the fireplace.

At last Harry shifted. He sat up, arms resting on knees, hands clasped as if in prayer. He was further encouraged by Viola not having thrown the box back at him. For the first time, with her, he felt in control. Instinctively he longed to make some extravagant gesture, throw himself on the floor at her feet, babble all the things that had been pent up in him so long concerning his love. But he knew any such action would be fatal, undoing all the good achieved so far this evening. What he would do, he thought, the resolution grim in his heart, would be to go very soon, as she requested. Show how reasonable he could be. But first he must put to her just one or two things.

'What you must understand, my beautiful lady, is that I'm a bit of a nutter, but I respond well when I'm treated well, as you can see. I'm not tearing up the carpets tonight, am I? I'm not throwing things about. I can be quite civilized, you know.' He smiled the charming smile that had endeared him to Hannah Bagle. 'I'm sorry, as I said, for my tantrums the other night, for bullying you over the telephone. But my lovely Viola, you can't know what it's like, this passion I feel for you. It's almost killing me.' He gave a small, self-deprecating laugh. 'Your face is constantly in my mind, your voice in my ears. I can't think about anything else, don't care about anything else. You can't begin to conceive of the torment.'

'No,' said Viola.

Hard little bitch, thought Harry, clasping his hands more tightly, *but I'll keep on smiling*.

'Look, I'm only asking one thing of you – it's not much. But give me a break. Have a bit of sympathy. Try to understand. And I for my part will try to act more reasonably. I won't pester you further, I promise. But in return, just out of human kindness, I'd much appreciate it . . .' His voice seemed to be near to breaking. '. . . if you'd let me visit you from time to time. Just to talk to you for a few moments. Like that, I can take new pictures of you away with me in my mind.'

He smiled again, stood up. The sag of his shoulders, the swell of his stomach, the tugging at his belt with ugly hands all conveyed his wretchedness. He was aware of this, looked to Viola for some reaction. And, wondrously, he detected some very slight interest in her eyes. Things were going better than he could have hoped for. He waited, but still Viola said nothing.

'Well, I must be going,' he said. 'I won't be bothering you for some time as I shall be away in Sweden, working. So that will keep me occupied while you're in Norfolk –'

'How do you know I'm going to –'

Viola leapt up, fiery, beautiful, so close to Harry he felt quite weak. He put out a hand, indicating she should come no closer. 'Calm down, calm down. I haven't been spying, I promise you that. Just keeping in touch. Any word of you makes the agony a little more bearable, you must see that. And I warned you: passion is a great spur to discovery. But I shan't be pursuing you to Norfolk again, have no fear. I shall wait till you get back.'

For all his gentleness, it sounded like a threat. Viola fell back on to the sofa, uttered a cry of fury curdled with fear. Harry knew he must leave at once. He went quickly to the door

'Take your brooch,' hissed Viola.

Not answering, Harry hurried from the room and down the thick stairs. Much had been achieved tonight. Perhaps he should not have mentioned Norfolk, but that was the only mistake he had made. One thing was quite definite: despite her shouts from upstairs about taking back the brooch, he had established himself as a new and intriguing man in Viola Windrush's mind. Of that he was quite sure. He banged the huge front door behind him, wishing it would shake the whole bloody palace of a house to its foundations. Pity he had forgotten to ask Viola how she felt about living in such a ridiculous place on her own, when ten homeless families could easily be housed there. But there was plenty of time. In his new position of strength, patience would surely come to him.

For all the success of the evening, by the time he reached his room Harry Antlers was shaking. He made himself a cup of tea to accompany a cheese sandwich, then took to his chair to review the evening, in film director's language, frame by frame. Viola's face, palpably beautiful, struck blindingly in his mind's eye, so that even though reason said she was a stupid, resistant, spoiled cow, he could not believe this. She was in fact as near perfect as you could find on this mean earth – and one day she would be his.

Lulled by the cheese, Harry had just turned his thoughts to the future penthouse for his loved one when the front door bell rang. He rose with some silly hope that Viola had followed him: her heart had turned, and here she was, offering herself to him in her entirety.

Harry opened the front door. A slight girl stood before him, blonde hair falling out of a scarf. Scarcely visible with her back to the glow of street lights, Harry's heart surged for a moment, believing his fantasy had come true. The illusion was broken as soon as she spoke.

'I'm Annie Light,' she said. 'Miss Whittle's great-niece. My mum sent me over with a message for you.'

Harry paused. Disappointment gathered in his stomach. He felt a sudden longing to talk to someone. Perhaps this stranger would do.

'Come in,' he said.

The girl followed him upstairs. Unasked, she took off her coat and scarf, laid them on a chair. She was as small as Viola, scared.

'Do sit down,' said Harry.

'I'm all right standing if you don't mind.'

'Shall I get you a cup of tea?'

'No thanks.'

'What's the message, then?'

Annie looked up at him, dull-eyed. She had too large a gap between her front teeth, but was quite pretty.

'It's my auntie – well, my great-aunt Marjorie,' she said, looking down. 'She's dead.'

'Oh?' said Harry.

'Yes. Dead. Few nights ago she arrives to see her sister, my grandmother, like, in a terrible state, with the cat. She didn't seem to be making any sense. Next thing: heart attack. They got her to hospital straight away. But she was dead on arrival. Just like that.'

'I am sorry,' said Harry. 'Very sudden.'

'Very sudden, yes,' said the girl. She paused for a moment, making some effort to remember. 'My mum said I had to tell you two things. She said great-aunt Marjorie's solicitor would be on to you soon about the rent and that, and selling up this place.'

'Quite,' said Harry.

'And then she said would I ask you if you knew if there was anything on my great-aunt's mind?'

'I'm afraid not. We very rarely spoke to each other. We had almost no communication.'

'Yes, well, she didn't speak to anyone much. She was that quiet. So it was unlike her to come round to me grandmother in such a dither. Something must have happened to upset her, that's what we thought. It's terrible, somehow, not knowing.'

'Well, I'm sorry I can't help,' said Harry.

'It, like, haunts us all,' said Annie.

Harry stared at the pitiful sight of her, forlorn shoulders

and scrunched-up hands. He cared not at all about the demise of his churlish landlady, and slammed down the small voice of conscience that accused him of possibly contributing to her death. But the sight of Annie served to inflame his feelings of self-pity: the unfairness of things in his life surged through him. He longed to weep on a shoulder – any shoulder. So when Annie then said, with a sniff:

'She was such a lonely thing, my old auntie, all her life,' Harry could contain himself no longer.

'We all are, we all are,' he whispered. 'We're all despairing, lonely creatures. What can we do?'

Annie, alarmed by the urgency in his voice, looked up.

'I don't know,' she said, sounding stupid.

'Comfort: comfort is all we ask of each other. And yet, where do we find it?'

Annie took a step back from him, by now much alarmed by the look in his eye.

'I must be going,' she said.

'Stay one moment.'

Before she knew what was happening, Annie was clutched in Harry's arms, crushed to his awkward body, listening to unintelligible murmurings as he nuzzled his mouth through her hair. He seemed to be strangely upset. But Annie, still frightened, felt a sudden pity for this stranger. The comfort he had spoken of seemed, magically, to be running through her.

For his part, Annie surprisingly in his arms, Harry sensed no relief: rather, her compliance only made it worse that she was not Viola. He kept his eyes shut, a picture of the girl who was not there in his mind. Fired by the beauty of this imaginative picture, he crushed the real girl more desperately, kissed her hard on the mouth, pushing back her head. He only had to start undoing her clothes, whisper a suggestion, and she would be his.

But, as suddenly as his desire had come, it left. Harry pushed Annie away from him, drained, disgusted. He saw that her mouth was red and bruised, and blood threatened a small cut on her lip. Her mascara had run, her dyed hair had fallen into dark partings. He wanted to be rid of her as fast as possible.

'I'm sorry,' he said. 'I'll see you downstairs.'

'That's all right.' The girl sniffed again, pulled on her coat. 'It's been a funny sort of day all round, matter of fact.'

Harry hurried her out of the house. She waved goodbye, friendly, saying that she'd drop by again one day to see how he was getting on. Harry considered this proposal nothing less than a threat. He must hurry to find new accommodation: he wanted no more Annies in his life, pestering him with stupid letters and declaring their unwanted love.

Viola had been so completely absorbed in the sudden thought of Edwin's return that when, in reality, he had been substituted by Harry Antlers, she had found it impossible to grasp the reality of the situation. Thus, while one half of her slipped into the old fear and anger that Harry always engendered, the other half was locked in contemplation of what might have been. As a result, she had no spare energy to chastise Harry and order him from the house. Anything to avoid a scene, she had acted in pathetically mild fashion, no doubt giving Harry reason to feel encouragement.

Most of the rest of the night was spent cursing herself for her own feeble reaction to Harry's violating her privacy once again. His sickening humility disgusted her as much as his violence, but she knew that if he now redoubled his efforts she had only herself to blame. She should have thrown the diamond brooch after him into the street. She should have . . . Wearily, Viola got up late next morning.

All the calm contentment of the last few days seemed to have disappeared. Those twin destroyers of a peaceful mind, rage and fear, agitated her limbs, making her restless. In no mood to continue painting, she could only think that a short talk to Hardley There, intimating, in the lightest way, some of her troubles, might be of comfort. She knew he would welcome an interruption from his moths.

But Edwin, Viola could see at once, when she met him on the stairs, was in no mood for other people's problems. Rather it was he who needed soothing. His blanched skin and unshaven jaw told of a night as sleepless as Viola's own.

'You'll never believe it,' he wailed, 'but I found one on the front steps when I got home.'

For a moment, with her slow morning reaction, Viola misunderstood him. 'A moth!' she asked.

'A *woman*. Imagine! Eleven at night. Waiting for me for hours, apparently. *Howling*.' He wrung his hands, moaning again. For the first time since she had woken, Viola felt like smiling. But she controlled herself.

'Did you invite her in?'

'Oh, well, yes. I had to, didn't I? She was making such a noise. Any minute the neighbours would have complained.' The thought of this possibility seemed to cause Edwin further distress. He sat on a stair, head in hands.

'What was her trouble?'

'Ah! Gracious me. She kept me up the best part of the night explaining. Apparently, I hadn't acknowledged some poetry she'd sent me. Well, I mean, obviously I wasn't encouraging her to send me poetry. God knows what *that* can lead to. Mind you, she's rather a good poet, I suppose. But as I keep on telling her, she shouldn't address the stuff to *me*. It's dangerous for married women to write poetry to bachelors. I keep *on* warning her. But she pays no heed. Reams of the stuff pours out, gets pushed through my front door. What can I do? She leaves copies all over her house, I gather. Very careless. It's only a matter of time till her husband finds out. Then what? I'll be unwillingly involved in some terrible scandal. Cited, or whatever. But how can I get rid of her? Every time I shut the door in her face her fixation only increases. Oh Lord, honestly . . .'

'But you must have done something to encourage her,' suggested Viola, intrigued. She sat on the stair above Edwin.

'Not really. We met at an AGM of the Hampstead Moth Society. We're in the same *world*, you see. Her husband writes for a scientific magazine – very well, as a matter of fact. Our paths cross officially. Too damn often for my liking. She said she had a lot of questions to ask me on some paper I'd written. I asked her out to lunch, thinking it would be a purely professional date. Not her intention at all, of course. Well, somehow, several more lunches happened.'

'Long lunches?'

'They did somehow stray into the afternoon, I'm bound to admit. But I made it quite clear that for my part there was no

146

possibility of things developing. But she heeded not a word. And now she's gone completely off the rails, threatening to leave her husband and children, give up her entire life to me. I don't want *any part* of her life, let alone its entirety. Oh, dearie me, married women are terrible, terrible pests . . .'

Viola, feeling a little foolish, patted his shoulder.

'You *are* a kind girl,' Edwin went on. 'In fact, this house is my only refuge. I was wondering if staying here a few nights might not be the solution? Then she couldn't possibly trap me again. She's no idea of the address.'

'I'm sure my uncle wouldn't mind,' said Viola. 'Why don't you stay for a week? You could go in the dressing-room. I won't be in your way because I'm going home for a while to be with my brother who's coming over from America.'

'Oh?'

It was hard to tell whether Edwin was disappointed by the news of her departure. But by now his feelings for her were of little consequence to Viola. Last night had been a one-night flight of fantasy, dead this morning. Edwin Hardley was a friendly, rather pathetic creature, driven by a complex web of insecurities that Viola felt no desire to untangle.

He moved into the dressing-room that night, and was there for the two remaining nights before Viola left for Norfolk. But she scarcely saw him. There were no more suggestions of dinner. From what Viola could gather, from their brief meetings on the stairs, the unhappy poetess was not the only lady in pursuit of his reluctant love. He crept about with a hunted look, indicating, with the merest droop of his weary eye, that he suffered from being the most wanted man in London.

Alfred Baxter, alone in the house in Norfolk, established a routine of work as hard as it had been in the days before his retirement. His self-imposed hours were long: eight in the morning till eight at night, with only short breaks for lunch and an afternoon cup of tea. The rewards were the results. Within a week the lawns were all mown, the borders weeded, climbing roses pinned back against walls, gravel drive swept smooth. Up on the roof two builders – men he had known as boys – replaced slate tiles, and waved to him from their ladders. So he felt there was company, should he want it. But on the whole he was too preoccupied with his work to require anything more than the occasional greeting. He had never been a gregarious man, and was not lonely.

No: he was definitely not lonely. But strange sensations, which he could not account for when he forced himself to think about them, made him uneasy. It was something to do with getting himself settled – that was it. Not so much in a physical way: that was all taken care of nicely, his rooms all shipshape and tidy, only the kitchen to paint. It was more a matter of settling his mind.

In detached fashion, Alfred regarded his problem – if so unidentifiable a thing could be called a problem, that is – as very peculiar. Here he was, in the perfect job at last, lovely house and surroundings, part of the coast he had known all his life, time usefully occupied, great respect for his employer Miss Windrush – and yet at times he found himself shaking, physically shaking. It was fine during the day, outside. But the evenings Alfred dreaded. Forced to give up his gardening by the dark, he would reluctantly go into his kitchen, fiddle about getting himself a pork pie and a piece of cheese, and eventually go to his chair in the sitting-room. Very comfortable it was, too, at the end of a long day. Good support to aching limbs. Nothing to grumble about in the view out of the windows, either. The limes, their shapes by now familiar, scarcely moving in the still summer nights, moonlight on their leaves. Alfred would sit in the dark, so that insects would not fly in to the light and annoy him, and Eileen would start up her tricks.

Trouble was, once her face began bobbing about he couldn't get rid of it. It didn't obliterate his view, exactly, but behaved like a transparent yo-yo, up and down, up and down, the solid things of the room showing through. Sometimes Alfred would smack his brow, crying out loud in protest, and shut his eyes tightly. But that was no good. The face merely danced in blackness, alone, decapitated.

Even worse – the thing that caused Alfred to shake – was that although he knew the vision *was* Eileen, the face was not as he remembered it in life. It was a decidedly nasty face, pinched, mean, unfriendly. The real face, the good and smiling

Eileen he knew and loved, would not return.

Eileen did not haunt him on her own. Some nights, when he returned to the sitting-room particularly late, she was joined by the girls. He had no visions of them, but could hear voices, laughter – all of them laughing, not just Lily, now. One particular night, summer lightning playing in the sky outside, lighting up the limes so that they looked like giant silver birds with their feathers all a-ruffle, he heard them *singing*. A mocking sort of song, it sounded, though Alfred could not make out the words. Alarmed by the strength of the hallucinations, he stood up and went to the open window, just as the church clock boomed a melancholy midnight. Alfred could not bear the sound. He slammed the window shut and ran from the room. He went through the door to the kitchen of the main house, sat at the table and threw his arms across the massive planks of pine. He lay his head on the wood, smelt the beeswax polish. Here, thank the Lord, there was complete silence. Not a voice to be heard, his wife's face vanished.

In time, Alfred grew calm. He raised his head, reason prevailing again. He had had one of his funny turns, that was all. Well, he should be grateful that was all he suffered. Physically, he was sound as they come, full of strength and energy for his years. But old men, he remembered, do sometimes have funny turns. Nothing serious. And if he had another one, well, he'd know what to do next time. Come in here straight away. The peace of the Windrush kitchen was something very strong. It acted like magic. It took away his fears.

Quite recovered, Alfred switched on the lamp on the dresser and looked gratefully round the room which had soothed him. It was then he remembered that Miss Windrush and her brother were expected in two days' time: *two days*. Alfred's look turned from gratitude to severe criticism. Why, with all the work outdoors he had not even begun on the house.

He glanced at the clock: almost one o'clock. Well, no time like . . . Besides, he didn't really fancy returning to his own quarters, yet. Alfred eagerly took cloths and brushes from the cupboard. He gathered dusty china plates, untouched for months, from the shelves: he washed, replaced, swept, polished, scrubbed and tidied all through the visionless night. For once, the swift dark hours had been a happy time.

149

10

When Viola and her brother Gideon arrived from London, their immediate delight in everything Alfred had achieved gave him great satisfaction. Much of their first day was spent going from room to room noticing things Alfred had never supposed would be noticed. Then they turned to the garden. They made a long, slow tour with Alfred, listening to his plans, praising what he had done so far. The vegetable garden gave them particular delight: Alfred had managed to rescue globe artichokes and asparagus from the undergrowth. Viola declared in great excitement they would have friends to dinner the next evening, with fruit and vegetables from the garden. Their enthusiasm was most rewarding.

But, privately, Alfred felt some concern about his employers: Miss Windrush looked pale after two weeks in London, while Mr Windrush looked positively unhealthy. Thin, strained. Well, that was city life for you. Alfred and Eileen would never for a moment have entertained the thought of living anywhere but the coast. Cities were poisonous: they corroded a man's guts, they shut him off from the rhythms of the earth, they were no resting place for a peaceful soul. Back in the kitchen, Alfred put the kettle on the Aga, found biscuits and mugs. He was determined to restore the Windrushes to the lively health he remembered in their childhood. In the meantime, he could hear footsteps and real laughter upstairs. The house had come alive again.

Maisie Fanshawe tucked a tartan rug round her father's paralysed knees. Despite the warmth of the evening, he felt cold. His skin was always cold these days. She dabbed a handkerchief damp with eau de cologne round his neck, and placed a new biography of Milton, open at the right page, on his lap. His eyes, fixed somewhere in the middle distance, took a long time to lower their focus to the book. The telephone rang. Maisie's father did not seem to hear it.

As the telephone ringing in their house was a rare occurrence, it gave Maisie a small start of anticipation. She could not have said whom she hoped might be calling her, but almost any outside voice would be welcome in the long, stuffy evening. She went to her father's desk, sat in his leather chair, picked up the old-fashioned receiver, very heavy in her hand, and shyly gave the number. It was Richard Almond.

'Maisie,' he said, 'here's an order for you. I'm calling for you at seven tomorrow evening. Please be ready. We're going out to dinner.'

Stunned by disbelief, Maisie giggled. 'Dinner?' she repeated. 'Where? Why?'

'Just dinner. That's all I'm going to say.'

'But, I can't. Father – '

'You know perfectly well there are a dozen people who'd be willing to look after him for an evening. So don't worry about that.'

'I suppose – '

'Fine, then. See you tomorrow.'

Maisie put down the telephone. In flippant reaction to the extraordinary invitation, her mind leapt to the new Fair Isle jersey she had been knitting herself to occupy the evenings. She would sew it up this evening: must have something new. Then she wondered why, after all these years, Richard should suddenly issue her with a mystery invitation. He was lonely, she supposed. Had a rotten life, really, what with Sonia . . . Perhaps he wanted to talk about her at last. Perhaps he wanted to try out a new restaurant in King's Lynn: he was quite a gourmet, Richard, and she was last on his list of possible ladies to accompany him. Well, she didn't care, really. For whatever reason Richard wanted to take her out she would be happy. To be spared just one evening with her silent father would be an infinite treat. But heavens above, what a disloyal thought! Guilt sprang within Maisie's thin breast. She stood up, fetched her knitting, returned to her chair beside her father.

'Richard Almond has asked me to dine with him tomorrow night, Father,' she said. 'I hope you won't mind. I'll arrange for Mrs Ray to come in and look after you.'

Her father made no movement. It was impossible to tell

whether he understood, or cared. Maisie, excitement mingling with her guilt, patted his speckled hand. Then she lifted it, kissed it gently, and returned it to his lap.

'Dear Father,' she said.

Gideon and Viola spent the entire afternoon in preparation. Gideon, who enjoyed cooking more than his sister, concentrated on mint and lemon sauce for a poached chicken, while Viola slowly chopped chives and polished tomatoes the size of marbles from the garden. At peace in their work, they scarcely spoke except to remark on each other's progress. The sun shone fiercely outside. But the thick stone walls and the flagstone floors of the kitchen maintained coolness within.

Now, evening, everything done, they sat in the garden awaiting their guests. Viola had changed into a lavender cotton dress that threw shadows of the same colour on to her pale cheeks. She took a sip of Pimm's from a tall glass, smiled as a protruding fuzz of borage tickled her nose.

'I can hardly believe you're here,' she said.

Gideon was sprawled in a deckchair, long legs slung apart, etiolated New York clothes replaced by old corduroy trousers and dark shirt. In contrast to his expression on arrival here, he now had the look of a relaxed man. His fine eyes lowered almost sleepily.

'Must find out about the tides from Alfred,' he replied. 'I'd like to go for a sail.'

'What, tonight?'

'Should be a full moon.'

They sat looking out to sea, the smell of night-scented stocks sweet behind them, that veil of fragile warmth peculiar to English summers light upon them.

'I realize I must come back here for good, soon,' said Gideon after a while. 'I kid myself, week after week in New York, there's no point in returning home. But of course I'm wrong. I only have to be here five minutes to know how wrong I am.'

'What about Hannah?' asked Viola.

Gideon thought for some time in silence.

'She wouldn't like it,' he said at last. 'She's a real New Yorker, only really happy there. I couldn't ask her to come with me.'

'So?'

'So, things will resolve themselves, I daresay,' he said, and they listened to the church bell striking eight.

There were footsteps on the path. Richard and Maisie, arm in arm, appeared round the corner of the house. Gideon leapt to his feet, went first to Richard. There was much jovial hand-shaking, while behind the laughter each man's eyes scoured the other, assessing the changes. Their prolonged greeting, Viola saw, gave Maisie time to contain herself as best she could. Richard had said nothing about Gideon being here: the shock unsteadied her. She stood clutching at the hem of her dreadful Fair Isle jersey, salmon pink and lime and yellow, sour colours in the quiet light of the terrace, blushing. Viola quickly handed her a drink. She took a deep, grateful gulp.

'Oh God,' she whispered, 'I never expected *this*.' She avoided looking at Gideon, cast her eyes towards the beach, the hollyhocks, the sky – anywhere but the two men so close to her.

In her narrow life, Maisie had learned no wiles. Amazed to see the man she had loved for years, unrequited, the shock was too all-consuming to think of a ploy to disguise that amazement. And when eventually Gideon left Richard, came over to her, hugged her, declared his pleasure in seeing her, the blush vanished from her face to leave her pale and lost for words.

'Gideon, you're *here*,' was all she managed to say.

Richard, meanwhile, busying himself with drinks, ignored Viola. He, too, was overcome by the pleasure of seeing Gideon again. But then he turned to her. She sat upright in a wicker seat, the pattern of its high back a halo behind her head. He spoke before he could stop himself.

'Christ, you look . . .' He bent down and kissed her forehead. 'Violetta, Violetta, why so silent?'

'It's your turn for Gideon,' she said. 'I've had a whole day of him here. I've got him to myself for a week to come.'

It was Gideon's evening. He sat at the head of the vast kitchen table, in his father's old chair, telling stories of New York life, making them laugh, master of the scene. Maisie sat on his right, entranced. The candlelight muted her jersey, and despite the wild grey fringe she was suddenly years younger,

153

smudgy eyes a-glitter, ungrounded by rare happiness. She did not trust herself to eat: picked at the delicious food, scarcely touched the champagne Gideon had brought, and dared but a few glances at him as he told his stories.

Seeing that the others were too preoccupied to be of practical help, Viola produced the food and cleared plates, aware that Richard's eyes were often upon her. Pouring the coffee, she noticed the laughter wane. Gideon's stories had come to an end. The four of them found themselves drifting into another key with the ease of friends who have known each other all their lives. Merry from the wine, delighted by the reunion, unanimously they seemed to pause, listen, feel: let the sensations break over them like music. At such times, thought Viola, the present is a positive thing, caught with both hands, grasped, felt, infinitely precious. So much of our lives we flail in anticipation or reminiscence. The *conscious* present is elusive, a rare thing, that strikes only in times of great crisis, or happiness. Here it was this evening, alive, trapped for an hour or so, luminous in reality as it would become in memory.

Viola looked about her, accumulating detail: three shadowy heads, two candle flames, firelight dimpling the walls, smell of strawberries and roses, hands round half-filled glasses, no one speaking, each of them resting with their private thoughts. And she knew that those moments, silently acknowledged by Gideon, Richard and the trembling Maisie, would be remembered by each one of them.

Gideon turned, at last, to Maisie.

'And you, Maisie,' he said. 'I've been hogging the conversation. I'm sorry. I want to hear about you. What have you been doing?'

Maisie looked straight at him, alarmed to be called upon. Then she glanced at Richard and Viola, hating the attention.

'I've been looking after Father,' she answered. 'He hasn't long to live now.'

Despite her protesting hand, Gideon filled her glass.

'I would like to see your father again,' he said. 'Could I come up tomorrow?'

At the thought of a further encounter with Gideon, Maisie blushed deeply.

'Oh yes. Of course. He'd love . . . I mean, he might not know you. It's hard to tell what he knows.'

'I'll be there for tea,' said Gideon, and Maisie's head trembled in disbelief.

Gideon then suggested, as the tide was out, a walk on the beach. So warm a night, he said, would otherwise be wasted. Richard declined. Viola kept her silence.

'I'll come,' volunteered Maisie, at last, her voice no disguise to her eagerness.

'Right, Maisie. You and I shall walk a mile up the beach. Come on, come on.'

Gideon was all impatience, up and off as if the kitchen suddenly oppressed him. The others hurried to follow.

'Violetta and I will come as far as the garden gate,' said Richard. Had it not been for all the years of small gestures that never added up to a fundamental change, Viola might have thought his assumption, that she would want to stay behind with him, bore some significance.

It was still warm outside. The violet sky was as deep a colour as ever it could turn on an English summer night fluttering with stars. They walked across the lawn, the four of them: Maisie and Viola ahead, the two men behind, in conversation about boats. Maisie's shoes were causing her anxiety.

'They'll be hopeless on the beach,' she said, trying to find something upon which to focus a more abstract worry.

'Then take them off,' suggested Viola gently, recognizing Maisie's condition.

Amazed by such an obviously good idea, all notions of practicality having deserted her tonight, Maisie slipped off her gloomy shoes at the gate leading to the marsh. She laid them neatly under the hedge. Her long, narrow feet gleamed like silver fish in the moonlight.

Gideon opened the gate, guided Maisie through it as if escorting an elderly aunt. Richard and Viola watched them for a while, as they made their way down the path, single file. When they reached the beach, Gideon took Maisie's arm again. Soon they became invisible in the distance.

Richard and Viola then turned away from the sea, looked in silence at the reassuring shape of the house, the massive

155

trees, the lawn chequered with squares of light from the various windows.

'That nightingale, whose extinction I predicted,' said Richard. 'I was wrong. Listen.'

Viola, listening to the birdsong cascade from some hidden place in the trees, remembered at once the conversation.

'You said fifty years. It's not even half that.'

'It seems a very long time.'

'Maisie told me the other day she hated that evening. She confessed she was furious with me because Gideon took me home early.'

'He took you home early because I failed in my duties.'

'You were whirled away by Sonia.'

'So I was.' They both smiled. 'Poor Maisie. I wonder if she's loved Gideon all these years?'

'Things of a certain quality don't fade,' said Viola. 'Hope can die, but a conviction that something would have been right, had it been given the chance, can exist for ever.'

'You're probably right,' Richard said.

They moved slowly over the lawn. Viola, straight-backed and head held high, looked sternly towards the house. She was aware that Richard, close beside her, walked at a slight angle, eyes upon her.

'I've a rotten memory,' he was saying, 'but there's another thing I remember about that night. Your dress. It was silver.'

'White,' corrected Viola.

'Well, silver by moonlight. Flowers embroidered on the hem. Daisies, I think.'

'Lilies.'

They laughed again. 'Silver lilies! That was it. Wet from the grass.'

'You showed some concern.'

'It was the prettiest dress I've ever seen.'

'My mother's.'

'And you looked . . . I have to confess, on our walk in the garden I had a considerable struggle with my conscience.'

'I don't believe you.'

'I swear it. I had a terrible desire to touch you.'

Viola stopped. '*Did* you?'

'I did. I promise.'

'Then you put up a very good show of being quite impervious to my lilies.'

'What else could I do? You were sixteen. My friend's younger sister. I was supposed to be looking after you.'

Viola gave a small sigh. She began to move again. 'The rules of a gentleman can cause wicked suffering,' she said, lightly.

'I'm sorry. Perhaps I should have given in to my instincts. But it would have been a terrible shock to you. I must have seemed so old. I thought you must have been very bored, lumbered with me all evening. That's why I released you by going off to dance with Sonia.'

By now they were back at the terrace. They sat on the iron bench, listening to the church clock striking twelve. Its chime seemed gentler than by day, the echo of each note shuffling furtively into the quietness of the night, fearful of disturbing. As Viola remembered the desolation of that moment Richard had left her for Sonia, she felt its pain.

'How much we miss through our disguises,' she said. She allowed herself a sideways glance at Richard. His expression was one of such bleakness that, with no thought of the consequences, she lay her head on his shoulder, to comfort.

'I've often wondered, Violetta,' said Richard, taking her hand, 'if I made a mistake that night. I've never liked to admit it to myself, because we both know, if I did, it's impossible to put right.'

'You still keep to the rules of a gentleman,' said Viola. She could feel him smiling, guessed it was the mocking smile he kept for use against himself.

'I do,' he said. 'But not quite always.'

Richard kissed Viola on the mouth. As they drew near that moment when a kiss takes flight, he pushed her gently from him, though still kept hold of her hand. They returned to the kitchen and began the job of clearing up. An hour later Gideon appeared, alone, having driven Maisie home.

'Maisie of Docking has changed,' was all he said. 'I wish we'd been able to have our sail.' Then he engaged Richard once again in talk about his boat. Viola left them, with a new bottle of wine, knowing they would talk long into the night.

The next day Hannah telephoned. From what Viola could hear of the conversation there was some dispute between her and Gideon. All that he reported was that she was complaining about London, boredom, lack of his presence: wanted him to return early and entertain her.

'But I'm not going to,' he said. 'I was adamant about that. I'm staying for the full week, as planned. There are masses of things for us to do. That includes Richard,' he added. 'God, it's good to see him again. And dear old Maisie.'

Harry Antlers, in Sweden, was full of disillusion. His stomach never satisfied by the ubiquitous *smorgasbord*, he was permanently irritable and melancholy. The activities he was bound by his contract to film he found distasteful: the amorous advances of various interchangeable blondes, far from satiating his vanity, only served to exacerbate the condition of his pining heart. He wrote Viola many letters describing in minute detail the hourly fluctuations of his misery and longing. Some of these he posted to her Norfolk address. Finally, in desperation, from the bleakness of his hotel bedroom, he rang his own answering machine. There were various messages from Hannah Bagle. She was in London as promised. Bored, lonely, longing to see him. Why wasn't he there? There were also three messages in a girl's voice that he did not recognize, and she did not leave a name. Harry could only understand that she wished to see him most urgently. In the hope that Hannah could temporarily deflect his wretched mind, he decided to return to London for the weekend. Somehow, he could always fiddle his expenses.

Richard took a much overdue holiday during the time of Gideon's visit, and joined him and Viola every day. Maisie was also included in their plans. Incredulous at her good fortune, she arranged a rota of people to care for her father in her absence, and wondered at her lack of guilt. But it was not often such happiness befell her, and she was determined not to miss a moment of the glorious week. It might, after all, be a memory she would have to live upon for many years to come.

The good weather continued. It was very hot, though a constant breeze from the sea diffused the burning of the sun. A daily picnic lunch was taken out on the boat: they swam, walked far along the beaches, dozed in the hollows of the dunes. Although all these expeditions began as a foursome, somehow the couples always divided for part of the day. Gideon, full of pent-up energy after so long in New York with no proper exercise, was always keen to walk. Maisie was eager to accompany him. She did not pretend otherwise, simply said she would like to come with him. Viola would stay silently guarding the sleeping figure of Richard, his cheeks quite sunburnt by now, the lines of fatigue cleared from under his eyes. She was happy merely to lie back beside him, head on a comfortable tussock, fingers weaving through the soft white sand, sun pouring through her, arc of cloudless blue filling her eyes, small rustle of the sea the only sound. Here I am with Richard, was all she thought. When he stirred, she said: 'First time for weeks, I feel quite safe.'

Richard sat up, yawning. 'That man still bothering you?'

'He's persistent.'

Viola had had two Express letters from Harry here in Norfolk – pages and pages of rampant passion, unnerving while she read them, reminding her of his constant menace. She had said nothing and burnt both letters. But they left a small flame of fear, somewhere in the depths of her, that would not quite die despite the distractions of the present.

'If he's a real nuisance you must promise to let me know. I'll deal with him.'

Richard patted Viola's bare knee, the first time he had touched her since the night he had kissed her. Viola smiled.

'How?'

'There are ways. Anyhow, promise me.'

'Promise.'

Richard removed his hand, turned and looked down at the beach. Viola followed his gaze. They could see two minute figures in the distance walking slowly through the shallows of the sea. Gideon's hand was on Maisie's shoulder.

'I wouldn't be at all surprised,' said Richard, 'if Gideon didn't find great relief in Maisie.'

'I'm sure he does. She's part of his old childhood pattern, like us. He doesn't have to make an effort. He's fed up with new faces. Part of this holiday is sticking to old ones. But poor Maisie. He's being nice to her years too late. God knows what she'll suffer when he goes.'

'Perhaps, in the end . . . Who knows?'

'I doubt it. Hannah's very demanding and very strong. It'll take him a long time to extricate himself from New York.'

'I'm sure he'll end up here.'

'Probably, but not for a long time.'

'And I'll take quite a large bet with you he'll end up with Maisie.'

'Nonsense!' Viola laughed. Gideon and Maisie: absurd thought.

But when they returned from their walk, Viola found herself observing them anew. There was a tranquillity about Maisie which obviously attracted Gideon. She was calm, responding to his gentle teasing with a quiet smile. Her supply of new clothes exhausted, in the last few days she had taken to wearing jeans and an old jersey. She looked years younger, despite the grey fringe. Her hands were beautiful, Viola noticed for the first time, and there was a sort of lonely dignity in her upright carriage. Often she and Gideon caught each other's eye, and just looked, a little surprised, as if surveying each other for the first time. Viola, who had been preoccupied by Richard's presence for five days, wondered that she had not noticed these things before. She let herself briefly imagine Gideon and Maisie settled in Norfolk, living in the house. Although that would mean moving herself, it was a pleasing thought. It would be good, then, if Richard's instinct proved right.

On their last evening, Gideon and Maisie went for a final sail. Richard and Viola stayed in their usual place on the terrace, flagstones warm beneath their feet. Alfred Baxter was clipping a hedge nearby. The snip of his shears pecked at the silence. In the evening light the patterns of finely mown lawn among the shadows was an intense green. Tomorrow's parting, not mentioned, weighed heavily.

'As a matter of fact,' said Richard, 'most unusually, I have to come to London next week. My old mother's birthday. I'm taking her out to lunch. She won't stir in the evenings.' He paused, looked at Viola. 'I wondered, if you weren't too busy, if you would come to the theatre with me in the evening?'

Viola, who had been dreading the return to London, and who had never received any such invitation from Richard in her life, accepted with alacrity.

'I shall look forward to that,' said Richard and, occupied with their own thoughts, they fell into silence for a while.

Viola, her eyes on the beach, suddenly remembered the dawn picnic she had encountered the day she left for New York. The memory made her shiver slightly, the luxurious shiver caused by recalling a fearful experience from the safety of a protected present. She heard herself telling the story to Richard.

'I'll never know the answer,' she ended. 'Some existentialist joke, perhaps. Some form of artistic happening. But whatever it was, it was chilling. I dreamed about those stiff ladies, their clothes blowing about them, for weeks.'

'Most peculiar,' said Richard. 'I hate unsolved mysteries.'

'Telling you, perhaps, will exorcize it.' Already the vision, now described, was less sharp in her mind.

'Hope so. No more bad dreams.'

'No more bad dreams.'

They could see Maisie and Gideon coming through the gate from the marsh.

'Has ever a week gone so fast?' said Richard, and stood to pour drinks for the approaching couple.

11

Harry Antlers, on his return to London for the weekend, found a letter from his late landlady's solicitor giving him notice to leave. The house was up for sale. This spurred Harry to ring several estate agents and urge them to find him a penthouse flat. There was also a note, in uneducated writing, that had been delivered by hand:

Dear Mr Antlers, I have rung several times and left messages. Please could you phone me when you come back? I feel very wretched and would like to talk to you again. Yours, Annie Light.

The mystery of the anonymous voice on his answering machine thus solved, Harry sat down, heavy with disappointment. Remembering the girl, dark roots to her divided greasy hair, cruelly unlike Viola after a superficial glance, he made a note of her telephone number and angrily screwed up her letter.

Harry was very hungry. There was no food in his kitchen, no energy to go to the shops. He contemplated driving to Norfolk and peering through the bushes at Viola, her brother, most probably her doctor lover. But he felt no enthusiasm for such a trip: were he caught, things might be awkward. Instead, he wrote Viola another letter. Then the telephone rang. Hannah Bagle.

'Harry? Hi. I've been calling constantly.' Her annoyance was plain.

'I'm only just back.'

'How are you?'

'Ravenous.'

Hannah laughed, misunderstanding him.

'We can easily take care of that. Why not come on over? I'm at a horribly loose end, you could say. I'll order you up a huge steak, French fries. Leave it to me.'

'I'll be with you in an hour,' said Harry, his stomach aching at the thought of the food.

In the damp silence of his room he had a feeble battle with his conscience, but it was a fight quickly resolved. Once Viola was his, he would never go elsewhere. Until then, if other beautiful ladies wanted him, if others would assuage his hunger, why should he deny them?

He drove quickly to Hannah's hotel. She opened the door of her suite to him wearing only a silk dressing-gown. His greeting was to tear the lapels apart, gaze upon her until his look shifted, even more hungrily, to the white-clothed table laid for two in the window.

'Food first, if you don't mind,' he said.

They remained in the hotel for the rest of the weekend.

Viola and Gideon parted in London. Gideon was to spend a couple of days with Hannah, then they would return together to New York. It was quite apparent the prospect of this return held little joy for Gideon.

'The week seems to have confirmed all my instincts,' he told Viola. 'Maybe it's been the lever. Perhaps I shall be back quite soon.'

'Wouldn't that mean a lot of extricating?'

'It would. But when I recognize the right time has come, I shall brace myself up for the severing.' He looked far from happy as they said goodbye.

For her part, Viola took care to conceal from Gideon her own low spirits on her return to London. Entering her uncle's house, the anguished figure of Edwin Hardley did nothing to cheer her.

'Oh, you've been *away*,' he groaned. 'It's been the longest week this summer.'

He carried her suitcase upstairs to the half-finished flat, made cups of coffee. Viola, in her melancholy, felt grateful to him.

'You seem sad,' said Edwin.

'Not really. I never like coming back to London.'

'It's time we had another dinner. I shall tell you funny stories about a gathering of moth men last week. How about this evening?'

Viola paused, thinking.

'Not tonight,' she said at last. 'I think I must . . . resettle myself. Besides, I'm terribly behind with all this.' Her eyes ran over the unpainted kitchen walls. 'But it's very kind of you. Perhaps next week.' Next week, once Richard had come and gone, there would be nothing further to look forward to.

'Very well.'

Edwin swilled out his cup under the tap, put it on a paint-spattered draining board. He glanced around for a dish cloth. Seeing none, he seemed struck with unease, unnerved by the fact that he was unable to accomplish his job.

'I shall wait to be summoned,' he said, with a courageous smile, and put out a hand to touch Viola's hair.

When he had gone, Viola reluctantly went to the bedroom. She knew the turmoil that awaited her: unpacked suitcases all over the floor, rolls of wallpaper waiting to be hung, stacks of pictures, unmade bed. She knew she should begin to establish some kind of order, but felt drained of energy. All she wanted was to shut her eyes and slowly, luxuriously, relive every moment of the week in Norfolk.

The room faced north. Despite the sun of the day, no warmth had reached it. In her thin dress Viola shivered. She sat on the cold, crumpled sheets of the bed and after a long time, listening to the absolute silence, feeling the weight of her body, she picked up the letter from Harry Antlers that had been waiting for her.

My beloved Viola, she read, *What are you doing to us? Can you really want to lacerate a man's heart so cruelly? Can you not understand the great love I have for you, and let me prove it to you? You resist, you scorn, you ignore : this surely must be out of innocence, because I cannot believe the creature I love would intentionally ruin a man's life. However, I have patience. I shall wait, for ever if necessary. Such love as I have is not concerned with time, but it cannot be scorned, or wasted. So know that I shall never give up. I am sorry you did not find that little diamond star acceptable : I shall relieve you of it soon. I am sorry they were not greater diamonds, but they will be one day. Hope you had a good time in Norfolk with your lover. Think of me. H.A.*

The old fear, almost quelled by the security of the week in Norfolk, shot back, dizzying. She felt a chill sweat, the stuff of her dress stuck icily to her back. She heard herself cry out loud, rending the silence of the darkening room. Such bleakness she had never known. She wondered where to turn.

Sated by quantities of good food at Hannah's hotel, and by her own generous provision, Harry was able to return to Sweden in reasonable calm. He was not a little intrigued by Hannah's apparent affection for him. Had Viola not existed, he reflected on several occasions, he might have been inclined to encourage her flattering desire. As it was, she was an agreeable vessel, and her infidelity would be useful ammunition some time in the future.

But the two lustful days with Hannah proved only a temporary antidote, inadequate balm to the real wounds of Harry's heart. Within a few hours of his return to Sweden, he had forgotten Hannah, was suffering again, more acutely than ever, from his love of Viola. His pain was further exacerbated by lack of filling food, and with no care for the standard of his work he hurried through the last days of filming. Sleepless nights were spent planning his next move. This was to be the taking back of the diamond star, as he had warned Viola in his last letter.

The week of agonizing in Sweden finally came to an end, and the evening Harry chose for his next visit to Viola he was in good spirits. In his absence the estate agents had found him a flat. It was not quite the exotic penthouse he had imagined, but at least it was at the top of a tower block in Notting Hill Gate, with large windows and a fine view. It was in good order, merely needing repainting. Harry had hopes that Viola would be tempted by such a place, would willingly leave the gloom of the great house in Holland Park. So, he felt, he would be bringing good news, which would mean an auspicious start. Also, she would be touched that he intended to take back the diamond star in response to her wish. This, surely she would feel, showed dignity and understanding.

Harry spent an unusually long time preparing himself, rejecting all his man-made fibre shirts for the only one of pure cotton. Then he set about his normal method of inducing some semblance of calm: a four-course dinner in an Italian restaurant. The fact that Viola might be out had not come into

165

his calculations. Instinct told him he would find her. With great hope of a rewarding evening, at last, Harry set off for Holland Park, stomach bulging.

He climbed the aristocratic flight of steps. The front door opened before he reached the top. A man stood there, carrying a briefcase. Of indeterminate appearance – in a seizure of suspicious fury Harry tried to imprint the lover's features on his mind, but they slipped from him even as he looked – the man was grey-skinned and anxious looking. Harry reached the top step, heart pounding.

'Ah,' he said.

'Were you coming in?' asked the man, hand on the vast gold door knob, clutching it as if for support.

'I was,' said Harry. 'Were you going out?'

Edwin licked his dry, grey lips.

'I was,' he said eventually. 'But in fact I've forgotten a couple of books, so I'm returning to the library for a moment.'

'Ah,' said Harry again.

He followed the lover inside, noting the odious width of his shoulders, the salmon pink polyester of his shirt. Viola's love for this creep must be quite blind to accept *that*. Harry would remember it, should it be necessary, to taunt her.

The two men stood in the dim speckled light of the hall weighing their mutual antipathy. It was an occasion that called for politeness above all else, Edwin thought. The hideous chap beside him, plainly deprived of public school good manners, should be treated courteously for Viola's sake.

'Are you looking for Viola?' he offered.

'I am.'

'I believe you'll find her in her flat at the top of the house.'

So *that* was it. Viola already had a penthouse – in Harry's estimation any top-floor flat was a penthouse – Goddamn the spoilt little bitch. And where would that leave his plans?

'She's waiting for me,' he managed to say. 'I'll go on up.'

He took a clumsy leap up the first two stairs, with an air of one familiar with grand staircases. In fact he was obliged to clutch at the mahogany balustrade to prevent himself from falling. Recovered, he sped on up three flights, the thick-piled alien carpet a deterrent to his impatient feet. The familiar sensation of a million pins piercing his veins was almost intolerable. He felt Edwin's scornful little eyes upon him. Indeed, Edwin's scornful eyes did follow Harry till he was out of sight. Then he made his own slower way to the library.

When the stairs ended at last, Harry found an ordinary door – there seemed to be an economy of mahogany towards the top of the house – half open. He paused, breathing noisily. He found himself to be hot, sweating, smelling. His plans, together with his intentions to present a calm and loving front, jeered through his head in tatters. The confrontation with the lover – dreadful, prying face of a medical man, he had – had quite unnerved him. His whole being seethed with outrage and self-pity.

But somewhere in the maelstrom of his despair a small voice of reason could be heard. Now, more than ever, Harry knew, it was essential he should contain himself. He must diffuse the wildness within, dwell on the moment later. If he was to win the heart of his beloved Viola, he should appear a rational man. He must pause and strive.

Sitting on the top stair, plump thighs supporting arms and head, Harry made the effort of a lifetime. Eyes shut, he willed pictures of tranquillity to flower in the darkness: slow clouds in a dull sky, grey rocking sea, a tablecloth of muted checks he had loved as a child – he remembered the comfort of twisting its soft stuff between his fingers. Music would have helped. Harry summoned Beethoven's Seventh to his ears, but the imagined notes were no match for the real sound of his own breathing.

Gradually, the sweat on his body dried, though the smell remained pungent. Cold, now, he opened his eyes. He had no idea for how long he had fought his battle. Time had been immeasurable. Harry stood, calm. The effort had succeeded.

He tiptoed through the door. Within the flat, he found himself in a narrow passage of bare boards. At the end of the passage was an open door. Harry crept towards it.

Peering into the room he saw Viola, back to him, kneeling on the floor turning the pages of a leather-bound photograph album. There were others in a pile beside her, open. The wall to her left was entirely taken up with newly painted bookshelves, half filled with books, ornaments, glasses, and two bottles of wine. There was also a large photograph of a handsome elderly couple in sporting hats. They smiled from an expensive frame. Parents, no doubt. (Extraordinary idea, displaying a photograph of parents.) The room, like the passage, was uncarpeted. The wall opposite the bookshelves was painted the kind of arrogant scarlet that evoked Harry's instant hostility, but he fought to control this reaction. The other two walls were as yet unpainted, though pots of scarlet paint on the floor indicated the end of their naked plaster state was imminent. There was no furniture, just two tea chests of objects wrapped in newspaper. No curtains in the single wide window. The darkening sun flared through Viola's hair, making it translucent as the fluff of dandelions.

'Hello, beloved lady,' said Harry, at last.

Viola's body snapped round to face him. Her beautiful mouth split into a hideous scream. She clutched at her ears through her hair, swaying. Harry felt himself smiling, seeing her as if through a sheet of protective glass. He squatted on the floor beside her. As he did so, he heard the rip of material: the zip of his flies had broken. Glancing down, he saw a tuft of white shirt protruding.

When the horrible noise of Viola's scream had subsided, Harry eased himself into a more comfortable position on the floor. He was not shaped for sitting happily on floors, and in this position he was at a disadvantage. He moved to support himself against the bookshelves, thus freeing his hands to try to disguise the gaping of his trousers. As usual, everything had conspired against him, but for the moment, adrenalin pulsing happily through his veins, he was in command of the situation.

'Calm down, beautiful Viola,' he said. 'I'm sorry if I should have taken you by surprise. I came merely to relieve you of the diamond star, as you requested. I'm sorry if it's been a burden to you.'

He could see Viola's heart pounding beneath the gossamer cotton of her jersey. He gripped his hands more tightly to prevent himself crushing the fearful creature to him. That would ruin everything.

Viola reached up to the bookshelves, took the small box with a shaking hand. She handed it to Harry.

'Now will you go?' she asked quietly.

'Thank you.'

168

Harry put the box in the pocket of his jacket with one hand, leaving the other to guard the split in his trousers. But the small exertion, combined with the strain of taut stomach against waistband, was fatal: the single hook upon which the sole responsibility of keeping the trousers together now lay, snapped. Viola's eyes joined Harry's in falling to the general disarray of flesh and sprouting shirt. Viola had the grace to smile. Harry, relieved, gave a grim laugh, patting and tugging to no good effect.

'Just my luck,' he said.

He realized that in some peculiar way this inauspicious happening had brought Viola closer to him than he ever had been before. They were briefly joined in mirth. The joke dispelled the anger and the fear. Heavens, thought Harry, the gods act curiously: but they had given him an advantage he must surely take.

'I'll go,' he said. 'Of course I'll go. Who am I to stay, unwanted?'

'You're unreasonably persistent,' said Viola, lightly, 'considering you must know by now that pursuing me is hopeless.'

'Ah, but there you're wrong. It's not hopeless, and I've only just begun.' Harry, too, tried for lightness: he did not want to scare her with what might sound like threats. 'My aim, of course, you beautiful, beautiful creature, is to make you realize *your* love for me, which up to now you've been fighting against like a wild cat.' Viola gave a small laugh. 'That's so often how real love starts. A great fight against commitment, against acknowledgement. But you must know, in your heart of hearts, you're as inextricably bound to me as I am to you . . . That evening in Norfolk, before I went berserk and did everything wrong, you standing there by the fire in your bloody great kitchen – you wanted me as passionately as I wanted you. I could *feel* it. Why else do you suppose I persisted, was eventually driven to violence by your stubborn refusal to recognize . . .?'

He saw her eyes widen. He was going too fast, too far, but she was still gazing at him, curiously. He still had her sympathy – just.

'Dear God, my love. Here I am, desperately uncomfortable on this dreadful floor, trousers split, ridiculous . . . loving you with all my heart, asking you just to think a little of my plight. You try to be so heartless. But you aren't, you aren't.'

He put out a hand towards her. She shifted away. He returned it to its place on the trousers.

'I'm sorry,' Viola said, quite nicely, very practical. 'But you've got it all wrong. You misjudged everything. You believe something that's patently not true. I'm sorry if I've hurt you, tormented you, even, resisting you. But how can I make you see the truth? You're a prisoner of some sort of wild delusion. It'll go, it'll die. Honestly.'

Harry swallowed. Paused. 'It won't,' he said at last. 'And it's you who are mad, as you'll realize when all these absurd preliminaries are over and we're a happily married couple with four children. However, you must take your own time to understand yourself. I shall wait patiently, constantly, wishing you well with your pink-shirted doctor downstairs.' His first mistake. Viola's eyes hardened. 'Well, whoever he is. Perhaps the doctor is in Norfolk? I get muddled, so many lovers . . . But let's not speak of them. Let's concern ourselves with us.' He pronounced it *uz*.

Viola looked as if she had much to deny in response, but decided to resist. 'Please go now,' was all she answered. 'I can see nothing I can say will make any difference to you. But if you really love me as you say, then perhaps you'll be kind enough to leave me alone, as I want.'

Perhaps you'll be kind enough to leave me alone : the triteness of the phrase swatted at Harry's mind-shattering passion as if it was an annoying fly. Oh, she'd learn, the girl: she'd learn. Though if this kind of patience, the infinite gentleness of his manner this evening, achieved no response either, then perhaps he would have to rethink his strategy once again.

'Very well: I'm going,' Harry said.

The performance of rising to his feet Harry was not able to conduct with the dignity he would have liked. He had to try to keep his trousers together with one hand, while pushing himself up from the floor with the other. He found it intolerable that Viola, who had leapt up quickly in a single youthful movement, should be looking down on his struggle. Mocking, no doubt. Seeing him as a figure of ridicule. But as quickly as such thoughts about her came to him, they were dispelled by a firm hand holding his, pulling. With the politeness of her class, she was helping him, though the help meant no more than just that, of course. No one like the upper classes to help an enemy . . . And there he was, now, panting foolishly, but standing, very close to her, the sky almost dark behind her luminous hair, her huge eyes confronting him with the wary sightless look of the blind. The brief physical contact, Viola touching him for the first time, had further confused Harry Antlers. He felt the approach of sentimental tears, and in that weakened state took the risk of saying one thing further.

'Viola Windrush, if you are never to be mine, then there is little point in continuing my life. I ask you to remember that.'

'Rubbish,' he heard her say, gently. 'You should never make such foolish threats. Please.'

The sympathy in her voice – no mockery there, Harry could swear – was his undoing. He flung himself upon her, crashing his mouth down upon hers – a brief chink of teeth, he heard, before her screams. He felt her writhing, struggling, scratching, shouting for help, scotching instantly his loving desire. Rage slashed over him: he felt his hand squeezing Viola's cheek, its soft pulp flashing him a memory of summer peaches he had tortured as a child, to bring forth the trickle of sweet juice – except that the juice he could see was blood. Blood! Dear God, here he was near to killing . . . Could nothing make her understand the love that lived behind his rage? And why would his hands not obey him, signalling what he really felt? With a great effort he tried gently to wipe the tracks of blood from Viola's cheek, but he could tell by a flick of her head he was rough, hurting again.

Viola was trapped against the window. From Harry's arms, curved crab-like, she could not escape. Wanting to roar his love for her, some indistinguishable abuse spewed forth, alarming him. He hit her on the bleeding cheek, saw her sway, moaning, left, right, left, about to fall. Then she splayed her arms out behind her against the window to support herself, and was still. Also, silent. She looked at him from the eye that remained open. Blood dripped from the corner of the other one, making a scarlet gash down her cheek, falling to spot the white of her jersey.

Silence, silence. Room nearly dark. Viola an immobile

171

poster stuck to the window, spectral. The silence crashed in Harry Antlers' ears, increasing the darkness in his eyes. Wrenching up the trousers, which were fast sliding over his hips, he lumbered across the bare floor to the pots of paint, kicked them over each in turn. Fascinated, he watched scarlet snakes sprout across the floor. Then he barged back to the bookshelves, both hands deserting trousers while he picked up the photograph of the parents with their nice kind smiles. He threw it to the ground. There was a crash of glass, miniscule splinters flew across the dark floor boards, glow worms in brief flight. He heard an intake of breath from the unmoving Viola.

'Not that . . .' she whispered.

'I'll destroy you, and everything that's yours.' This was a thick cry Harry did not recognize as his own. By now his arms were full of books. He threw them about the room, watching them land like clumsy birds in the red paint, their pages sprawled pathetically.

Shouting obscenities, Harry threw books more wildly, with both hands. In his preoccupation, he did not notice that his trousers had slipped below his knees. He took a step. They slid to his ankles. They fell.

From the small stone pebble of her mind, whose one eye could see but hazily, Viola Windrush watched Harry Antlers grovelling on the floor. He was both weeping and moaning at the same time, tears and spittle joining in the deep runnels at the sides of his mouth. His words were slurred, barely understandable: something about begging and forgiveness and madness, and Viola's fault. He crawled backwards and forwards, an obscene monster baby, a caged and spent tiger, trousers twisted round his feet, flashes of appalling underpants beneath the drooping shirt.

Some infinitesimal part of Viola's mind registered that had she not been involved in this melodrama, she would be able to appreciate the black humour. Men in the depths of their wretchedness can be shockingly absurd. She was reminded – in halting thought that came in single words – of an amateur production of Shakespeare, in which a slain man had not been able to bring himself to die, rolling round and round the stage in an extravagance of last breaths. The audience had laughed. Viola stretched the tight line of her clenched mouth just a fraction, and tasted blood.

'Get up,' she managed to say. 'You're a horrible sight.'

She thought: why am I here? A sane woman, pinned to my own window, bleeding, silent, forced to watch so degrading a scene? And why do I feel nothing, nothing?

The weeping and crawling continued for another couple of lengths of the room. But then, like an actor whose part is over and who must gather himself for his bow, Harry Antlers stood up surprisingly fast, considering the state of his trousers. Viola shut her good eye against the sight of thuggish thigh and bandy calf. Harry held on to his trousers with one hand, blew his nose with the other.

'You can call the police, my love,' he said. 'It won't matter. This is the end.'

Viola, opening her eye as he spoke, and seeing his loathsome face greasy with tears, shut it again. Thus she only heard him shuffle from the room, down the passage, and bang the door behind him.

When he had gone, she lowered her arms from their place across the window, dead, bloodless things which felt huge as balloons. She made her way through the dark passage to the bathroom, switched on the light. In the small mirror above the basin she observed the damage to her face. She bathed her closed eye with a sponge of cold water, wiped away the blood. She told herself she must find the energy to go downstairs and telephone the police. But, leaving the bathroom, savage pain began to fill her head, and such deadly tiredness accosted her that it was a wonder she made it to the bedroom. There, she pulled off her clothes and fell on to the bed. Blackness absorbed her, instantly.

12

Two flights beneath Viola's flat, Edwin Hardley was suffering a perfectly horrible evening. He tried to convince himself that in his favourite chair with an article on the Prosperine hawk-moth in his hand, his thoughts could be deflected. But no such miracle occurred.

Three things were troubling him. The first – and this was the merest graze of anxiety on a skin thickened by available women – was that a nubile young painter was waiting for him in her flat for dinner, and she had no telephone. She would have to accept a note of apology next day.

Second, the man who Viola was apparently expecting, and of whom she had made no mention, had looked extremely un-desirable. Well, the light in the hall had been very dim, fair enough – it would have been impossible to observe in detail. But Edwin had received a strong impression of squatness, ill-bred thickness, and unusual ugliness. Edwin himself, for instance, would not have been happy about meeting such a chap alone in an alleyway on a moonless night. An instinctive fear, on Viola's behalf, had fretted at his stomach. With no forethought he had told the lie about returning for a book. Now, on reflection, he knew he had made that decision with good reason.

The third worry was a nameless one. That is, pressed, Edwin *could* have put a name to it: but that would have been an ungentlemanly thought, an undignified confession even to himself. Especially, it seemed quite clear for the moment, as Viola and he were merely affectionate friends. All the same, fighting against the very *suggestion* that he could be . . . taken that way, made Edwin restless. He put down the dull book. Paced the room a while.

When the library clock struck eleven – which meant Viola's visitor had been with her an hour – and he had not been called upon for help or company, Edwin decided it was time to go.

This thought was quickly replaced by another one: that would be a most cowardly act. Villains struck at midnight – how could he ever forgive himself if he fled an hour before Viola needed him? No. He must stay, her protection.

The fearful novelty of the evening had put all thoughts of food from Edwin's mind. A drink, however, was another matter. As pictures of rape and violence upstairs multiplied in his mind, the thought of a drink became imperative. Edwin went quietly to the drawing room, fetched whisky and a glass, and returned to the comfort of his armchair. There, one ankle twirling, he drank three glasses of whisky with unnatural speed for so cautious and moderate a drinker. By the time the alcohol had reached the third or fourth stages of benign effect, and he was beginning to think there would be no harm in having a short nap, the library clock struck twelve.

At that very moment, as he had known he would, Edwin heard a muffled scream from upstairs. He leapt to his feet, ran a wild hand through his greasy hair. Courage, engendered by the whisky, so rampant within him only a moment before, now abandoned him with distressing speed. More screams, distinct this time. Edwin gave a small jump, muttering 'dearie me', clinging to the wing-back of the chair for support. His head was a bright haze. Then, merciful silence.

As Edwin looked about him, he perceived the library furniture and the hundreds of books in their shelves had taken on an unnerving life of their own. They floated hither and thither through Edwin's confused vision. He tried to anchor them back into their old positions with no success. They spun and danced about him, so that he was forced to hesitate a long time before taking a single step. But despite the disadvantages Edwin suffered, a firm and noble part of his mind deliberated with great determination: rescue Viola he must. Bold body-guard, he. He thumped his own chest, a gesture he could not recall ever having made before in his life, and made himself smile.

After some time Edwin made his uncertain way to the door, bending and swaying to miss the objects that seemed to be hurling their way towards him. At last he reached the vast door, pulled it ajar, leaned heavily against it. Now he could hear, with sickening clarity, moans, screams, and the violent thuds of objects landing angrily. 'Dearie me,' Edwin whispered to himself once again, and recognized with extraordinary cool wisdom, considering the havoc of his head, the fact that he would never be able to leap upstairs and rescue poor Viola unless he allowed himself a short rest.

Somehow, he found his way back to the chair, sank into it. There, he urged himself to listen to the good reason which was pressing its way into his wretched head: a man should not interfere. That was definitely it. Interference could lead to terrible confusion and misunderstanding. After all, it was possible Viola was enjoying herself. Some girls, he had heard, liked a rowdy time, a bit of horseplay. Who was he to . . . ?

At which point the whisky obliterated the reason, and Edwin Hardley fell into a deep sleep.

The library clock woke him at four. Confused, stiff, with aching head and dry mouth, he looked at the empty bottle of whisky beside him. Then he fingered the empty glass, longing for water. After a while, the events of the night, and his own behaviour, came back to him. He moaned gently, protecting his eyes from the gash of grey in the sky, with a shaking hand. Remorse is powerful at dawn.

Edwin mustered all his strength. He stood, smoothing his rumpled hair and clothes, small tongues of anxiety lapping within him. Once more he went to the door – a less precarious journey this time – opened it, listened. Silence. He made his way to the kitchen, drank two glasses of water. Then, forcing back thoughts of what he might find, he crept upstairs to Viola's flat.

Its door was shut, but not locked. First, he went to the sitting-room. At the sight of the devastation – for a moment he thought the red paint to be blood – he gave an anguished cry and ran to Viola's bedroom. He found her, in a dressing-gown that seemed to have been pulled on carelessly, lying on the bed. Flinging himself down beside her, Edwin opened her folded arms and pressed his head to her heart. It was beating firmly. Weak with relief, he stared down at her pale profile – head on one side, the other side buried in the pillow. She seemed, thank God, not to be harmed. Gently, he made to return her arms to their former position. But they resisted, then rose up: Viola's hands were on his shoulders. Her visible eye opened.

'Hello,' she said. 'I'm sorry, I don't look too good, do I?' She spoke thickly, like one emerging from an anaesthetic.

'What nonsense you talk,' whispered Edwin. Suddenly he cared no more about the violent activities Viola and her lover had been engaged in. In the dim light she did not appear ravaged, but beautiful. And now she was alone, warm: it was his turn. After all, he needed her to assuage the terrible night she had caused him. He pulled up the blankets.

Viola, shifting through pain and sleep, recognized a pallid light in the window, the soft voice of Hardly There. Some time later she felt a new warmth, of blankets, limbs, flesh. She was dimly aware of a faint struggle with clothes, a soft hand on her hair, and on her brow, the friendly voice saying 'There, there,' over and over again. She was just conscious of a slight, surprising sensation, not altogether disagreeable: the merest hovering above her, it seemed, before the weight rolled away.

Then, never having been fully woken by the fluttering of Edwin Hardley, Viola returned to a dreamless sleep.

When Harry Antlers emerged from the house in Holland Park, the warmth of the night was gentle upon him, evaporating the last of the mingled sweat and tears on his face. He felt calm, sane, exhilarated. Despite the exertions of the last few hours he was full of energy, and knew that sleep would be impossible.

He drove to a telephone kiosk, found Annie Light's number in his diary. The process of telephoning her was an awkward one, conducted with one hand, while the other secured his trousers. She took a long time to answer. Then, her voice was confused with sleep.

'This is Harry Antlers. You know, Harry Antlers. I'm coming round to see you.'

Annie gave a small squeak of gratitude and told him her address. She was in bed, she explained.

'Stay there,' ordered Harry. 'That's just where I want you.'

Ten minutes later, clutching his trousers with both hands, Harry barged up the scurvy path that led to an uncared for terraced house similar to the one which he was shortly to leave. He found the front door ajar, pushed it open. Annie was waiting behind it in her nightdress. There were no lights. The hall smelt of wet cat and boiled fish, familiar smells. Annie, a dim blade of whiteness in the dark, put a trembling hand on Harry's arm.

'Good thing me mum's working nights, this week,' she whispered. 'Dad won't hear a thing. He's out cold, as usual.'

Harry was in no mood for conversation. This was not the time for explanations, or the nicety of preliminaries.

'Upstairs,' he grunted.

Because Annie refused to put on the light, Harry was spared details of her room. The darkness also concealed the rumpus of his shirt and trousers, and sight of her greasy hair and ratty face. He was aware of a hard, narrow bed that smelt of cheap scent. Annie, in his arms, was rigid with some imbecile love for him, muttering how she'd thought of him day and night, idiotic declarations of passion straight from the pages of a romantic novel. Briefly amazed that he had had so powerful an effect in such a short meeting, Harry told her to shut up: he wanted to get on with it. She eagerly complied.

Harry crashed through Annie, thinking only of Viola, her shut and swollen eye, bemused face, scarlet blood on white jersey, arms outstretched against the London sky. Annie's stupid moans of ecstasy spurred him to put on his jacket very quickly once it was all over. (The sweaty shirt he had not bothered to remove.) Her pleas for him to remain a while were of no avail. His business finished, Harry's only thought was to leave as soon as possible. The activities of the night had made him ravenous.

'I'll be in touch, one day,' he snarled, and left the ravaged girl to make sense of things in the dark.

Harry's next stop was at an all-night cafe in Shepherds Bush. There, he ordered three eggs on toast, bacon, sausages, tomatoes, several cups of tea. The food acted as a quick restorative, filling aching caverns that had made a honeycomb of his body. By four o'clock, dawn sky silvering pearls of condensation on the cafe window, revenge was sweet within him. To celebrate his new idea, Harry ordered a fourth cup of tea and two currant buns.

Viola woke at midday. Getting up was a slow and painful business. Having confronted the horrible sight of her face in the bathroom mirror, and dabbed her bruises with witch hazel, she forced herself to assess the havoc of the sitting room. There, she knelt on the floor slashed with scarlet paint, fingering the contorted shapes of her books. She did not think of returning them to their shelves. Then she picked up the smashed picture of her parents. The glass was a web of cracks – she traced a finger over them – but the photograph itself was little damaged. She replaced it on the floor. Later, she would set about putting the room in order. For the moment, she had no energy.

Viola left the brightness of her flat for the duskier regions of her uncle's quarters. Grateful she had somewhere with no memories of the night to go, she made herself a cup of black coffee in his kitchen, took it to the soothing browns and greys of the drawing room. She ensconced herself in the depths of a velvet chair by the window, the telephone on a small table beside her. In a moment she would ring the police. In the meantime, she concentrated on the pattern of sycamore leaves outside the window, dull green against a dull sky. An hour or so went by. She ached against the cushions. She may have dozed.

Then Edwin Hardley was beside her: he must have crept so quietly over the carpets she had not heard him enter. His face was stricken, a look Viola recognized when he spoke of the ladies who hunted him. He was crouched on the floor beside her, clutching her hand. He seemed to be in a state of much anguish.

'What's the matter?' she asked.

'Matter?' he cried. 'Dear God, what's the matter with *you*?'

Viola fingered her closed eyes. She essayed a small smile.

'Slight disagreement with a hunter,' she said.

'But, last night – well, I suppose it was more like dawn this morning, I came up to you, found you asleep . . . Didn't you hear me?'

Viola frowned: dim memory of some vague visitation. Edwin, troubled, had blushed.

'You were on your side,' he went on. 'I can only have seen the unharmed side. Oh my God. Let me ring a doctor.'

It was then Viola remembered she would be seeing a doctor tonight: Richard was coming to take her out. She gave a small moan.

'I'm all right,' she said. 'No need for a doctor. It's only bruises and a headache. I'm filled with aspirin and I've bathed the eye. Sorry I look so awful. Perhaps you could buy me an eye patch when you next go out?'

'Oh Christ. This is unbelievable. Of course, an eye patch . . . I'll go in a moment, and get us something for lunch. But please let me call a doctor.'

'No.'

'The police, then.'

'I'll call the police this afternoon.'

In truth, Viola knew it was unlikely she would do so. The thought of being questioned, of involving the law, and the publicity of a traumatic court case were more than she could bear to think about.

'What happened?' Edwin was on the window seat now, legs crossed, an ankle twirling. Viola shrugged.

'It's quite hard to remember, at this moment, exactly what did happen. Some form of dispute got out of hand, obviously. But what gave you the idea of visiting me at dawn?'

'We-ll. I met this . . . *man* on the doorstep. He looked a bit menacing.'

'*That's* how he got in.'

'He said you were expecting him, so who was I to detain him?'

'Quite.'

'Anyhow, at the risk of interfering, I had some funny instinct I should stay. I didn't like the thought of you being alone in the house with him. So I returned to the library for the evening.'

'That was very kind.'

'Not of much use, in the event. Sleep, unfortunately, overtook me.'

Viola smiled. 'You didn't hear anything?'

'Well, I'm bound to say I did. A few thumps and cries. But then I thought perhaps . . . well, you know. You might have been enjoying yourselves. People have their different tastes, don't they?' Edwin had blushed again. 'I was about to go home when I heard the front door slam. So I crept up, just to make sure you were all right. I'm sorry if I . . . I had no idea. I mean, your bruises were turned away from me. It was scarcely light.' He paused. 'I'm sorry if I woke you.'

'You hardly did.'

They both smiled at the joke, looking at each other for a long time. Viola was struggling to remember. Then Edwin leapt up, patted her hair. In the grey summery light, muted further by the shadows of the room, he looked exhausted.

'Now, you just stay there,' he said. 'I'm off to buy lotions and potions and eye patches and lunch. We're going to have a picnic lunch, right here.' Again he patted her hair, kissed her very gently on the nose. 'And then you might find yourself doing a little explaining. I think there are probably some things that will have to be sorted out. We can't have any more such . . . carryings on, can we?'

'You're very kind,' Viola said again. She was grateful and tired, glad of Edwin's protection.

'I hope you'll forgive . . .' he added quietly.

'For what?' murmured Viola, fighting against sleep.

Later, Edwin woke her with a tray of lunch. They ate smoked trout and ice cream, and drank a bottle of iced white wine. Sitting on the floor, Edwin told funny stories about the gathering of moth men he had attended last week. Viola found herself laughing. Dear Edwin: spindly on the carpet, the mildest of gladiators, the most charming of companions when safe from pursuit by desperate women. She liked him. She was glad he was there.

Lulled by the wine, Viola dozed most of the afternoon in the warmth of the armchair. Her only struggle was to keep at bay pictures of the evening before. At five she was woken by the telephone. It was Gideon in New York.

'Violetta? You all right?'

Viola paused, decided a transatlantic telephone call was no place for explanations. Besides, he sounded exuberant.

'Fine,' she said.

'Good news. I'm coming home. The return here hasn't worked out too well. I've just got to wind up a few business things, then I'll be with you.'

'Will you be alone?'

'Absolutely. I'm afraid we reached a crisis point. I had to tell Hannah I no longer – '

'Good.'

'Quite. Hope you'll be able to spare a few days in Norfolk while I sort myself out?'

'Of course. In fact I'm going there for a few days next week, when the flat is finished,' said Viola, making up the plan as she went along. 'Catch a few more days of summer before I get a job.'

'You might look up Maisie,' said Gideon. 'She'd like to see you.'

'I will. I'll tell her the good news.'

Gideon's turn to pause. 'She already knows, matter of fact,' he said.

'Oh?'

Viola sat up in surprise. But there was no time for further questions. Elated by her brother's news – something to look forward to once Richard's visit was over – she returned to her flat, for once not regretting the lost day. She began to prepare herself as best she could for the evening.

Heavy from his enormous breakfast, still clutching at his trousers, Harry Antlers left the café at six in the morning. The ebullience of a few hours earlier had left him. A profound wretchedness seeped through the cushion of food in his stomach. He no longer cared, as he shuffled ungainly down the street to his car, how foolish he must look.

An early sun, sharp-edged, rose in the sky above the buildings of Shepherds Bush. Still the watery colour of a moon, it hurt Harry's eyes. He cursed summer, light mornings, the general brightness of the world. To add to his pains, city sparrows, perky little bastards, were tweaking about the place as if auditioning for a Disney film. Their ghastly cheerfulness and piercing squawks damaged Harry's ears. He longed for silence, dark, the oblivion of sleep. But sleep, he knew, even now, would not be forthcoming.

When eventually he opened his front door, he was greeted with a smell so vile that he was forced to bury his nose in his handkerchief. It occurred to him, on his melancholy way upstairs, the innards destined for the cat that he had cast upon the floor had never been removed. The smell had insinuated itself into his flat, too: quite definite, today, whereas yesterday it had been a mere hint of the stench to come. Unwelcoming though this homecoming was, therefore, the idea of clearing up putrefied lights after such a terrible night turned the lump of Harry's breakfast into an alarming swill. He felt tears returning, his trousers falling again. Locking himself into the bathroom, he lit the Ascot heater, whose whistling gas flame was the only friendly sound he had heard in the last twenty-four hours. Next, in something of a frenzy, he dabbed his bottle of Jungle Man Aftershave on every available soft surface: towel, bathmat, candlewick lavatory seat cover, and simulated silk dressing-gown that hung on the back of the door. He then relieved himself of the offending shirt and trousers, plummeted into the steaming bath. Rotten meat smell at last quite overpowered by Jungle Man, Harry was able to breathe deeply in relief. Gradually, the nausea subsided.

Some two hours later he was eating a second breakfast in an unsalubrious café off Oxford Street. He wondered if that vilest of bitches, his beloved Viola, was suffering due remorse. If she was tormented by imaginings of Harry hanging dead from his knotted socks, that was the least she deserved. More likely, in her accustomed and unfeeling way, she was sound asleep. Well, her luck was running out. Harry decided to reflect further upon those matters when his head was clearer: though God knows how he could be expected to get a good night's sleep among the smells of rotten meat and, he presumed, rotting peonies.

He spent the day with his film editor in a small, dark and airless room watching beautiful girls degrade themselves in indecent positions and he remembered, briefly, his skirmish with Annie Light. At least she loved him, poor wretch. Might be someone to fall back on, one day, if all else failed. As long as she never turned on the light he could probably keep fancying her in a purely salacious way.

Harry's unappealing film also reminded him of the money that had made it worthwhile: he decided to take a further look at his penthouse flat, later, and put in an offer. He could not abide his present quarters much longer. A sudden longing to be an admired man again came upon him. Fame had had its sweetness once: he longed for its return. He would work with his old energy, repeat his early success, earn a new fortune and give it all to Viola. The penthouse would be the first step towards his happy new life of riches and power. Soon, once more he would be a man so irresistible that even the obdurate Viola would be bound to succumb.

Harry was pleased by the second viewing of the flat. It seemed to have great potential.

'By the time I've painted the sitting room a fiery red,' he told the agent, 'every glossy magazine in the country will be clamouring to photograph it.'

'Why, I'm sure they will,' the agent agreed, impressed by so much confidence. With some excitement, Harry made his offer. By 5.30 it seemed reasonably sure the flat would be his.

That matter dealt with, next loomed the imminent problem of the long evening ahead. Very tired by now, Harry wanted only two things: a hamburger, and to be near Viola. He would like to catch a glimpse of her, make sure that her eye was not seriously damaged. He would like to ask her forgiveness once again: beg for one last chance.

Too weary to think with any clarity, Harry drove to Holland Park, stopped his car fifty yards from her house. He wrote her a short note, but the humble, loving tone he strove for was inexplicably lost in the writing. Having slipped it through the letter box, Harry decided he would sit in the car for a couple of hours, watching. Just in case. Just to be near her. Then, he would eat.

When Viola fell asleep after her second glass of wine, Edwin returned to the library. It was his intention to make up for the lack of morning's work, but he found himself beaten. Too many things conspired against him.

He sat at the round table, piled with books for comfort, and tried to take stock of the disparate matters jostling his weary brain. First – the only clear part – he was infinitely glad the assault upon Viola had not been more serious. Had she appeared worse, he would have insisted on sending for a doctor, whatever she said. As it was, her cuts and bruises were plainly superficial, though she would definitely have a black eye.

Next, the unknown assailant. The outrage Edwin felt about this mysterious man he had tried hard to disguise from Viola. It was not up to him to pass judgement on her friends and, strangely, Viola had conveyed no hard feelings against him. Perhaps she had been too shocked and tired. Edwin had tried to press her a little for some sort of explanation, but with no success. She had repeated she did not want to think about any of it for the moment, and naturally he had respected her wish. He had urged her, though, very strongly, to summon the police. You could not let such an assault go unreported, he said: for her future safety she must prosecute so dangerous a man. But again he had met resistance. In time, she had said, with a weariness of spirit he could well understand: in time.

It occurred to Edwin that he felt more fear on Viola's behalf than she felt for herself. The idea of the violent thug pursuing her further chilled his flesh. He himself lacked qualifications as a bodyguard. Besides, he could not spend night after night in this library, a sort of volunteer coastguard waiting for danger signals. When Viola was stronger, therefore, he would have to press her further to organize some sort of protection for herself and, indeed, for him.

The third worry was a great billowing mist that almost obscured all other thoughts, important though they were. It was a matter so delicate that Edwin strove not to put it into words. Yet, cruelly, the words pounded at him, tormenting.

Did Viola know, or not? Should he tell her? And if he did, how would she feel?

The unanswerable questions made him shake like a man beyond his years, while the stuffy, summer air of the library was cold on his hands. Worse, the particular questions led to more general ones, dragged from the darkest corners of his soul, a place he was never anxious to frequent. Could it be that, as the most conscientious and overworked lover in London, he might also be the most unremembered? Could it be that he was so much in demand simply because, due to his *lightness of touch*, as it were, girls, scarcely aware of his impact, asked him to return to make sure of his existence? Oh God, the thought. He cradled his head in his arms. The unfairness of the Creator: it was intolerable. For within him, he had always known, crouched the most robust of lovers. But this inner man was a most cowardly chap. Faced with reality, his inspiration would flee with cruel speed, leaving Edwin to his own feeble devices. These, he also knew, were no more than a kind of disappointed, disappointing hovering. Immemorable.

Always frightened of his own inadequacy, Edwin had begun his amorous pursuits at a late age. What he had lacked in quality of performance, he had made up for in quantity. Girls, girls, girls. Streaming through his life, shouting their love, so that many times he had almost convinced himself that he *was* that heroic inner man who had struggled to the surface. But he knew this was not true. He knew it would never be true, and that always he would have to go on searching, for ever finding disappointment. On this black afternoon, hating himself, the whole bleak state of the truth set before him, Edwin Hardley quietly wept.

He was disturbed at 6.30 by the front door bell. Instantly alert, he leapt up, scorning himself for the wasted afternoon. Viola had said nothing about an expected visitor this evening. She was upstairs, presumably asleep. Well, here was her bodyguard's chance. Tonight he would comport himself in more heroic manner: go down and deal swiftly with the violent maniac. For self-protection, he armed himself with a small brass poker.

On his way downstairs, Edwin was conscious of his thumping heart. He hurried, trying to ignore it. In the hall, he found a card on the doormat. Picking it up, he strained his eyes in the perennial dim light to read:

Beloved Viola, Forgive me if you can and think of me when I am no more. Ever yours. H.A.

That, thought Edwin, was the sort of melodramatic rubbish Viola was certainly not going to be allowed to see. He tore up the card, shoved it in his pocket. The bell rang again, making him jump. He clutched the poker, quite prepared to slug the brute across the face at the first glimmer of menace. Slowly, he opened the door.

A very agreeable looking man stood there, eager face,

slight smile, but worried lines round bright green eyes. Edwin let the poker drop by his side. The man, plainly well-mannered, pretended he had not observed Edwin's curious weapon.

'Am I at the right house for Viola Windrush?' he asked.

'Oh my goodness, you certainly are,' answered Edwin, very confused, and strangely nervous considering the gentleness of this new visitor. His mind snapped into a flashback of the evening before: the whole performance of the Entry of the Unknown Visitor once again, except that the nature of the visitor was very different.

'Do come in,' he heard himself saying. 'And go on up to the top floor. That's Viola's flat.'

'Thank you so much.'

When the stranger had climbed the first flight of stairs, Edwin, making a great effort, followed him, then made his way back to the library. It had been his intention to take out the young painter whom he had let down last night. But such weariness, such sickness of spirit came over him as he sank into an armchair, that he knew he would have to disappoint her once again. Strangely enfeebled, now that his intended valour had been thwarted, Edwin only wanted time in which to think. Viola would need no protection from this man, that was clear. But perhaps it would be wise to stay nearby, just for a while. He was puzzled she had said nothing about going out tonight, but then she was never one for revealing her plans. Unlike ninety per cent of the girls he knew, Viola was reticent in talking about herself. Dear, funny Viola. So pale . . .

Edwin himself felt considerably pale, too. He needed music to restore his tranquillity. He chose a record of a Schubert quartet, let the familiar sounds sponge over him, smoothing away all thought, leaving him a tired and empty husk, splayed out in the chair near his books. Thus began his second night of vigil.

Viola heard Richard running fast up the stairs. She met him in the passage, dark enough to conceal the shock of her face.

'Richard! Richard, listen. I warn you. I look a bit of a mess.'

Richard had kissed her on her unharmed cheek. His eyes had now grown accustomed to the dim light. He saw the eye patch, pushed Viola almost roughly from him, pulled it off.

'What on earth has been happening? What have you done? Quick: let's go to the light.'

They hurried to the sitting room, still strewn with collapsed books, upset tins of paint. At the window, severely professional, Richard observed the swollen eye. He touched it gently.

'Violetta . . .' Frowning, his eyes danced round the room. 'I'll be back in a minute. I'm going to get my things. That eye needs bathing. I've something in the car that'll help till we get to a chemist.'

He was gone. Viola touched her own face with cautious fingers. She thought about how this first evening in London with Richard should have been: herself waiting prettily for him, drinks ready, flat in some order if things had gone to plan, hours of pleasure ahead. As it was, she felt suddenly weak, shaky. She would have to muster all her strength to sit through *Hamlet* and dinner: a poor companion for the one for whom she most wanted to be otherwise.

Harry Antlers, from his concealed position, had seen a car with a doctor's sign draw up at Viola's house. He had watched the doctor, a well-dressed looking bastard, obviously one of those millionaires from Harley Street, ring the bell. There had been a long pause, and then another ring, before the door opened. Presumably Viola had taken some time coming downstairs. That meant, at least, she was not confined to bed. Harry had strained to see her as the door opened, but caught no glimpse. He decided to wait till the doctor left, in case he could catch sight of her then.

A short time after the doctor's entry, Harry observed him scurrying back down the steps very fast, leaving the front door open behind him. He had the look of a very worried man. It was also a fierce look, as far as Harry could tell from such a distance, as if the doctor had some cause to be angry as well as concerned. He snatched a medical bag from his car and hurried back up the front steps, slamming the door impatiently behind him.

It was then the truth came blindingly to Harry. Viola was

gravely ill. Although it was all her fault, he, Harry, was responsible.

He started the engine. There was no point in sitting here any longer. The only thing he could do now was to go back to his vile flat and carry out the idle threat he had written on the card. He had a large supply of sleeping pills. If he did not stop to think, it should not be too difficult a process.

Dreading the smell that would greet him more than the act he was almost determined to commit, Harry let himself into his deceased landlady's house once again. It took him some moments to take in the magical transformation that had taken place in his absence.

For a start, there was no more smell. Harry sniffed several times, to make quite sure. Rather, there *was* a smell, but a new one: disinfectant. Curious, incredulous, Harry went to Marjorie Wittle's kitchen, peeped in. It was in a state he had never seen it before: pristine, with shining surfaces and polished floor. No sign of meat or flowers.

Wonderfully confused, but also fearing that this was some mad hallucination brought on by lack of sleep, Harry made his way upstairs. He noticed the thick drifts of dust, lodged for so many months on the scrawny carpet, had disappeared. His bathroom and kitchen were both equally clean and tidy, though there was still a faint trace of Jungle Man in the air. Shaking with disbelief – this surely was some trick of the mind sent to punish him – Harry went finally to his sitting room. Again, a room transformed. And there, on the table in the window, was a plastic cup holding three wallflowers. Propped up beside it was a note. Harry snatched it up, read wildly.

Dear Harry, My mum gave me Aunt Marjorie's key and sent me round to tidy up a bit. She said the agents wouldn't like it all dusty. Was it in a mess! I did my best. I hope the smell has gone. I took the liberty of doing your rooms too. Hope you don't mind. Thank you for the most wonderful night of my life. Please let there be others. I love you. Annie Light.

Harry read the note several times. As he did so, the shadow of death seemed to evaporate. Some stubborn new hope descended upon him: this had been an act of God, physically

189

carried out by a girl, showing him the way. After a large dinner and a good night's sleep in a sweet-smelling room, Harry would go forth with new heart. In the end – he knew not how, precisely, at this moment – he would win his Viola, and they would spend the rest of their days in peace. Meantime, he would choose himself an expensive French restaurant . . .

Harry let the pleasure of such plans for himself sink in for a while, then his thoughts turned perfunctorily to Annie Light. In a way, he supposed, it could be said she had saved his life. He had to be grateful for that. And there was no doubt she loved him. Poor lady: even if Viola had not existed, he could never return that love. A ratty girl with silly hopes. Still, he would not abandon her completely, just yet. Annie Light, he felt, might one day have her uses.

Richard bathed Viola's eye, insisted she swallow a pill. Viola did not enquire what it was. But on the way to the theatre she felt her limbs begin to relax, though her head still throbbed. After the play they had a simple, one-course dinner at the Savoy Grill. Feeling stronger, Viola found herself telling the whole story of Harry Antlers' pursuit, and the climax last night. She also told him of Gideon's plan to return home for good, of which Richard approved strongly. He judged it not the time to make any comment on her predicament. When her tale was over he talked lightly of their week in Norfolk, which already felt long past, and told amusing stories of one of his oldest patients who refused to die.

When they returned to the flat, well before midnight, Richard insisted Viola should go straight to bed. While she did so, he said, he would clear up her books, replace them in the shelves. Otherwise their spines would be damaged beyond repair.

Viola obeyed quite readily. Once in bed, propped up among the pillows, she felt much better. She called Richard. He appeared with a glass of whisky for himself, water for Viola. He gave her two more pills.

'They'll help you sleep,' he said. 'I'll leave some more, too, for the next few nights.'

'Thank you.'

Once again, Viola obeyed without protest, swallowing the pills with a gulp of water. She would have done anything in the world Richard wanted. She wondered if he had any notion of her compliancy.

Richard sat on the bed. His look was grave.

'It's now my duty, Violetta,' he said, 'to give you some professional advice. Something has got to be done about the activities of this maniac before he does any worse damage. What are your plans?'

'None, just at the moment. I did intend to ring the police this afternoon, but somehow I hadn't the energy . . . all it would involve.'

'Dear, silly girl, you should have rung them the moment he went last night. Having left it so late, they won't be much interested. They won't regard it as a very serious matter if you let so much time elapse before reporting it.'

'No, I suppose not.'

'You must get on to your solicitor in the morning, go and see him. You must get an injunction taken out against Mr Antlers. He must never be allowed near you again.'

'All right.'

'Are you taking in what I'm saying?'

'I think so.'

'Because it's very important. You must understand, you're the victim of a man's obsession: a man whose mind is severely disturbed. I've known several similar cases. In each one, the victim has always tried to be rational, relied on the aggressor's reason prevailing in the end. But you see, that's not how it works. Do you understand? Common sense, logic, rational dealings, are not the answer for one whose mind is disturbed. Heavens, I of all people ought to know, oughtn't I? No, they need help. And meanwhile, it's imperative you have some form of protection, Violetta. I don't like the idea of your being here all alone, vulnerable. A man obsessed overcomes all barriers. He could easily get in. I think you should come home for a while, till your eye has recovered. Besides, you're probably suffering from shock, you know. You need a few quiet days.' He paused. 'You need to feel utterly safe. Alfred would, of course, guard you well. If you liked, I could move in for a few days, too. Make sure you were all right.'

For the first time since her attack, Viola was near to tears. She felt her mouth twitching in her fight for control.

'Thank you,' she said. 'But let me think about it. My plan was to finish everything here – just a matter of a few days, despite the setback in the sitting-room – then I was going to go home and get things ready for Gideon, anyway.'

'Why don't you let me drive you back tomorrow?'

Viola shook her head. 'I can't, really. It's very sweet of you. But I'll come soon, I promise.'

'You're being dreadfully stubborn.'

'I'm sorry.'

'*Please . . .*'

'No. I refuse to allow him to interrupt my plans.'

'Then you must make me one promise.' Richard sighed. 'If this bastard ever threatens you again, in any way whatsoever, you must let me know *at once*. I shall come immediately, and deal with him myself.'

'I promise. Absolutely.'

'Wish I wasn't so far away.'

'Wish you weren't, too.'

There was a very long silence between them. Richard finished his drink. Then he took Viola's hand.

'Violetta, let me ask you one more thing, impertinent though it may be. Are you, in any way at all, attracted to this man?'

Viola's visible eye, beginning to droop with the sleepiness that was descending, widened in shock at the suggestion. She managed to smile.

'Are you mad? You should see him. He's totally abhorrent. He fills me with a deep revulsion I've never felt for anyone in my life before.'

'Has he no charm, no endearing ways, whatsoever?'

Viola thought hard.

'I suppose he might have for some. His bulldozing ways, his wild passion and energy. But not for me.'

'And you've never done anything to encourage him?'

'Not knowingly. In the very beginning, in New York, I agreed to help him with his play. I was flattered he should ask, I suppose, and foolishly agreed without really thinking. Later, I retracted my offer, of course. He considered that my first betrayal. Since then, I've done nothing, nothing, but beg him to leave me alone and try to convince him his feelings are totally unreciprocated. He seems to think it's only a matter of *time*, till I come round to realizing the *truth* – which is: did I but know it, I love him as much as he loves me. In that way,' Viola went on, 'he's very good at making me feel as if *I'm* the one who's mad. Last night, for instance, at one point I began to doubt my own sanity. Perhaps I was deluding myself, after all, I thought. Perhaps he knew something I didn't, and I was being very dim, not seeing it. But then, watching him slobbering about the floor on all fours, I thought, No: *he's* the one out of his mind. Surely. But it was an unnerving moment.'

'The great art of the expert bully is to make his victim feel guilty of madness,' said Richard. 'I've seen it often.'

'I have to admit,' went on Viola, feeling the relief of being able to tell Richard everything, and wanting to say just a little more before she fell asleep, 'I don't attack him back. I try to be calm, polite. Perhaps you could call that encouragement. I did scream in fear when he first turned up last night, but then I controlled myself. I've no doubt he's able to see how frightened he makes me. Perhaps that urges him on.'

'The coward's spur,' said Richard. He was still holding her hand.

'Well, he's caused me to live in daily fear. Isn't that silly? I never imagined a time would come when I would wake up every day dreading the hours ahead. Nothing can ever quite put that fear out of my mind, not even that lovely, protected week in Norfolk.'

'So I observed.'

'Did you? I imagined I looked very happy and cheerful.'

'You did, in a way.'

'Well, now, you know what? Now more than anything in the world I long for peace. I long to wake up in the morning unafraid of the day. Unthreatened peace would be the greatest luxury I can think of. I wouldn't even mind a boring life so long as I was unafraid.' She sniffed. 'Oh, heavens, Richard. I've gone on and on. I'm so sorry. And I can't say any more. I'm falling asleep.'

'Good. I'm going to leave you now. I'll ring you tomorrow evening, make sure you're all right.'

'Thank you. And for this evening. I'm sorry I wasn't . . .'
'Goodnight, my love.'

Richard kissed her good cheek. He stood up, looked down upon her until he was quite sure she slept. Then he left the room, closing the door, and began the long descent downstairs.

Edwin Hardley, strangely restless despite the hours of music, heard Viola and her friend returning. An hour later, he heard the friend depart. Relief, exhaustion.

Slumped in the armchair, the fact was Edwin had had a most exhausting evening. He had not even dared to revive himself with a drink, for fear of repeating last night's shameful performance. While he had managed to put the searing thoughts of the afternoon aside – other, more *local* speculations had come upon him in their droves.

Viola, it seemed, was their cause. Imagining her dining in some superior restaurant (by heavens, he would take her somewhere better next time) with her well-dressed friend, the question had suddenly struck him: do I love her? Or if I do not love, is this not an uncommon devotion, or affection, that might well be confused with love?

Love had been an elusive thing in Edwin's life, always one woman away. Never having experienced its sureties, he could not be quite sure how to gauge its tricks. There had been moments when he had liked to think *this* was it, here he was, feeling heady as millions of others. But no sooner than he had analysed any such delight, slippery as a worm the conviction slipped from him, leaving him alone with his broken vision. What's more, he had on occasions felt the faintest twinklings of unease – nothing greater than that – at the thought of others dallying with his girls: but last night was certainly the first time in his life he had felt . . . Even to himself he could not spell out the loathsome word. So maybe Viola had touched some part of his psyche previously undiscovered.

Edwin shuddered at the thought. For all about him those who pledged their hearts were forced to change their selfish single lives, and that was usually a disaster. Edwin tried hard to imagine changing his own life for Viola. Sharing a small flat with her, for instance. Having to move some of his books out of her way. Meeting her friends. Being forced to accompany her occasionally to forlorn parts of the countryside, that seemed to mean so much to her. Agree to children . . . God forbid. No: it was all a preposterous idea, brought about by lack of sleep. And yet, what was this unaccustomed restlessness, that even music and his beloved moths could not seem to calm?

When Edwin heard Viola's friend depart, he decided it was time for him, too, to go home, try to catch up on all the lost sleep. He was confused to find himself, therefore, creeping upstairs rather than down. Fascinated by the force within him in whose command he seemed to be, in detached manner he watched himself creep into Viola's flat, open the door of her bedroom, move to her bed.

By the light of the full moon he was able to look at her beautiful face lying back on the pillow, hair awry, poor swollen eye a blackish colour. She breathed deeply. Edwin's eyes went to the bottle of sleeping pills beside her bed. The idea came to him that he could slip in beside her without disturbing her. There, head on her breast, he could sleep for hours. Once again, she might never know.

But even as he reflected, the foolishness of his plan rasped through Edwin. He was a gentleman, after all. Gentlemen do not take such unfair advantages or unwise risks more than once. With regret, he would leave her sleeping. He left her room.

His secret visit, unfortunately, had done nothing to calm his blood. Sadly, by the light over the front door, Edwin found himself scanning his address book. There were girls all over London longing for nocturnal visits. The problem was merely one of choice. When considering the recipient of his tired state, he had to choose one who would be full of sympathy, and not likely to make too many demands.

His finger paused at an address not far from Holland Park. Edwin hailed a taxi, wondering at the fickleness of man, and continued on his way.

13

Though not for one moment did Alfred Baxter cease to appreciate his good fortune in working for Viola Windrush, the week after she and her brother left he found something of an anti-climax. The comings and goings engendered by their visit, the laughter, the carefully prepared meals, the frequent appreciation of all his work in the garden, had been a constant pleasure. Their apparent happiness, thought Alfred, had brushed off on to himself. Besides which, being kept so busy, there had been no time to dwell on the mystery of Eileen's elusive face, and the haunting voices of the girls were never heard again.

But alone once more, wife and girls returned in their strange forms. No matter how hard he worked in the garden, Eileen's face flew back and forth in Alfred's mind, a silent pendulum, taunting him with an expression he could have sworn he never knew when she was alive. This imagined face was pinched, mean, accusing. It did not smile. The eyes were unforgiving. It was filled with dislike.

Sometimes, Alfred thought it must be the heat that was affecting him. He would break off from his digging, sit on a bench in the shade of the limes, take off his cap and wipe his balding head with a large handkerchief. He would listen to the flutter of the leaves, and sniff the distant smell of sea. With some pride he would then let his eyes dally among the lovingly cared for herbaceous border, the massed white roses, the velvet-eyed pansies and starry pinks that edged the stone paths. He alone had rescued the garden, and the transformation gave him a satisfaction that could not be denied. But no matter how much he filled his eyes with flowers and leaves and sky, the unpleasant face of Eileen remained in his vision.

At the end of his day's work, she was replaced by the chatter of the girls. After his tea, once Alfred had retired to his chair in the sitting-room, hoping for a peaceful evening, they would begin their gossip. He could not make out exactly what they said, though sometimes odd sentences came to him so clearly that he would look round and be surprised to find himself still alone. It was the tone of the girls' talk that made him shiver: he had the distinct impression they were in some way against him, mocking – like Eileen, accusing. In fitful dreams, at night, they lined up in court and interrogated him. He could see they were shouting, but he could not hear the questions. When he was unable to answer, they laughed and jeered. Night after night Alfred woke up sweating and afraid. Dear God, he prayed, what did I do to them that they should punish me like this?

After a week of solitude, Alfred could bear evenings in his own sitting-room no longer. Instead, he took the liberty of passing the hours in the Windrushes' kitchen. There, he would drag up a chair to the fire, which he liked to light despite the warmth of the evenings, and read his paper or do his crossword puzzles. In peace. Merciful peace. No one followed him there, and by day Eileen's face was less persistent. Alfred felt the balance of his mind gradually returning.

One evening he came across a report in the local paper that Admiral Fanshawe, Maisie Fanshawe's father, had died. It gave the time and place of the funeral. Alfred, remembering the Fanshawes had been good customers in the old days, felt he would like to pay his last respects. He had not, by his own volition, taken a day off since he had been there, so he would feel no guilt in going to the funeral on Friday. He would like to say a word of condolence to Miss Maisie, who had been here recently. Yes, Admiral Fanshawe's funeral would make a pleasant outing.

On Friday morning Alfred went early into the garden and gathered a bunch of white roses. He was not much of a one with flowers once they were cut, but he managed to gather them into a reasonably tidy-looking spray. Eileen would have laughed at his effort, no doubt: but he was not ashamed, and the smell was wonderful. Alfred wrote a small card to accompany the flowers, and placed them in water while he dressed.

For the first time since the morning he left the shop, Alfred took out his navy serge suit and a plain cream shirt. He found the sad black tie that he had bought for Eileen's funeral, but nowhere could he lay hands on his old black bowler. This was a much-loved and well-worn hat, purchased when Alfred was made church warden forty years ago, brushed and used most Sundays since, until the sale of the shop. The hat had also accompanied Alfred on his many journeys with Eileen to cathedral cities. It had been respectfully taken off as they had entered some great portal, and put to rest on a chair beside him while Alfred prayed for strength to do his duty and love his neighbour. The fanfares of stone arches, flaring hundreds of feet above his head, always made Alfred feel strangely naked. He was glad when he could replace the hat once more, outside.

The loss of the bowler – in the move, Alfred supposed – was something of a shadow on the bright day. Luckily, inspiration came to him: in the many hats in the cloakroom, surely a suitable replacement could be found. In the circumstances, he felt, Colonel Windrush would have understood, and approved the loan. Alfred hurried off, found what he needed almost immediately – a most superior bowler, a size or so too big, perhaps, and in need of a good brush, but otherwise perfect.

With clean handkerchief sprightly in his pocket, white rose in his buttonhole and the Colonel's hat bobbing on his ears, Alfred set off in some excitement for the bus stop. He enjoyed the long wait in the sun, sniffing at his funeral spray, admiring the shine of his shoes, and the general feeling of wellbeing. He enjoyed the ride on the bus, the view of harvesters in wide fields, the grey line of sea becoming fainter and fainter. But by the time the bus arrived in Docking, the sun had disappeared in an overcast sky. Very appropriate, thought Alfred. Climbing down the steps, he felt the first drops of fine rain.

The village church was half full, mostly elderly people. Alfred was a little shocked to see many of them had not bothered with funeral clothes: some of them were in positively cheerful dresses and scarves, and some men wore no ties. But perhaps that's how it was these days: perhaps showing respect for the dead through sombre clothes was an old-fashioned idea.

Alfred found a seat with a good view of the altar and settled down to enjoy the music. There was a nice show of flowers, though he himself had never had a fondness for gladioli. But the lilies were magnificent: probably from the Fanshawes' own garden.

After a while a small group of Fanshawe relations were escorted up the aisle by the vicar, and shown to the front pew. Miss Maisie was the tallest, and very thin. Unlike the others, all in black, she wore a neat coat of grey flannel, cut on almost military lines, Alfred thought. She wore grey stockings, grey shoes and gloves, and a hat that was no more than a puff of dotted net, half concealing her eyes. It reminded Alfred of a bunch of *gypsophila*. Very pretty. He trusted the word was not out of place on such an occasion.

From where he sat, Alfred had a fine view of Maisie Fanshawe's profile and high shoulders, bony through the grey flannel. The coffin arrived, the service began: Alfred knelt, sang, listened, prayed with the congregation. But the conscious part of his mind he found entirely preoccupied by the sight of the Admiral's daughter. There was something about her, he could not for the life of him explain what it was, that held his complete attention. She was, in some way, like the Windrushes' garden, *transformed*. Alfred turned his mind back to the pictures he had of her, so recently, on her visits to the Windrushes: an awkward-looking lady, really, in clothes that never looked quite right, like Miss Windrush's, and grey hair that made her older than she really was. She had seemed cheerful enough, but had – how could he put it? – no *presence*. That was it. Nothing about her that made you look again. Rather pathetic, was his impression, really: the downcast air of an eternal spinster.

But now, so great was the change, here in the church, that Alfred found it hard to believe he was looking at the same person. Her pale bony cheeks, flecked with tiny shadows from the dotted net, were – well, not exactly beautiful, but arresting. The mouth, significant before for its definite downward curve and damson lipstick, was colourless, perhaps to disguise in its corners the hint of a smile. It occurred to Alfred that relief, obviously, was what had caused the change: that was it, sheer relief. After all, it had been well known the poor girl had had to look after her paralysed father for many years. His passing on, for all its sadness, must also afford her secret joy. But there again, it wasn't just her sense of freedom that seemed to burn through the slight grey figure: it seemed to be something more positive than that. She had about her the sort of calm exhilaration that you see on the faces of lovers when one is forced to catch an early train and the other, bidding him farewell, knows she will be following shortly.

The service over, the funeral procession moved out into the graveyard. Most of the villagers then dispersed. Only a small group of relations and friends made their way to the open grave. Alfred was undecided what to do: he would not like to offend the Fanshawes by intruding in a private occasion, but on the other hand he felt to leave now would be to cut his outing short. Settling for a compromise, he placed himself behind a tall gravestone some way from the coffin. Thus he could silently join in and observe, but cause no offence.

Alfred pulled the bowler well down over his ears, watched the almost invisible rain spread a gossamer sheen over his navy serge. The funeral group intoned their prayers, eyes cast down into the gaping earth. The severity of black yew trees, behind them, was dimmed with rain: the sky was a solid grey, church and gravestones were grey stone and, matching them in her grey flannel, Maisie Fanshawe shone like an ethereal being, a dove among crows. Once again, Alfred stared and stared, trying to put his finger on what it was he was seeing.

Once the ceremony was over, Maisie detached herself from the others as if she wanted to be alone for a few moments. Unknowingly, she approached the gravestone behind which Alfred stood, half concealed and at attention. He took his chance.

'Miss Fanshawe,' he said, stepping on to the path and raising the bowler. 'May I offer my condolences?'

'Oh, Mr Baxter. Thank you. It was good of you to come.'

She looked surprised to see him. They shook hands. Her eyes, smudged through the *gypsophila*, were not mourning eyes, but sparkling.

'Your father was a fine man, if you don't mind me saying,' added Alfred. 'And a very good customer.'

Maisie smiled. 'I'm glad his suffering is over,' she said. 'Now, it seems to be raining harder. Would you like to join us back at the house for a drink and something to eat?'

Alfred, taken aback by such unexpected kindness, hesitated

in his acceptance. But Maisie insisted. She tugged at his arm, laughing. 'Come along. You need something before your journey back.'

Then, amazingly, Alfred found himself in step with her along the path, some distance from the others. He felt her high spirits, dancing within her slight form. It was as if she had been untouched by the death, the rain, the grey.

'I suppose you're getting into order for the return,' she was saying. 'Isn't it a nice surprise?'

'What's that you're saying, Miss Fanshawe?' Alfred was confused.

'Didn't you know? Well, as a matter of fact I only heard myself last night. Gideon is coming back. For good. Isn't that lovely?'

'Good heavens,' said Alfred. 'I suppose Miss Windrush has been ringing me and I haven't been there. She may be trying even now!'

'No matter: she can ring again.'

'And when will he be coming, if I may enquire?'

'Some time in the next few weeks. He sounded as though he intended to stay in Norfolk quite a while, this time.'

'Just what the doctor ordered,' said Alfred, very pleased, observing Maisie's light grey shoes almost skipping on the gravel path.

'Exactly,' she agreed, and they reached the house.

Alfred spent a most agreeable hour in the company of some polite Fanshawes, partaking of thin pink meats and garden salads, and he found himself accepting several glasses of sherry and white wine. Maisie Fanshawe herself ate nothing, but saw to it her guests were as happy as could be expected in the circumstances. She rustled from one to another of them in a grey silk dress that put Alfred in mind of Eileen's honeymoon silk. A diamond dust of rain was on her nose – again, like Eileen's wedding day. Her dotted net was pushed back to reveal happy eyes and a private smile.

All the way back in the bus Alfred thought of Maisie Fanshawe, wondering what it was about her. Strange thing was, it seemed to be something he recognized: some look he had seen, been warmed by, many, many years ago. Funny he couldn't put a name to it. Perhaps it would come to him, like the answers in his crossword puzzles, sudden from nowhere, making sense of the clues.

Hannah Bagle quickly observed the change in Gideon on their return to New York. He was preoccupied, distant, restless. The things about her he used to appreciate – her efficiency, cooking, beautiful clothes, well-informed mind – he seemed not to notice any longer. It came as no surprise to her when he announced he was returning home for good, which meant farewell for the two of them.

Hannah took the news calmly, inwardly furious she had not taken her chance and been the one to do the breaking off. She was practised at leaving but did not care to be left, however unsatisfactory the arrangement had become. And she had to agree with Gideon the best of their relationship had passed. Some vital energy had gone astray, died, whatever, to be replaced by irritation and apathy. Ah well: their measure of time having come to an end was no great cause for regret in Hannah. Her weekend with Harry Antlers in London lingered excitingly in her mind: maybe she should now take her chance to visit him for longer, and persuade him to return with her to New York. But should that plan not materialize, there were always others. Plenty of others.

Thinking Harry might display some interest in the news – Hannah guessed his affair with Viola was not progressing as well as he claimed, she rang him from her office. She explained the situation. His voice was dull in response, tired.

'So,' said Hannah, 'Gideon will be back in a couple of weeks. I understand he's going to jolly old Norfolk for a while. Hope he has himself a ball. Your Viola, I understand, is going there next week.'

'Is she?' Harry's voice brightened with interest.

'Funny, the English way of loving some old seaside dump. Yeah, she's going on down there, she told Gideon. Doesn't like London in the summer. Didn't you know?'

'She may have told me. I probably didn't take it in.'

There was a long pause. Hannah took her chance.

'Which leaves the way open for you and me, honey. I've reason to be over myself, quite soon. We could get together again.'

'Maybe,' said Harry. 'I'm going to be busy moving. I've found my penthouse.'

'That's terrific. I could help. Viola all right?'

'Fine.'

'You sound tired.'

'Just overworked. Offers for films and plays have been streaming in, somehow. Difficult to know which to do.'

Harry glanced at the letter he held in his hand: a single offer to direct *Measure for Measure* for an autumn festival in southern Ireland.

'That's terrific,' said Hannah again. 'It's nice to know I'm in with a famous director.' Her words were strangely cheering.

Having finished editing his film with extraordinary speed, Harry occupied himself with the move to his new flat. This involved buying furniture, china, linen, everything: he owned almost nothing but books and records. Unaccustomed to choosing such things, his searches round the shops confused and irritated him. He found himself in a perpetual state of frustration and bad temper, breaking off more and more frequently to fill himself with soothing snacks. His only means of judging any piece of furniture or household object was by its price. If it was very expensive he thought it must be all right, and took it. Thus his film money dwindled in a matter of days. Sliding towards an impoverished state increased his general despondency. Completely desolate, one evening, he turned into a French restaurant he could not afford, with the intention of eating and drinking till his troubles receded.

He stood at the door, eyes refocusing in the gloom, waiting to be shown a table. It was then he saw, in a distant corner table, Viola and the scholarly-looking worm who had opened the front door to him. A waiter approached. Harry fled into the street.

This was the first time Harry had set eyes on Viola since the evening that had gone so wrong. Since then, he had sent her a series of letters, varying in tone and assurances (*I swear I have not laid a finger on anyone since the day we met, more than can be said for you and all your lovers*) but he had made no attempt to meet her. The unexpected sight of her, this bleak evening, was the final undoing of a desperate, ravenous man. The revenge which he had contemplated in Shepherds Bush at dawn, but rejected later, now screamed back into his heart. This was it: the time had come to hurt Viola as much as she had hurt him.

As Harry hurried along the street in search of another restaurant, rage and venom so contorting his features that people stepped away from him, the calculating part of his mind was coolly at work. Thanks to Hannah's recent invitation, a plan formed quickly in his mind. He would have to hurry, though: make sure he had moved into his flat, when the deed was done, so that no one could find him. Today was Friday. Viola would be going to Norfolk tomorrow, of that he could be certain. In private celebration, Harry ordered spaghetti, two steaks, baked potatoes and a whole bottle of good wine.

The brief sight of Harry destroyed the pleasure of dinner for Edwin and Viola. Viola's reaction was one of pounding heart and shaking hand: panic, fear, the desire to run away. They left halfway through their sorbets. Viola clung to Edwin's arm the whole way back to the house.

She had planned to go to Norfolk that afternoon. But Gideon had rung to say he had booked a plane on Sunday evening, a week earlier than he had expected. So Viola changed her mind, decided to wait for him over the weekend, and drive him to Norfolk on Monday. Edwin, hearing the changes of her plan, had invited her to dinner tonight. He had also come up with a whole list of agreeable suggestions as to how they should pass the weekend.

Back in the house, they fetched themselves large glasses of whisky, went to the library. They both preferred the comfortable clutter of books to the austere tidiness of the drawing room.

'I shall stay here in the dressing-room, tonight, and the whole weekend,' said Edwin. 'If that man's on the warpath again, you need someone to protect you.'

Viola smiled gratefully. Her face still ached when she moved it.

'Perhaps a little music would unwind us,' said Edwin.

He put on a record of a Brahms quartet. They lay further

back on the same sofa. Edwin took Viola's hand. She did not resist.

The inspiration of the music filled Edwin with a deep longing – for what, he could not precisely define. Comfort, perhaps. Peace, perhaps. Viola, almost certainly.

When the music was over, Edwin sat up, still holding her hand. Warmed by the whisky he felt bold and happy.

'Do you know what I think?' he asked.

'No,' said Viola.

A dozen declarations, in a hopeless tangle, knotted in his head. He sighed.

'Dearie me,' he said. 'Well, perhaps one day . . . In the meantime, I shall take it upon myself to guard over you when you're here. It's the least I can do in return for your Uncle David's kindness.' He went to refill their glasses, then picked up one of his books. 'I shall insist you go to bed in a few moments,' he went on, with mock fierceness, 'but I shall also insist you spare me just a minute to look at this. I've found the most wonderful seventeenth-century engraving of the *Smerinthus ocellata*, the Eyed Hawk Moth. Look at those fierce eyes painted on its wings! When it fears it's going to be attacked it raises the wings. They look like the face of an owl, or a cat, and the predator is scared away . . . Just what I need as your bodyguard.'

They both laughed. Edwin went on to tell Viola about the cautious nature of the Oak Processionary Moth, whose larvae have extraordinary habits.

'They're the hippies of the moth world,' he explained. 'They live in communal webs in the trees. During the day they travel to other trees to eat their leaves. They move, head to tail, in long processions – sometimes twelve metres long, spinning a silk thread to guide themselves home again. You'd be surprised by the infinite wisdom of the humble moth.'

Safe in Edwin's world of gentle creatures, Viola found herself enjoying the rest of the evening, her mind happily diverted from thoughts of Harry Antlers.

It was by now the ragged end of summer, late August. The long hot days were coming to an end. The sun, when it moodily appeared, gave off an irritable heat as if to spite the dregs of its own high season. There were frequent clammy showers in London. Storms of thin thunder by night, summer lightning.

On the Saturday marked for the execution of Harry Antlers' plan, rain fell heavily all day. But Harry's mind was not on the weather. He was busy trying to make some order of his own flat, in which he intended to spend that night. His new plan had made it essential that he never return again to his old address. This meant moving sooner than he had intended – a matter of loading his car with his few possessions, and unpacking the many things that had been delivered. Surprisingly, the activities of the day, which he had been dreading, gave him pleasure. He was proud of his view and his expensive furniture. A little disappointed, perhaps, that the place looked so small, once the stuff was arranged, but he would continue to call it a penthouse. A penthouse would be some compensation for the odious behaviour of his beloved lady. His own home at last, it was but a beginning of greater things . . . Full of energy, Harry ate quantities of fish and chips in his soulless kitchen, and felt rising within him the heady mixture of determination, resolution and revenge.

It was raining hard in Norfolk, too. Alfred Baxter, with only the weekend left to prepare the house before the arrival of the Windrushes on Monday night, set about his favourite job of cleaning the silver. He lit the fire in the kitchen, for it was quite cold, made a pot of tea, and hummed to himself, as was his habit, while he polished.

His mind was still on Maisie Fanshawe. Funny thing was, thinking about her so much since the day of the funeral, Eileen's nasty face had not been giving him so much bother. It was as if all Maisie's gentleness and goodness had blotted out the badness of Eileen, which Alfred still could not remember in real life, but which had haunted him so after her death. Thinking of Maisie gave Alfred the same shivery feeling as looking at a sunset, or walking through the door of Lincoln Cathedral: a sort of private communion with something that understood. He still could not be sure of the reason for her elation at the funeral – indeed, he sometimes thought it might have been his imagination, the impact of a rare outing. But he was no longer concerned about its cause: merely grateful for the warm effect it had had upon him. In his nightly prayers he now thanked the Lord for so strange a blessing in his old age. He also approached his Father on the delicate subject of timing. Dear God, he said, why was it not your will that I should have met someone like Miss Fanshawe when I was at an age to do something about it? Why should you have chosen to show me, too late, what I have missed all these years? He pondered these questions many times. As yet, the good Lord had not given him an answer.

At the end of the day, the silver completed and returned to its cupboard, Alfred went upstairs. With the rain still battering so hard, he wanted to check all the windows were firmly shut and there was no leaking since the new repairs to the roof. The thundery sky made it very dark upstairs. Alfred switched on several lights, checked every room. He had it in mind to put flowers in Miss Windrush's room before she arrived, by way of welcome. His funeral spray had given him confidence when it came to cut flowers. That was another thing: Maisie Fanshawe had written a very nice letter thanking him for the roses. A beautiful spray, she had said.

Downstairs again, Alfred went to his part of the house. With the Windrushes coming home so soon, he felt he should revert to spending his evenings in his own sitting-room. It was not inviting, there. Unlived in for several weeks, it was cold, damp and gloomy, though through the windows the lime trees were a searing yellow-green against the blackish sky. Alfred made himself a cheese sandwich. He boiled the kettle. As it began to whistle he heard the mocking laughter of the girls coming from the sitting-room. At least, he thought he heard it: he could not be quite sure, for when the noise of the kettle died down there was absolute silence. He may have been confused, but it was enough to cast aside all his good intentions about keeping to his own quarters. A stormy night was not the sort of night on which a man should be alone listening to the ghostly laughter of his former girlfriends. Alfred hurried back to the fire.

In the high-backed comfortable chair, crossword puzzle on his knee, a cup of tea beside him, Alfred soon put himself to rights. The flames from the apple wood were warm upon him. He had Monday, and all the delights of a lived-in house again to look forward to. Yes, he was a man of good fortune, thought Alfred, and may it please the Lord to let things thus continue.

He listened to the rain chipping at the window, and the grumbling of thunder. Maisie Fanshawe glowed in his mind, an indefinable colour like early dew. She smiled at him through her *gypsophila*, and he smiled back, with tears.

At seven that evening Harry Antlers opened his brand new formica kitchen drawer and studied the collection of brand new carving knives and kitchen implements. After much deliberation he chose a knife-sharpener, a long steel implement with a heavy handle of carved bone, which had made it very expensive. Harry tested it in his hand. He liked the feel of it.

When he had placed his chosen weapon in a plastic bag, he gathered up two apples, a packet of biscuits, a hunk of cheese and a bar of chocolate to be added to the bag. These were in case of urgent hunger on the journey, despite a three-course supper in an Indian restaurant. Harry had no intention of experiencing for a second time the pains he had suffered on his first journey to Norfolk.

He set out into the pouring rain. Just his luck, he thought, the heavens should be so against him whenever he wanted to visit Viola in her loathesome seaside house. But, with the curries filling his stomach, he was not really disconcerted. He rather liked the rhythm of the windscreen wipers slashing through the lemon pearls of water, the slooshing noise of the tyres as he drove fast through the London streets.

There was an extraordinarily clear picture in Harry's mind, so precise that he was convinced it had been sent to him by way of a message. It was a picture of Viola, happy in her monstrous kitchen. He knew, quite surely, she would be there. Less definite in Harry's mind was whether or not she would be alone. He guessed, judging by her general promiscuity, she would probably be entertaining her doctor lover. In which case the doctor would be dealt with by the brand new weapon. In fact, Harry hoped the lover would not be there: he did not contemplate murder but, unused to armed attack, his plans might get out of hand. Besides which, the lover might well recover from his wounds, thus more closely bonding him to Viola.

No: Harry's aim of attack was something he supposed might hurt Viola more than a few blows to one of her many admirers. He had noticed through his tears, that dreadful night in London, the only thing that had seemed to pierce Viola's hard little heart – the smashing of the photograph of her parents. Harry had reflected on this fact, and suddenly it had all become clear to him. What she was, plainly, was a materialist of the worst order. What mattered to her were things, places. She knew nothing of love or charity: there was not an ounce of goodness in her. (God only knew why he loved her.) But she was moved by *things*. Things, therefore, were his target. Smash up a few things that meant most to her, and she would see what it felt like to have a broken heart.

Harry arrived at the Norfolk village as the church clock was striking ten. He spent some time driving round to find a concealed parking place away from the house. There was no one about on such a wet night: the elements were, after all, on his side.

He finally chose to park in what appeared to be a deserted track leading to the marsh. He finished off the food, then realized he had foolishly left nothing for the journey back when he would certainly be in need. Cursing his stupidity, he put the knife sharpener in his pocket and got out of the car.

In crime stories, Harry remembered grimly, the villain always makes one silly mistake: his was to have forgotten his mackintosh. The force of the rain surprised him. It soaked through his thin jacket in moments, while muddy puddles seeped through the synthetic leather of his shoes. Angered by these unexpected handicaps, Harry made his stumbling way towards the house. There was no moon, just darkness, all the more disagreeable for being warm.

He came at last to the drive of the house, saw two lights upstairs. They indicated Viola was preparing for bed. Good. That would leave Harry free to smash up the kitchen – he knew that trusting country idiots like her never locked doors – and get away easily. He went down the front drive, round to the back door that led directly to the kitchen. There, to his consternation, he found more lights. This must mean that though Viola was probably upstairs, it must be her intention to come down again and switch them off. Harry swore.

For a long time, standing under the mulberry tree for shelter, he wondered what to do. His eyes were fixed on the lighted kitchen window, some twenty yards away. There was no sign of life. Perhaps Viola was in the bath. With the soaking sleeve of his jacket Harry wiped at the rain on his face. Curiously, his violent intentions had subsided a little. He thought perhaps he should wait until all the lights went out. But then a loud crack of thunder brought him to his senses. He jumped, enraged again: must get on with the business with no more thought.

A dripping figure, Harry moved slowly towards the window. Overhead, the thunder crackled and rumbled, and he thanked the heavens for their aid. Like this, his entry would never be heard.

A yard or so from the window, Harry stopped. He could now see the high-backed chair drawn up by the fire, turned away from him. He could also see a small part of a man's bent head, and his arm.

So that was it, the bitch. The lover waiting downstairs while she prepared herself for him. Well, she would get no fun from him tonight.

Harry crashed through the back door, half blinded by rain in his eyes and the light after darkness. Thunder filled the room. Harry felt himself hurtling towards the chair, catching his hip on the corner of the table as he went, causing a sharp pain. He heard his own roars climbing against the thunder, saw the startled flash of an old man's face, open mouth spewing forth a pitiful cry. The rough bone handle of his weapon gave courage to Harry's hand. He slashed at the cowering head, over which defensive hands fluttered feebly as fledgelings. The skin at the temples broke like egg shell. It was so easy. So easy. Serve the baby-snatching bastard right.

In the room of laughing thunder, Harry watched a thin claw of blood spout from the head fallen over the side of the chair. The blood gathered speed and density, began to drip on to the flagstone floor. Harry moved backwards, one hand on the table. The thunder stopped, quite suddenly. In the silence he thought he could hear the drip of blood, but it may have been rain from his own clothes. The quiet unnerved him. He gave a feeble slash with the knife sharpener at the only two things on the vast pine table: a bowl of white roses and a pot of home-made strawberry jam. (Naturally home-made, scoffed some part of Harry's mind.) They fell over, a small noise. Roses sprawled in spilt water. Jam oozed from broken glass. The old man did not move.

Harry Antlers ran.

An hour later, driving home from a late call, Richard Almond passed the house. He was surprised to see a lighted window upstairs. Viola had sent him a card to say she and Gideon were returning late on Monday night. Perhaps there had been some change of plan.

Richard drove past the house, thinking he would ring in the morning, when he found himself stopping the car. He had a strange feeling that he should just check everything was all right. He knew all too well the ruthless energy of those possessed. Harry Antlers would stop at nothing. If Viola had arrived early, pursued by the madman, she would need more than Alfred Baxter's protection.

Alarmed by his own thoughts, Richard skidded into the front drive. Viola's car was not there. He rang the front door bell, shouting his name through the clatter of rain. He did not want to alarm anyone by so late a call. He waited, ringing and shouting, for some moments. Then he went round to the back door. It was open. The kitchen lights were on.

Richard's appalled eyes leapt from the spilt jam to the spilt blood. In a moment he was pushing the unconscious figure of Alfred Baxter upright in the chair. It was at once apparent the old man was alive. Shallow breathing, profuse bleeding. With remarkably quick fingers Richard snatched a dishcloth and bound it round Alfred's head to quell the flow of blood for the few moments while he fetched his case from the car.

A short time later, having made his patient as comfortable as he was able and covered him with rugs from the cloakroom, Richard went to the telephone in the hall. First he rang for an ambulance. Then he called the police.

Harry Antlers drove slowly and calmly back to London through the rain. He stopped only once, on the outskirts of Newmarket, to throw his knife sharpener into a field. Hungry though he was, he judged it unwise to relieve his hunger at a transport café.

By three in the morning – having made sure no one observed his entry into the block of flats – he had bathed, put on dry clothes, and consumed an early breakfast of eggs and bacon. His only regret was that he had not had more time for wrecking the kitchen. Still, incapable though she was of loving, even the hard-hearted Viola might suffer some punishment on hearing of her elderly lover's attack.

A very small worry nagged beneath the fried eggs: the bloody old man had looked curiously dead. The blow, Harry was sure, had not been hard, nothing to a younger man. But he had not counted on Viola's taste for geriatrics. Some time, he would try to find out how serious the damage had been.

But for the most part Harry's mind was wonderfully clear of thought or conscience. He imagined he must be a true villain, feeling like this, and the reasons for his villainy – ugly face, dreadful childhood – were not his fault. Juries were very sympathetic to such cases these days. Not that the incident would ever get to court. For Harry was about to carry out the final part of his plan.

He rang Annie Light. Once again, sleepily, she urged him to come round. Having granted her the compliment, this time, of undressing completely, Harry insisted on a serious talk before they indulged in anything else. They clung to each other in the narrow bed.

'Now listen, Annie. If you love me as you say you do, and you must know by now the feeling is pretty mutual, I want to ask you to do something for me that might make a whole difference to my life.'

'Of course, Harry. Anything. *Anything*.' Annie wriggled, impatient.

'I don't want you to ask me any questions. What's been happening is no concern of yours, and never will be.'

'No.'

'But I want you to *extend* tonight in your mind. Should anyone ask you questions about what you were doing this evening, I want you to say you spent the *whole* evening with me. We went for a drive, came back here. You can admit we made love, if necessary.'

'What sort of people might question me?' asked Annie. 'Are you in trouble?'

'No, my love, I'm not in trouble. But I could be without your help. It's all far too complicated to explain. Just trust me: I need your help.'

'Of course,' said Annie.

'So if by any chance one day the police –'

'*The police?*' Harry felt her fear.

'I love you, Annie.'

'I'll do anything you like.'

'You swear you will keep to your story?'

'Of course. I'd do anything in the world for you. You know I would.'

She had relaxed at last, silly little thing. Harry thought he could count on her, though plainly she would need a little encouragement from time to time.

'I was so touched, the way you cleared up my flat,' he whispered. 'The flowers.'

'It was nothing.'

'You mustn't be frightened by the police. It's a very small chance it'll ever come to that.'

'No. I'll do my best.'

'Swear I was with you all night?'

'Swear. Wish you had been.'

'You will be. Another time.' Harry braced himself to seal her promise. 'I've always loved you, you must know that,' he said.

Early on Saturday morning Viola and Edwin left the house to visit the Tate Gallery. They were out for the rest of the day and went to a film in the evening. Thus Richard, who had been ringing continually, was not able to get hold of Viola till very late that night. She at once rang Gideon in New York with the news, and rose at dawn on Sunday to drive to Norfolk. Her farewell to Edwin was very brief: she woke him in the dressing room with a hurried explanation. She could give him no idea of when she would return, she said. Perhaps

213

never, to her uncle's house. Horrified by her various bits of news, Edwin leapt from his bed with uncharacteristic speed. With no conscious thought he ran to the library, snatched up the engraving of the Hawk-Eyed moth and thrust it into her hands.

'Hurry,' he said, 'and take this.'

'But its your precious moth with the fierce eyes —'

'I'd like you to have it. Off you go, now.'

He put up a hand to pat her hair. But she was gone, shouting something about trying to remember the moth's name. Edwin, clutching at his pyjamas, ran after her.

'*Smerinthus ocellata*,' he called down the stairs. But .the front door had slammed. He doubted if she heard.

Richard met Viola at the house. Having told her all he knew, in greater detail than on the telephone, they drove to the hospital to see Alfred. He was recovering well and was expected home in a week or so.

'The police can't get much out of him,' said Richard, on the way there. 'He remembers very little about the whole thing. He keeps saying the man was very wet, as if he'd been in a river, and very fat. He remembers seeing the buttons of his shirt were undone. He had no clear picture of his face except that it was nasty. Nothing else has come back to him. The police are coming up this afternoon to see you,' he added. 'They wanted to know if you might have any ideas.'

'You told them nothing?'

'Nothing. I thought it was up to you.'

'It's quite plain. Harry Antlers was out to kill either me or my imaginary lover.'

'He's overstepped himself,' said Richard. 'It's a traditional end for those suffering from his particular affliction. You'll put them in touch with Mr Antlers, then?'

Viola paused only for a fraction of a second.

'Of course,' she said.

'I know, quite positively, I've made the right decision,' said Gideon. 'My life is here, not in America. It's a tremendous relief to be so sure.'

It was Monday night, late. Viola had waited up for him.

They sat by the fire with bread, cheese and wine. Gideon was full of the adrenalin of one who has made a long journey and is not yet ready to sleep. They had talked at length of the assault on Alfred, the obvious fact that Harry Antlers was the culprit. Viola had discussed her own attack, horrifying her brother. Now, they turned to their plans.

'And what about you, Violetta? When the flat is finished will you live there? I hope not. I don't want you anywhere on your own till that maniac is put safely away.'

'I've been idle long enough,' said Viola. 'Getting a job is my first priority. But not in London. I don't want to be there any more. Ever.'

'No. You could be here.'

'Only for a while. There's no work, here. Perhaps I should go abroad.'

'It might help,' said Gideon, 'if I told you about an even more important decision than coming home.' He twirled his glass, spinning his wine. 'I'm going to marry Maisie of Docking.' He laughed, seeing Viola's face. 'That is, I can't be *quite* sure of that: but I'm going to ask her tomorrow.'

Viola, speechless, found delight in the idea slowly coming to her.

'I've thought about nothing else since I left here,' Gideon went on, 'and it seems to be the only decision in my entire life about which I've not had a single doubt. She's the one for me. The only puzzle is why I never realized, years ago . . .'

'She was different, then.'

'She was. Well, we've left it a bit late, but not too late. We'll get married in the next month or so, live here as much as we can. I'm sure she'd want that. Though I shall probably have to be in London a few days a week.' He studied his sister's face again. 'But you, Violetta – and I know Maisie will agree – you're not going to be turned out of your house. You can stay here for as long as you like.'

'That's very kind of you,' said Viola, 'but I would never do any such thing. Quite impossible for everybody. Really. But if you could perhaps buy me out, then I could find myself something else. I rather fancy the West Country.'

Gideon smiled down at her.

'Of course I'll buy you out if that's what you want. But

215

wouldn't that be a lonely life? The West Country would be far away from us.' He paused. 'And Richard,' he added.

'So it would,' said Viola. 'But you know me. I like my aloneness.'

Gideon got up.

'Well, there's time to think about it all. Now, I must get a few hours sleep before the proposal. Do you think she'll have me?'

Viola laughed.

'Not a single doubt.'

'And you think it's a good idea?'

Viola rose, too, and embraced her brother.

'The best idea you've ever had,' she said.

Now that the pain in his head had almost gone, Alfred was rather enjoying himself in hospital. Everyone made a great fuss of him, changing the bandage over his eye very gently, propping up his pillows, constantly enquiring after his comfort. They intended to take out his stitches in a few days time, then he would be allowed home.

He had had visitors every day. The first time the police had questioned him he had still been quite drowsy, and remembered nothing of what they had asked him or what he had told them. Since then, they had been several times. But he was not able to give them much help, try as he might. The fact was the picture in his mind was very unclear. Trying to remember did nothing to help. One moment he had been imagining Maisie Fanshawe – he had omitted to furnish the police with this detail – the next, an ugly mug of a face had loomed above him, shouting. After that Alfred knew nothing till he woke up to find himself surrounded by the flowery curtains of a hospital cubicle. So, regretfully, he had not been able to be of much use to the police. He only hoped they caught the bugger. Shouldn't be at large, a maniac like that. It was a very good thing, though, and Alfred thanked the Lord for His blessing, that *he* had been the one to be attacked rather than Miss Viola.

She herself had been to see him every day, sometimes with the gallant Dr Almond. They brought roses from the garden, and books and jars of honey and jam. They were kindness itself. What a fortunate man he was.

Then, the day after his return, Mr Gideon and Maisie Fanshawe came. Alfred could hardly believe it when he saw them walking down the ward towards him.

'Well, I never,' he muttered to himself, straightening his pyjama top.

Maisie Fanshawe sat by his bed and gazed at him with marvellous concern, so that he felt he was basking under a bright sun. Dressed in a lovely pink, this time, she still had that funny radiance about her, so it hadn't been his imagination at the funeral. When her eyes were not on himself, Alfred noticed them swinging constantly across the bed to Mr Gideon. Beautiful, she was, sort of, thought Alfred. But it was not an uneasy thought.

They asked all about the attack, and were evidently pleased to see him so well on the way to recovery. Not until a few minutes before the end-of-visit bell did they then tell him their own news: they were to be married very shortly. What's more, Norfolk was to be their home, and Alfred's job and flat were there for the rest of his life, should he want them.

Alfred gripped each one by the hand, unable to speak, overjoyed. Not in a million years would he ever have imagined Mr Gideon going for such a *quiet* lady, but how right he was. Alfred, had he been able, could have assured him how right he was.

When they had left, promising to return next day, Alfred lay back on his pillows. Although he was delighted by their news, and looked forward to serving them to the best of his ability for many years to come, they soon went from his mind. Lovely young couple though they were, they were replaced by the person who had been occupying most of Alfred's thoughts since he had regained consciousness: Eileen.

Yes, Eileen was with him again, laughing and smiling and sweet as ever, just as she had been in real life. He tried, just once, to remember the disagreeable face, the face which had gone wrong in his mind, somehow, in the last few months: but it would not return. And another thing: he had a dream one night about the girls. Turned out they had enjoyed their picnic so much they had been taken short by the incoming tide and drowned. Somehow, in his dream, he wasn't sorry.

Just realized they had gone. Awake, he never gave them another thought. He heard no more laughter.

Funny thing, really, thought Alfred, sniffing the white roses. Old man gets a blow on the head, and it brings back his wife. Brings her back just as she always was, his dearest Eileen. So in a way, and Alfred would confide this to no one in the world but the smiling Eileen – he couldn't bring himself to feel that hard about his attacker. Poor man. Perhaps he had never known a happy life, or what it was to love.

14

The first visitors to Harry Antlers' penthouse were two plain-clothes policemen. They were received with cool courtesy, and tea in the brand new Worcester cups. Harry conveyed no surprise at their visit. He merely wondered how they had tracked him down, considering he was ex-directory and had given his address to no one, but he supposed they had their ways.

The interview, he thought, went very well. Privately relieved to hear the old man was alive, he showed concern at the plight of Alfred Baxter who was, said the police, 'living in the house'. This news ignited fury in Harry's breast, for he had never supposed Viola's lover was actually *installed*. To quell his agitation he quickly ate several digestive biscuits and maintained his outer calm. No, he said, he had never met the Baxter man or heard of him. He himself had only visited the house on one occasion, and Viola Windrush had been on her own.

The police then questioned him, in most delicate fashion, about his own relationship with Viola. Was it true there had been some harassment?

'Ah, that,' said Harry, giving a pained smile. 'Well, you know what women are. They get these fancies in their heads . . . Make up incredible stories when they're spurned.' He sighed. 'I'm sure you know what I'm getting at.' He sounded so solemn, pained, and full of understanding, the two men exchanged a glance that might have been of sympathy. One of them wrote a very short sentence in his notebook.

Finally, he was asked in the nicest possible way if he could prove to them where he was and what he was doing on the night of the attack. Harry's eagerness to oblige, he later considered, might have been the only moment he went slightly over the top. He jumped up and fetched his diary, rummaged through the pages.

'Think I was probably somewhere Miss Windrush –' he gave them a look – 'wouldn't like to hear about. I trust you'd be discreet in this matter?' They nodded. Harry's finger jabbed a page of the diary. 'Yes! Here we are. A.L. 7.30.'

'What, may I ask, sir, is A.L.?'

Harry assumed his conspirator's face.

'A.L., Inspector, is my girlfriend, Annie Light. To put it simply, it's a matter of mutual love. Not, as is the case with Miss Windrush, a case of your unrequited. On the night in question, we met at 7.30. We spent the evening together. Then, well – you know how evenings with the girlfriend are inclined to end?'

He thought one of the policemen allowed himself the faintest smile.

'Could you give us Miss Light's address, sir? We'd like to have a word with her, confirm all this.'

'Of course.'

Harry supplied her address and, also by heart, her telephone number which he had taken the precaution of learning that morning. He felt confident in Annie. Since their last night together, he had spoken to her several times, tutored her on what precisely to say. Only yesterday he had sent her a dozen yellow roses, with the promise that if she was interviewed, and all went well, he would take her out to what he called a champagne dinner, plus much else besides. So there were incentives for Annie. Harry was not afraid.

The policemen thanked Harry for his trouble and said they hoped they would not have to be in touch again. Harry urged them to come any time, often as they liked. Nice to see them.

Once they had gone, he felt it appropriate to congratulate himself on a brilliant performance. The brand new fridge being stuffed with delicacies from an expensive shop nearby, he was able to celebrate in his favourite manner.

A few days later he heard from Annie the interview had gone according to plan. The police believed her, definitely. To prove to himself there was some honour in his heart, Harry took the girl out to dinner and did indeed buy her half a bottle of inferior champagne. Promising there would be many more such occasions, he visited her narrow bed for the last time. The next day he arranged for his telephone number to be changed – Annie did not know his address – and sent her more roses proclaiming his undying love. But Annie's use was over. He never saw her again.

The next visitor to the penthouse was Hannah Bagle. She had flown over on an extended business trip, which meant she would be occupied by day, but have many a free night, should that be of interest to Harry.

She sat on his low, pale sofa – not unlike her own in New York – looking, thought Harry, just the sort of girl most men would give their eye teeth to have in a penthouse: dressed in a cream satin shirt slung with gold chains, long silky legs flowing over his new carpet. She was sinuous, alluring. Harry found himself opening his one bottle of good wine, boasting of its year.

'So tell me,' he said, 'what's been happening? You and your lover parted on good terms?'

Hannah looked down into her drink, modest.

'Not at all,' she said. 'Unfortunately not. I would have liked it that way, as you can imagine. But it wasn't to be.' She sighed. 'No, I'm afraid poor Gideon was pretty cut up about the whole thing. I didn't mean to hurt him, of course I didn't mean to. But the thing had come to its natural end, as far as I was concerned. It would have been pointless to go on. So I just had to take the bull by the horns and tell him goodbye.'

'Difficult,' said Harry.

'And now, you know what? Almost as soon as he got here he called me to say he was getting married. Next week. Can you imagine?' She laughed. 'The quickest case of rebound I've ever heard in my life. Some middle-aged spinster, I gather – though he didn't put it quite like that – who's never been out of Norfolk. Taking her last chance, poor old thing. Well, good luck to them.' Hannah raised her glass. 'I think it's all very funny.'

'Quite,' said Harry.

'Poor old Gideon. He was so British. I hope he's happy. Such odd things seem to please him. That week in Norfolk when we came over, remember? Apparently he and his sister spent most of their time in a boat. He said it was wonderful.

Well, we all have our different pleasures.' She fiddled with the top button of her shirt, finally leaving it undone. 'And you, Harry. How are you and the elusive Viola?'

'She's in Norfolk for a while. Helping prepare for the wedding, I dare say.'

'Most probably.' Hannah gave a small laugh. Her pale cheeks had turned to apricot. Harry had never seen her so desirable. 'Shall I tell you a cute idea that came to me? I thought it might be quite amusing if you and I went to the wedding.'

'*What?*'

'Sit down. Let me explain. Not officially, of course. Just take a peep, from a distance. I could feast my eyes on the country wife, you could get a glimpse of your beloved Viola.'

'It's a very mad plan,' said Harry, recognizing in this beautiful woman something of his own deviousness.

'Well, think about it. It might be entertaining.'

'It might indeed. And as you can imagine, I know the layout up there pretty well.'

Hannah stood up, slunk towards him.

'Well, then. Besides, I'd like to get a glimpse of this *Norfolk* that Gideon was always going on about.'

Harry took her hands.

'Norfolk stinks,' he said.

Many of those who had been at Admiral Fanshawe's funeral now came to see his daughter married. Alfred Baxter, an usher with no more than a bruised temple and a mending scar, had seen to it the church was billowing with flowers from the garden. Miss Windrush and he had arranged them the previous day, and now the smell of roses, pinks, lavender and honeysuckle had gathered like a whole summer into the cool grey stone of the church walls.

Richard Almond was best man, very handsome in his morning coat. Alfred liked seeing him and Miss Windrush coming down the aisle together, after the bride and groom. They made a fine couple. Would that things could have been different, but no doubt the Lord had His reasons.

Outside, a crowd of villagers had gathered at the gate. Some distance away, a short fat man and a tall blonde girl, both wearing dark glasses, strove to be inconspicuous among a small group of elderly people.

'Seems he's married his grandmother,' Hannah observed.

Harry agreed, though his eyes were not on the bride. He was watching Viola, in a lavender dress much like the one in which he had first seen her, and a straw boater with dancing white ribbons. She went to a car with the best man. Admittedly, the best man gave no indication of being anything but polite to Viola, but the fineness of his tired face caused a jealous shaking in Harry's legs.

'Come on,' he said. 'I know a good vantage point for the next part.'

Hannah, thoroughly enjoying herself, followed her co-conspirator.

The small reception, as Harry had discovered from one of the villagers, was to be held on the lawn of the Windrushes' house. It was a warm September afternoon, gentle breeze from the sea fluttering through flowers and skirts and ribbons. Alfred was proud of the garden. He had put in a great deal of overtime, since his return from hospital, and he thanked the Lord he felt fit as a fiddle. The roses were clinging to their prime: a week from now any breeze would shake their petals to the ground. But this afternoon every rose head was firm, scenting the soft air.

Alfred Baxter, while hurrying dutifully around with trays of champagne, managed to spend much time admiring the bride. In cream satin, which emphasized the delicacy of her bones, to Alfred's delight she wore another dotted veil – white this time, naturally – which was as near as you could get to real *gypsophila*. She shimmied about the lawn among her guests, holding her husband's hand, smiling, smiling. Alfred recognized the look: a development of how she had been – though properly sad to outward appearances, of course – on the day of the funeral. So *that* had been her secret: Mr Gideon. Well, she deserved him. She had had too many years on her own. Nice to think, at last, she'd found herself one of England's gentlemen.

In the course of his duties at the reception, Alfred was urged to partake of several glasses of champagne himself, and after a while his own wedding day merged happily with the real one. As Maisie Fanshawe glided about the garden with her husband, he saw himself and Eileen in a state of similar enchantment all those years ago. The only difference was that he and Eileen had been less fortunate with the weather. It had been raining. Eileen's pretty face, smiling at him here among the guests, was sprayed with diamonds of rain, just as he remembered. And then he came upon her with her old woman's face, the sweetness of it unclouded, still smiling at him. As Alfred raised his glass to toast the young couple, he knew quite certainly Eileen was near him now for ever, good as he had always known her to be, and he thanked the Lord.

Sometimes Viola drew away from the guests, looked back at the whole picture, securing it for the future. She recognized the day as the end of an era. She wanted to preserve its essence: the air, light with roses, the trembling trees dappling the lawn, the smiling faces and nostalgic hats, the solid protection of the house behind them. Once, she turned towards the marsh and sea, and for a mad instance thought she saw the face of Harry Antlers peering through the hedge. She knew it was a silly fantasy brought about by the champagne, but her heart began to pound in its accustomed way. She turned, to find Richard at her side.

'What's the matter?' he asked.

'For an awful moment I thought I saw Harry Antlers spying through the bushes.'

They both laughed. Richard looked about.

'Imagination, this time,' he said.

'I hope so.'

'When are you off?'

Viola took a small sip of champagne. Her eyes, huge over the rim of the glass, were violet against the pale sky.

'Very soon.'

She had found a cottage in the West Country, an isolated corner of the land sheltered by the Downs, which she would transform slowly over the years.

'You must let me know where you are,' said Richard.

'Of course.'

Richard sighed, looked out to sea.

'Weddings,' he said. 'Weddings.'

Viola looked at him. She had drunk enough to make her bold.

'They make one think,' she said.

'They do. They sadly do.'

Gideon and Maisie were approaching, a shining galleon through the waves of friends.

'Come on,' said Richard, touching Viola's arm. 'I must go and do my duty: the toast. We must drink to the bride and groom.'

He lifted his own glass fractionally in the direction of Viola, then drank, emptying it, shutting his eyes.

'They don't seem to have many friends,' observed Hannah. She had a ragged view of the proceedings through a thick hedge. Her high heels were sunk in marshy earth. She was hot and uncomfortable.

Harry, from his superior position lower in the hedge, had recognized Alfred Baxter from his wounds, and was fascinated. He watched him hand a glass of champagne to Viola, watched him talking and laughing with all the ease of an old lover. How could Viola bring herself . . .?

'That,' he said, nudging Hannah, 'that small one there with the balding head, is another of Viola's admirers.'

'Don't be ridiculous,' she scoffed. 'That's some kind of servant. Look, he's taking the tray round to people.'

Harry plunged his face so far into the bush his cheeks were scratched by thorns. But no discomfort could interrupt his studies.

'By God,' he said at last, 'I do believe you're right.'

At that moment, Viola, who had disengaged herself from the crowd and moved alone towards the hedge, her eyes on the sea, looked straight at the small gap through which Harry was carelessly peering. In sudden terror, he dropped to his knees, pulling Hannah with him. Through the thickness of the bottom of the hedge, he could now see only Viola's shoes, suddenly joined by those of a man.

'Time we left,' he said.

On the way back to the hidden place where Harry had parked the car, Hannah suggested they paid a short visit to the beach. Harry was reluctant. Too many matters were pressing to be turned over in his unhappy mind. He wanted to get back to the safety of London as fast as possible. But Hannah was persistent.

'Come *on*, Harry, for heaven's sake. We've driven all this way. Now we're here, I want to see a bit more of this Norfolk. The wedding wasn't much of a show.'

Harry agreed to half an hour. They settled themselves, after an awkward walk in unsuitable shoes, in the curve of a dune.

'This isn't bad,' said Hannah, brushing sand from her silk trousers.

'The place is a dump,' said Harry. Somehow, sand had crept into his socks. He looked across the beach. The tide was far out. He could see the black ribs of an old wreck. Despite the warmth of the air, he shivered.

'Your Viola looked all right,' said Hannah.

'She's a lovely lady.'

'Gideon was putting on a cheerful face.'

'His class are very good at disguising,' agreed Harry. Then a wayward thought came to him. 'I wonder how he'd feel, your ex-lover, if you and I went off together?'

Hannah laughed. 'What an idea! But you're not a free man. There's Viola.'

'Quite,' said Harry. 'But supposing I were free?'

Hannah laughed again, a little puzzled.

'Why, that'd be salt in the wound all right. He'd go mad.'

Harry strove to find a more comfortable position in the sand. He was very hungry. He put his hand in his pocket, searching for the last of his fruit gums. Coming across a small box, he drew it out. Opened it. It was the diamond star.

'My, that's pretty,' said Hannah.

'It's for you,' he said, handing it to her. 'Here, take it.' A wonderful plan was beginning to form.

'You're kidding,' said Hannah.

'No. I mean it.'

'For me? Really?' Hannah pinned it to her silk breast. 'It's marvellous. Heavens, Harry, that's the kindest thing.'

'Well,' he said, 'it's just a small tribute to a very beautiful lady. There'll be others.'

'Listen, you're sounding serious!'

'I am serious. I'm dead serious. I wouldn't give a diamond star to a lady unless she meant . . .' Harry's voice almost broke. Cursing the lack of fruit gums, he controlled himself. 'Hannah, will you marry me?'

With great surprise, Harry watched her rolling about the sand, bent knees caught in her hands, laughing in a way that was highly amused, though he failed to see the joke.

'*Marry* you, Harry? That's the greatest. Oh, that's quite something. For a moment, I almost took you seriously.'

She knelt, then, before him, gently touched his ugly face with a luminous hand. Behind them, the sun was falling.

'Did you?' he said.

'What's in store for you and me,' she answered, 'is one hell of a good time. Don't you think?'

At that precise moment, Harry recalled later, Hannah's silvery face almost touching his, his bottom uncomfortable in the sand, a kind of mist lifted in his brain. It was then that he knew the demon of Viola had gone from him: his love for her was dead. But rising from the gap she left was the most beautiful creature on earth. He wanted her more than life, and he would get her. He would try his utmost to set about it in a tranquil fashion: he had no doubt he would succeed. Then, together, they would go to southern Ireland while he made *Measure for Measure*. They would return to New York while he directed a hit on Broadway. In London they would buy a bigger penthouse. He would be the envy of all men, including her ex-lover Gideon. Viola herself would not be unmoved. The adrenalin of his new plans charging his veins, Harry heaved himself up.

'Come on, my love,' he said. 'Time to go.'

Hannah stood beside him. They looked at the darkening beach and sea.

'Oh, Harry,' Hannah said, 'I forgot to tell you. While you were showering, there was a call. The police, they said.'

Harry laughed. He had no worries now.

'The police?' he said, and touched her diamond star.

227

EASY SILENCE

Angela Huth

'A lovely novel – both witty and menacing . . .
strongly recommended'
Daily Express

The Handles, happily married for many years, have
reached the point in their lives where easy silence, an
acceptance of each other's ways, is the norm. Grace has
her painting, and the children's reference book she has
long been working on. William has his music, and his
string quartet, even if his name isn't quite spelled like the
great composer.

Then Grace encounters a young man, Lucien, who adopts
her, haunts her, threatens her – and provides her days with
a bittersweet frisson. And William becomes so besotted by
his new viola player, he decides to murder his wife . . .

'A wry tale of marital harmony threatened'
Marie Claire

'Delicious black comedy'
Woman's Journal

'Angela Huth is at the top of her form . . . a brilliantly
comic social exploration, with overtones arbitrarily and
mischievously grotesque'
John Bayley

Abacus
0 349 11136 7

LAND GIRLS

Angela Huth

The West Country in wartime, and the Land Girls are gathering on the farm of John and Faith Lawrence.

Prue, a man-eating hairdresser from Manchester; Ag, a cerebral Cambridge undergraduate; Stella, a dreamy Surrey girl stunted by love; three very different women, from very different backgrounds, who find themselves thrown together, sharing an attic bedroom and laying the foundations for a friendship that will last a lifetime . . .

'Angela Huth's riveting novel . . . is evocative and entertaining'
Mail on Sunday

'A good story, told with wit and a keen observation of detail'
Times Literary Supplement

Abacus
0 349 10601 0

NOWHERE GIRL
Angela Huth

Estranged from her second husband, Jonathan, Clare Lyall is less sure than ever about the role men should play in her life. Her first husband, Richard, was much older than her, and his casual disregard for youth, gradually hardened into indifference. And Jonathan, if anything, was too easy – too attentive, too concerned, and just a little pedantic.

So when she meets Joshua Heron at a party, the offbeat Clare isn't exactly thirsting for love. But she *is* mildly impressed when Joshua stubs her cigarette out on his thumb, and swayed still further by the advice of her new friend, the indomitable Mrs Fox. 'Take a lover,' she says, 'it's better to have a lover when young than neurosis when you're old . . . '

Gentle, wistful and wry, *Nowhere Girl* is a beautifully controlled love story.

'Huth's controlled, elegant style has been compared to Jane Austen's, but her talent is entirely original'
The Times

Abacus
0 349 10630 4

WIVES OF THE FISHERMEN

Angela Huth

Ravishing, extravagant, flirtatious Annie MacLeoud and
kind, plain, virtuous Myrtle Duns cannot remember a time
when they were not the most loving, rivalrous and unlikely
of friends, unflinchingly loyal to each other in the harsh
climate of the Scottish fishing village which is their home.
Their friendship has been tested many times, most of all
when Myrtle embarks upon the great love affair of her life,
while the beautiful Annie finds only disappointment. Still
the friendship survives, until a horrifying accident destroys
the equilibrium, and exposes the secret sadness, jealousy
and betrayal each has hidden over the years.

'An elegantly plotted tale which owes something to Aesop
and something to Jane Austen . . . the characters are
rendered with such skill, and the timing of the narrative is
so expert, that the story is genuinely engrossing. Angela
Huth's undemonstrative brand of excellence has rarely
been seen to better effect'
Sunday Telegraph

Abacus
0 349 10851 X